Praise for

FIVE YEARS AFTER

"The future has never seemed more chilling or more believable than in *Five Years After,* a riveting dystopian page-turner from one of the masters of the genre."

—William Martin, award-winning, *New York Times* bestselling author of *The Lost Constitution* and *December '41*

"Forstchen is a rare storyteller who not only entertains, but also conveys a vital message." —Ward Larsen, winner of eight major awards and *USA Today* bestselling author of *Deep Fake*

Praise for the John Matherson series

"With *One Second After,* William Forstchen redefined and elevated the genre of apocalyptic fiction." —Kathleen O'Neal Gear and W. Michael Gear, award-winning, *New York Times* bestselling authors of the People of the Earth series and *Dissolution*

"The only thing more terrifying than this masterfully crafted story is the possibility of it actually happening—and not a damn thing being done to protect us."

—W. E. B. Griffin and William E. Butterworth IV, *New York Times* bestselling authors, on *One Second After*

"Forstchen is the prophet of a new Dark Age. The wise will listen."
—Stephen Coonts, *New York Times* bestselling author, on *One Year After*

"A riveting cautionary tale." —*Booklist* on *One Second After*

"An entertaining apocalyptic thriller."
—*Publishers Weekly* on *One Second After*

William R. Forstchen

FIVE YEARS AFTER

TOR PUBLISHING GROUP New York

FIVE YEARS AFTER

Copyright © 2023 by William R. Forstchen

A Forge Book
Published by Tom Doherty Associates / Tor Publishing Group
120 Broadway
New York, NY 10271

www.torpublishinggroup.com

Forge® is a registered trademark of Macmillan Publishing Group, LLC.

The Library of Congress has cataloged the hardcover edition as follows:

Names: Forstchen, William R., author.
Title: Five years after : a John Matherson novel / William R. Forstchen.
Description: First. | New York : Tor Publishing Group, 2023. |
    Series: A John Matherson novel; 4
Identifiers: LCCN 2023942505 (print) | ISBN 9781250854568 (hardcover) |
    ISBN 9781250854582 (ebook)
LC record available at https://lccn.loc.gov/2023942505

ISBN 978-1-250-85457-5 (trade paperback)

Our books may be purchased in bulk for promotional, educational, or business use. Please contact your local bookseller or the Macmillan Corporate and Premium Sales Department at 1-800-221-7945, extension 5442, or by email at MacmillanSpecialMarkets@macmillan.com.

First Forge Paperback Edition: 2024

Printed in the United States of America

0 9 8 7 6 5 4 3 2 1

*For Mary Frances Flora, who showed such infinite patience,
and Linda Franklin, who shall be missed*

And I looked, and behold a pale horse: and his name that sat on him was Death, and Hell followed with him. And power was given unto them over the fourth part of the earth, to kill with sword, and with hunger, and with death, and with the beasts of the earth.

—Revelation 6:8

It mattered not from whence it came . . . [T]he strange temper of the people of London at that time contributed extremely to their own destruction . . . Our breaches [were] fomented, ill blood continued, prejudices, breach of charity and of Christian union. . . . Another plague year would reconcile all these differences; a close conversing with Death . . . would skim off the gall from our tempers, remove the animosities among us and bring us to see with differing eyes than those which we looked on thing with before. . . . I recommend it to . . . all good people to look back, and reflect duly upon the terrors of the time; and whoever does so will see, that it . . . was not like appearing in the head of an army, or charging a body of horse in the field; but it was charging Death itself on his pale Horse; to stay indeed was to die, and it could be esteemed nothing less.

—Daniel Defoe, *A Journal of the Plague Year*

I will show you fear in a handful of dust.

—T. S. Eliot, *The Waste Land*

PROLOGUE

This is the BBC Home News, broadcasting tonight to our friends in the former United States of America.

It has been five years to the day since the current conflict started in the former United States with the EMP strike initiated by forces that are still unconfirmed but believed to be connected to North Korea and Iran. An in-depth analysis of the ongoing struggle and its origins will be broadcast in the following hour on BBC America, but first, the news.

The reconstituted government of America will meet in an emergency session starting this week at the provisional capital at Raven Rock, Pennsylvania, the former underground command center near Gettysburg, Pennsylvania. President Robert Scales will attempt to expand the scope of his government in the face of growing resistance from various groups located in Atlanta, and other anarchist groups east of the Mississippi.

Tensions continue to mount in the Pacific as the Chinese government continues to claim that Taiwan and the provisional government in South Korea are engaged in a plot that the Chinese claim includes the use of biological weapons.

Rumors continue to circulate of the threats of another EMP strike launched by several dissident groups. President Scales stated yesterday that the United States Navy still has a nuclear strike force, which allegedly consists of four nuclear-capable submarines, and that any EMP strike, from any country, targeting another, will be viewed as an unacceptable threat to the government. Whether or not that government is still actually a functioning entity is increasingly open to speculation and will be the subject of an analytical report at the bottom of the hour.

And now a message for the Northern California independent republic of Mount Shasta: "The chair is against the door. Repeat, the chair is against the door."

PART I

We but teach bloody instructions, which,
Being taught, return to plague the inventor.

—William Shakespeare, *Macbeth*

CHAPTER ONE

For the moment John Matherson felt at peace.

He looked over at his wife, Makala, and their one-year-old daughter Genevieve, nestled up between them, asleep in her father's arms. Makala glanced over at him and their sleepy child and silently mouthed *I love you*. And his world felt complete.

The spring graduation concert was nearly finished. In a moment he'd have to stand up and deliver a closing benediction as president of Montreat College. Tori Gasper, a graduating senior, came up to the front of the gathering and all fell silent. Besides being the valedictorian, Tori was beloved for her gently pitched soprano voice. She nodded to the pianist accompanying her, and began.

"Try to remember the kind of September . . ."

No matter how many hundreds of times he heard that song, it always hit hard. It was, he felt, the anthem for the world they now lived in, for all that they had lost in this tragic world in the years after what everyone now called "the Day." As always, the opening line triggered a deep, warm memory.

It was five years ago, on that fateful day, that he had met Makala. In those first hours after the EMP attack, he was not yet sure what had happened, and with his mother-in-law, known as Grandma Jen, and Jennifer, John's daughter with his first wife, he decided to drive into the town of Black Mountain to see what was going on in the village. But his car wouldn't work, though Grandma Jen's old Ford Edsel started right up, which was one of the first clues that whatever had happened was beyond a mere local power failure.

Nothing was moving on the interstate, every car stalled; more of a warning to John of what would prove to be true, that it was an EMP that had shut things down. It was there that Makala, standing beside her stalled BMW, had asked for help.

John had sensed danger, however; that more than a few who would approach him for help might also very well take his car— with daughter and mother-in-law inside—so he refused and sped off, leaving Makala behind.

They would later laugh that this first encounter was a hell of an introduction and the next morning he was quick to offer an apology for leaving her stranded.

Makala was now one of the most trusted and loved citizens of Black Mountain. As the nurse in charge of a cardiac surgical unit down in Charlotte, she was an invaluable asset, helping with the refugees and citizens who within days were overloading the town's medical facilities.

It would be Makala who was at John's bedside for days when a simple cut on his hand turned deadly with septicemia, and saved his life. But more important to John than what she did for him was the way she became part of his daughter Jennifer's life as well. Jennifer was a type 1 diabetic in a post-EMP world where, beyond the insulin he'd managed to get on that first day of chaos, no more life-saving medication would follow. As the months painfully dragged out, and the supply of insulin that John had stockpiled for his diabetic daughter began to fail for lack of refrigeration, it was

Makala who was by her side as well until the last tragic day of his daughter's life.

There was a day when Makala had accompanied John to his college to see how things were faring. Standing together in the campus chapel, they listened as a student, who would later die fighting to defend the town, had practiced that song and it was on that day John realized he was falling in love with Makala.

Tori continued to sing *The Fantasticks* classic.

John stirred from his musings. He looked over at her. She smiled wistfully, for of course she knew what he was remembering, the song always triggered his memories. Sliding closer, she took the still-sleeping Genevieve onto her shoulder, then reached out and took John's hand and squeezed it.

Her eyes were bright with tears, one of them coursing down her cheek.

"What is it?" he whispered.

"I don't want you to go. I want you safe here."

"I know" was all he could manage to say.

Tomorrow he would leave, not sure how many weeks or months he'd be gone. Maybe forever.

In the morning he would travel to Raven Rock, the underground citadel near Gettysburg, Pennsylvania, that was now the seat of a government. Or at least an attempt at creating a government.

He was the vice president. But vice president of what? A real government, a shadow government, or just a chimerical dream of Bob Scales? In any case, he, somewhat against his better judgment, had accepted a position and title based on what was called an "electoral vote," voted on by less than a hundred men and women in the shattered remnant of what once had been the original thirteen states of a new republic called the United States of America.

It was impossible to actually bring the twenty-six senators together when most road travel was problematic at best, and in more
than a few cases near suicidal. A few had tried to come to Raven
Rock but were never heard from again. Two women senators from
Rhode Island who tried to make the journey, complete with a four-
man armed escort, were found crucified on an interstate just outside
of New York City with signs on their crosses declaring they had not
repented to the new Messiah. Whatever the fate of the guards was,
John hoped it had been quick. The meetings of government were
therefore held on short wave radio, but even then rarely was there a
quorum. It was, John thought, a helluva way to try and reconstitute
the government of what was idealistically called the New Republic
of America.

The college had thus become far more the center of John's life
after Makala and the new baby.

With 170 students, it was actually surviving. The school had re-
trenched, like everything else did in their lives, after the Day. There
was no longer any chartering institution, no state mandates—
basically nothing more than the fact they called themselves a college. They now offered just one degree. Their catalog called it a
bachelor's degree in Life Skills; John called it a degree in survival
and rebuilding for a post war America.

They offered, as any real college should, a few courses in the old
traditional sense: history, English lit, and so on. John felt even at the
worst of times, there was still a need for such things. That the hu-
manities were as valid now as they had been in places like Paris and
Cambridge six hundred years ago. In arguing to keep such courses,
he cited stories of POWs in World War II and concentration camp
inmates who still tried to carry on with some cultural foundations.
Along with his other duties, he found time to teach a course on
basic American history and another on the Constitution and what
he hoped would again be their system of government, and a third
course on Democracy versus Totalitarianism. All three became

mandatory courses, and he hoped something of them would rub off and someday, perhaps decades from now, these beliefs would again bear fruit.

But it was the pragmatic needs of this time that had to take precedence. Alongside such traditions of literature and government, the college offered what could almost be a degree in and of itself for those students who became EMTs and worked at the clinic in Black Mountain.

That program was run by Makala. John had—more than a little bit seriously—wanted to give her the title of dean. She'd just laughed, thinking it far too pretentious, and said if she had to use a title she preferred to be simply "Nurse Makala," or her maiden name of "Ms. Turner." The medical course covered the gamut, from how to sterilize and bandage a flesh wound up to emergency field surgery for gunshot wounds that even a beginning doctor would find challenging.

Given the continuing role the students had of also being the town's rapid mobilization force and the border guards at the pass for I-40 and the crest of the mountain on Route 9, such training was needed. Just a few months ago, half a dozen raiders had crept in at night on a pig raid, trying to steal a few hogs from an isolated farm belonging to the Stepps, whose clan lived up on the North Fork. The raiders were killed, but not before killing two watchmen, one of them a student, and wounding several others. A student medic's quick thinking on a compound fracture of the thigh and severed femoral artery from a shotgun blast saved the life of one of the Stepp children. Thereafter, if rations were thin at the college at times, all she had to do was hike over to the North Fork and come back the next day with a full stomach and usually a juicy smoked ham to share with her friends.

For people like the Stepps, the Wilsons, the Franklins, the Robinsons, and the Burnett group on the far side of the Black Mountains, life had in general reverted to the nineteenth century, and the adjustment was, in fact, hardly an adjustment at all for some.

A team of students worked in "practical chemistry" under the tutelage of Brad Bennett, one of the few surviving professors from before the Day. They were now producing ether and antibiotics, and worked a still to produce antiseptic alcohol—and, when John's back was conveniently turned, some illegal moonshine for late-night parties up in the woods. Cannabis was grown as well for a variety of uses, including help for cancer and chronic pain, and John had to turn a blind eye as well to the "recreational" use that more than a few indulged in, but doing so on duty was not tolerated. They were also the ones who manufactured the black powder for the assortment of old muzzleloaders found in the town. Modern cartridges had been all but used up over the last five years, and the dwindling supply was strictly reserved for military use. One of Burnett's people, a maker of flintlock rifles before the war, was backlogged a year in advance for his fifty caliber Pennsylvania long rifles.

A production facility had been created for making this black powder, with a major component of that coming from Bat Cave, twenty miles south of Black Mountain. Hundreds of thousands of bats had lived in the caves for thousands of years, and therefore tens of thousands of tons of bat guano was piled up dozens of feet deep. Guano meant nitrates for saltpeter, the main ingredient, which was then combined with sulfur from a hot spring in Asheville and wood charcoal. Lead was plentiful, of course, from thousands of old car batteries. They manufactured so much black powder it was now a trade item to the communities that still survived in the mountains of the Carolinas and Tennessee.

A careful survey of every dwelling in the area had produced a few hundred black-powder weapons, most of them reproductions, but even a few originals from the Civil War. Many people now hunted with flintlocks and quickly learned they had but one shot, and to make that shot count. More than a few at the college were now deadly marksmen at two hundred yards, and what was left of the roving bands knew that Black Mountain was a place to avoid.

In the first months after the Day, anyone who had a gun had taken to the woods to hunt, many a town- and city-dweller just assuming that any day they went hunting would result in enough meat on the table to last for weeks. In little more than a month the woods were all but hunted out for anything bigger than a squirrel. After what was now called the Starving Time, and the die-off from starvation and disease, and the battle with the Posse, those who survived gradually returned to hunting, now with flintlocks or bows. Deer were finally making something of a comeback, along with a plentiful abundance of wild geese, whose old flyways were now all but devoid of humans and thus flourished. Wild boar were actually becoming plentiful to the point of being a nuisance.

In the first months after the Day, more than a few pigs had escaped from farms, especially in Swannanoa and below the Old Fort gap, and they'd flourished up in the hills, reverting back to their predomesticated state. Hunting them with bows and spears had almost become a sport. A few venturesome students, after reading *Lord of the Flies,* would go out armed only with spears, and of course some bootleg moonshine and pot, chanting "Kill the pig!" They would return in the evening hooting and hollering like Neolithic hunters of old, most of the campus turning out to cheer on their triumphant return.

The "granola eaters," as some students referred to them, would look on in disgust as the pig was roasted on an open fire, and at times the celebration would get out of hand with dancing, and more than a few couples retiring to the woods for other activities. John had voiced his concerns about the whole thing taking on a pagan aspect, but then again, with all the pressure those students were under, he would find an excuse on such nights to conveniently remove himself from the campus. Makala was disgusted with these displays but knew as well that it was definitely a pressure release. Still, she would mutter for the students not to come crying to her if one of them got gored. One of them finally was gored and darn near killed, and of course she bandaged him. Then the spear hunting stopped for a while, though not for long, the injured student roaring in triumph as he led back a successful hunt a few months later.

Beyond all their other responsibilities, students had to participate in military drills, mandatory for everyone except those who were disabled, on sick call, or could rightly and honestly claim conscientious objection and then served instead as medics. The drills were held every Saturday morning, along with two weeks of full-scale practices and maneuvers every spring and fall after the harvest was complete.

John no longer participated in those. Students who had survived the Day and fought in the war against the Posse and the few dozen minor skirmishes since then were the veterans now and had taken over, led by Kevin Malady, their head of militia on the campus, and Josiah Stepp, a combat vet with most of his time spent in the Middle East. He had come back with a Silver Star and two Purple Hearts. Josiah supervised the training in town. He was the one who started the tradition that students wounded in the Posse fight and other actions could wear a purple ribbon on their jacket, and those officially noted by Kevin Malady for valor wore a coveted gold ribbon.

All new students went through a boot camp at the start of the year, learning the usual requirements of firearm safety and after that, training. Woe betide a student who did not count any weapon, even a flintlock, as always loaded or behaved with one in a reckless manner. Last year a student was shot in the shoulder and darn near killed by a student laughingly saying "It ain't loaded" as he pulled the trigger. The victim survived, but lost her arm in spite of Makala's efforts; the malefactor was drummed out of the campus never to return and the lesson held strong for all who witnessed that ceremony. After completing target practice, at first with the flintlock weapons, the students then graduated to a cartridge-firing weapon, though actual live firing was restricted to just half a dozen rounds per student per year. Come the fall, unless they somehow managed to get a resupply, they would be reduced to just dry firing. But then again, John had reasoned, half a hundred flintlock rifles, and even the town's half dozen muzzle-loading cannons, could be a deadly force. Such weapons had won for America at Oriskany, Monmouth, and Yorktown.

Ammunition was only one of dozens of scarcities that had taken hold in their community that they'd had to find a way around. Salt was another. They were dependent on an old saltlick forty miles away, and several times a year a party was sent out to spend a week boiling down the precious mineral and lugging the fifty-pound bags back home. Going out on the "salting parties" was a sought-after diversion that went to top students who could skip studies, camp out, have some fun parties, and just enjoy the change of pace and scenery.

As for food, there was finally enough, but balancing it for nutrition was always a challenge, as Makala constantly struggled with an increasing cadre of trained students and more than a few surviving old timers from the town. The struggle to bring nutrients back to a semblance of normal was finally working. So many things to worry about, so many things facing his community in a truly daily struggle to stay alive, in this the fifth year since the Day.

With Makala leaning on his shoulder, the baby still asleep, John stilled his thoughts. Things, for the moment at least, were working out.

Tori entered the last refrain of the song, his favorite part:

"Deep in December it's nice to remember . . ."

The words stirred John from his reverie. Once she was done, he'd have to get up to offer the closing benediction and blessing to the graduates, their proud families, and of course the rest of his community.

The final stanza drifted away.

Many in the audience had joined in, shedding tears for a song that had become "their" anthem in this brave and still at times frightening world that was now their reality.

The song drifted away into silence that was broken only by a few sniffles and quiet weeping. John looked over at Makala and forced a smile. She shifted little Genevieve, who started to whimper a protest at being stirred awake, but then rested against her mother's breast and went back to sleep.

John Matherson stood up and stretched, his frame still lanky even though he was pushing fifty. But then again, everyone was thin now—maybe one of the few health benefits created by what had happened. He unconsciously scratched his short, graying beard; nearly all men were bearded now. With electric razors gone and safety razors long gone, only a few tried to continue with the ritual of shaving. Makala said John's new habit of tugging on his whiskers for a few seconds before speaking made him look Lincolnesque. Students seemed to appreciate the gesture as well, saying it made him look distinguished and thoughtful.

He never did like going up to the podium on the stage, feeling it put a bit of a barrier between him and his audience. Standing in front of them was less formal, more like a neighbor talking to friends, so he stopped at the base of the stage, turned, and stood silently for a moment, not aware that he was still tugging on his whiskers.

He looked over at Tori and smiled. "As always, Tori, you have such a beautiful voice. And congratulations on being this year's valedictorian. You've done a magnificent job."

He looked back out to the audience, to Tori's mother. She beamed with delight. Tori was one of the lucky few in that her mother had also survived the Day and now was sitting in the audience, eyes brimming with tears of pride.

He lowered his head for a few seconds to gather his thoughts, and started softly.

"Reverend Black, could I ask for our traditional prayer in re-membrance of all those who have passed since that Day, five years ago today, when our lives changed forever."

Black started into a short prayer and John looked at him, filled with concern. He remembered Black before the war, young and vibrant, even in his mid-fifties, always smiling and looking like he wasn't a day over forty. His wife, Portia, was a charm—John always said she looked like Sally Field's twin sister. The years, the tragedy, had taken a deep toll on Richard. Gone was his youthful-ness. His hair had gone prematurely white, and like nearly every-one else he had lost any excess weight.

All of them looked like the fading daguerreotypes of Civil War soldiers and their families from 160 years ago: wiry, frames taut, slender, their clothing from a day before dry cleaning and wrinkle-free fabrics causing them to look rumpled. Richard was like that now too, but there was something deeper, an almost infinite wea-riness of the soul. A younger generation now coming of age were survivors adapting to the world around them; it had become their norm. But for an older generation, who had long ago come of age before the war, a generation accustomed to the internet, markets crammed with food, the latest miracles of medicine and science and entertainment that they had of course taken for granted, for all of them, it was hard not to be haunted by the past. Just this morning at breakfast, Makala had cracked open one of their last precious K-cups, a gift from Jim Bartlett from over the mountain in Burnsville who had found a wrecked truck loaded with them and actually used them as currency. Makala had made two cups of coffee, adding a few drops of honey for sweetener. That was now luxury.

CHAPTER TWO

Reverend Black finished his prayer, his voice barely above a whisper, and sat down. John again had the audience.

"Well, that's about it then, my friends. Tonight we'll have something of a feast, thanks to our intrepid hunters who came in yesterday with two deer, and our food-gathering teams who have provided lots of greens and other delights."

He paused for a few seconds and tried to look straight-faced. "The wild boar roast was two days ago. For those of you who missed it . . ." He paused. "Well, I'm glad you did."

That drew some appreciative laughter and a few comments given in sotto voce, which John of course chose to ignore.

"All here are invited to the feast. There'll be appropriate music, dancing, and Paul Hawkinson has strung some electrical lights, and as long as it doesn't rain we'll have them on as well. So everyone, come. Okay?"

The audience applauded, some stirring, half standing up, as if the ceremony was over and the time of celebration would begin immediately.

"Remember, though," he quickly added. "Drill as usual for

everyone starts the day after tomorrow. I need not tell you it is mandatory, of course."

That was greeted with the usual groans and muffled comments.

"I do have one final thing to note, and I think most of you are aware of it. I am leaving tomorrow morning for Raven Rock, just outside of Gettysburg. Maybe it wasn't so much of a coincidence that place was built there more than half a century ago. The Civil War general Joshua Lawrence Chamberlain, who you've all heard me talk about at one time or another, who received the Medal of Honor for his regiment's gallant stand on Little Round Top, back on that hot July day in 1863, would later describe that storied battlefield as 'the vision place of souls.'

"There is some doubt that our attempt at forming a new and lasting government will meet with success, and some are saying it is impossible. I shall try with all that is in me to see that this government will still take hold and flourish.

"We shall see." He stood silent for a moment, and with lowered voice said again, almost to himself, "We shall see."

He looked out at the graduating class and all who had gathered to celebrate and support them. "I therefore ask you for your prayers as I leave this place to help make one final bid to create a permanent government that shall again flourish. A hundred and sixty years ago, as this nation tottered on the abyss of what would become our tragic Civil War, Lincoln appealed to his fellow countrymen and said:

"'The mystic chords of memory, stretching from every battlefield, and patriot grave, to every living heart and hearth-stone, all over this broad land, will yet swell the chorus of the Union, when again touched, as surely they will be, by the better angels of our nature.'"

As he spoke the words of Lincoln, his voice was somber, but clear and ringing. Makala had told him more than once that at such moments he seemed almost to be the embodiment of that man.

He lowered his head for a moment of silence, joined by the rest of the assembly.

"God be with you as you leave this sacred chapel," he told them. "To those who have graduated, it is time for you now to go forth and serve so that together we shall see a rebirth of a country dedicated to the proposition that government of the people, by the people, and for the people shall not perish from the earth."

He looked over at Makala, who was beaming at him. She stood up and stepped to his side, their baby still asleep as they walked out of the chapel.

A lone voice started to sing, and by the time he was out the door, Tori was joined by others singing the "Battle Hymn of the Republic."

CHAPTER THREE

John watched as Makala recycled yesterday's coffee into the percolator and set it on the hot woodstove that filled up half their kitchen. Several of his students had spotted it in an abandoned house far up on a Montreat back road, decided it would make a grand Christmas present for the president and his wife and child, and hauled it down the mountain on a horse-drawn cart. The thing was a bit of a monstrosity, a nickel-plated expression of high Victorian gaudiness, complete with hot-water tank. It was ugly as sin but Makala loved it, and on cold winter days it filled the kitchen with a cheery warmth. The problem was that on a warm early-summer day, even with all the windows open, using it made the kitchen almost unbearable. When summer really hit, she would move the cooking, just as in colonial days, to an outdoor shed with a wood-fired grill.

The coffee started to perk, the sound of it a warming reminder of John's boyhood at his grandmother's home, where there had been a stove not unlike the one he now had.

The morning's luxury even included two eggs and home fries, now that potatoes had become a real bumper crop. It promised to be a halfway decent year for all crops, with just the right amount of rain and sun, and no late frost this year to threaten the apple, peach, and pear trees. But there would be no toast until the wheat was harvested in July, so John had to content himself with corn bread.

Eggs, potatoes, and coffee on the table, Makala settled in by his side. It was still an hour before dawn, and Genevieve was still asleep. He had peeked in at her and felt a stab of painful memory.

No matter how much he truly loved Genevieve, he almost couldn't bear to watch her sleep, because she looked so much like his lost daughter Jennifer. The Jennifer of what seemed so long ago had slept like that, clutching her Rabs the Rabbit, who had gone dingy gray with love like the Velveteen Rabbit from the book he had read to her so many times. Rabs had looked over Jennifer's grave from John's office window for more than year after her death, until he had finally parted with this keepsake and placed the rabbit's tattered remains in the prayer porch next to the main walkway on campus.

This little shrine to his lost daughter had become a respected fixture on campus. Students would leave little notes under Rabs, sometimes a prayer of comfort for John, and it always touched him deeply.

There was a little part of him that imagined, at times, that Genevieve was a reincarnation of Jennifer from before the war.

He'd never much liked corn bread but gladly devoured the eggs and home fries. Makala sat in silence, coffee cup in hand, barely taking a sip.

"I still don't like you going off like this," she finally announced.

The debate was now on, John realized. He drained half of his cup and set it down.

"Go on, tell me what's on your mind," he said, trying to sound comforting and reassuring.

"John, why go?"

"Because I feel I have to."

"John, just listen to me. I've stayed silent since you got the letter last week from President Scales that he needed you up there. But I do have a right to tell you what I think."

"Of course you do," he replied.

She looked at him, now a bit cross. "Am I detecting some sarcasm this morning?"

"Not at all, really."

She paused for a moment as if gathering her thoughts or wondering if he was indeed being sarcastic.

"I know you made up your mind the moment you got that letter from him. He said he wanted you up at Raven Rock, and I think you jumped at the chance to go."

"Not really, no, actually. I didn't jump. Did I see it as my duty to an old friend? Yes, I did, and that's what motivated me."

"You really want me to believe you."

"I wish you would."

"John, I know your loyalty to General—" She paused and corrected herself. "President Scales, but honestly, John, to what end?"

"Call it my sense of duty to a man I've known for decades, who was once my instructor at the War College. A friend who stood by me when . . ."

His voice trailed off. He knew that she understood the love he had felt toward his first wife, Mary, who had died so tragically and in fact horribly from breast cancer more than a decade ago. That there had been someone long before he knew Makala. That he did indeed love Makala intensely, but still, Mary had been his wife before her. She had not been an ex who was divorced away from him; Mary had in fact died as he held her. Mary had been the mother of two children, Jennifer and Elizabeth, long before Genevieve. Elizabeth was living now on a farm outside of Swannanoa with her husband and John was grandfather to her two young children.

Makala accepted all of that, of course. There was not a shadow of a departed wife between them. But at this moment, memories of the way Bob Scales had become a mentor, confidant, and friend in a time of crisis over the death of his first wife, might be better left unsaid.

Makala reached across the table and took his hand.

"John, I understand that. Bob and you have a bond that I fully appreciate. But that is why I'm questioning it now. Is your attachment to Bob influencing how you see your duty?"

He was silent, not sure how to respond.

"John, we've talked about it before. Bob is kind of, and I say *kind of* deliberately, the president of what you call the New Republic of America. He claimed legitimacy from so-called state electoral colleges that voted for its creation in a wave of enthusiasm after the taking of Raven Rock.

"He nominates you to be his vice president. Perhaps well and good, John, but I think it's fair to say it has been something of an empty office since."

John found himself remembering John Adams, and so many other vice presidents through history who saw the role as nothing more than sitting quietly, waiting for a president to die. Maybe a few of them, down deep, hoped that whoever was above them would go off and die or be assassinated, but most held the office with quiet dread that they just might get that call. He recalled Harry Truman's comment that the presidency fell upon him like a ton of bricks. It was a burden he as well did not want.

"So, John, I'm asking you, why does he suddenly need you now, today, up at Raven Rock?"

"All he said was he wanted to see me."

"And you go running to him because of that?"

The way she said it made him bristle slightly, ready with a retort that he was not running because some master called him.

"I am going to him because I trust him. I've always trusted him. I have to go."

"And if I ask you not to?"

"Why would you ask that of me?" His words were cold. Months

could go by without a cross word between the two, but he felt now as if she was pushing him.

"Don't ask me," he finally said.

"Why, John?" She tried to laugh but it came out strangled, and he realized she was on the borderline of tears. "John, we have a good life here now. You, Genevieve, and me. You are respected by all, you are the president of a college, what more would you want in this life?

"This whole New Republic, or Second Republic, or whatever you want to call it is a chimerical dream. We both know the chances of it taking hold are just that, little better than a dream. God bless Robert Scales, I truly mean that, John." She paused. "But there is something more at play here, and I think we both can sense that."

He didn't reply, letting her get everything off her chest.

"There's something dangerous afoot, John. Too many different forces are at play beyond our control. Stay here, John. Tell Bob something, anything. Be a little more diplomatic and stall for time and see what then plays out. You can always go later if you want, but for now I'm asking you to stay here and be safe."

They sat in silence for several long minutes, Makala finally pouring some more water into the percolator to make a third, very weak round of coffee that came out as pale as tea.

He drank his share of it in silence, and then they heard a car in the distance.

"I better get my bag," he finally said, standing up.

She sat without comment as he went into the bedroom, picked up his flight bag. He stepped into the nursery. The baby was still asleep. Leaning over her crib, he kissed her lightly on the forehead. She stirred but didn't wake up.

When he came back out to the kitchen Makala was on her feet. She was wearing her favorite rumpled and worn bathrobe, stained on one shoulder by one of Genevieve's bouts of upset stomach.

He came up and hugged her closely. She had nothing on under

the robe and for a second he was tempted to reach down to squeeze her backside and pull her in tighter, but he knew that was not what she wanted at this moment. She just wanted to be held.

He kissed her on the neck and she sighed.

"You really got to clean this robe," he said, trying to laugh. "It's getting a bit rank from the baby."

"Oh shut up, you idiot," she replied, and he knew that they would never part on a cross word even now.

The jeep, an original World War II vehicle owned by his friend Maury Hurt, was out in the driveway.

He did give her an ever-so-slight squeeze, and she tried to laugh.

"When you get back, John," she said, and then he was out the door and climbing in the passenger seat.

"The plane is already waiting for you down on the interstate, John," Maury told him.

"Okay, let's go."

As they pulled out of the driveway, John looked back to see Makala in the doorway.

"You know something, Maury, that woman can drive me crazy, but hell, I can't live without her."

CHAPTER FOUR

Their plane was an antiquated Bonanza, painted in military blue that was starting to chip and fade. John had never felt comfortable in Bonanzas, which had a well-earned reputation for being a bit squirrely, and when piloted by someone without much experience could be killers.

This pilot was in his twenties. He chatted on for a while about civilian flight training before the Day and how he'd eventually wound up volunteering to serve the new government forming at Raven Rock.

"I was in Harrisburg and walked all the way down to the Rock, knocked on the door, said I was a pilot, and they let me in. Guess I'm regular air force for the Republic now, which here in Raven Rock is Six Black Hawks, two Apaches, a mixture of some civilian planes like this old Bonanza.

"They chose me to go down and fetch you. This plane has just enough range to get from the Rock to your place and back on a single tank of gas. Gas is premium stuff now. You must be high priority for them to top off the tank. Yes, sir, we might be running on dry by the time we get back, but no headwinds, a bit of a tailwind up aloft, we'll be okay."

He was definitely not reassuring and John wasn't in the mood for talking. Eventually the pilot fell silent.

As they crossed over the Black Mountains and came into the upper reaches of the Shenandoah Valley, John sat back and enjoyed the view as they crossed over Lexington, Staunton, and continued northeast.

The Civil War historian in him awakened as the Massenet Ridgeline came into view, where Stonewall Jackson had once played his cat-and-mouse game with three different Union armies who were trying to corner him.

From their height of 12,000 feet, the limit they could go without oxygen on board, he could look down off his port-side wing to see New Market, to his right Front Royal, and straight ahead the battlefield of Cedar Creek.

It seemed an eternity ago that he had walked those fields, and again there came a memory of Mary when they were both college students and he had taken her on a tour of battlefields, which she at least pretended to show she had a desire to learn about. It was a happy memory, that first trip, camping out under the stars in that fabled valley. He forced himself not to think of it, because it suddenly seemed that the plane engine was developing an intermittent stutter in its beat.

"I've got the mixture leaned out," the pilot announced. "I wouldn't sweat it. It misses occasionally, but no big deal."

As they crossed over Winchester, the pilot cut the throttle back a few hundred rpm, and the altimeter started to slowly wind down.

"Piece of cake, sir, we'll make it to the Rock with a gallon or two to spare."

As they crossed over Sharpsburg with the city of Frederick to their right, they started running into turbulence.

"Morning thermals," came the answer to the unvoiced question, and he could tell they were, in fact, starting to run rough.

"Don't you think that . . ." John started to ask, but his pilot held his hand up.

"I got it" was all he said. John could see ground past Frederick that was all so familiar. There was the road going up to Emmitsburg, and beyond it the twin hills of Big and Little Round Top, the old Emmitsburg Road cutting through the middle of the battlefield of Pickett's Charge.

It still thrilled him to see these places, even if it was just a glimpse from the air. How many times had he walked that field? He smiled at the memory of riding horses on that field below with Bob Scales, now the president but back then the commandant of the War College, he a colonel attending a semester of training there. Bob had his eccentricities, one of which was his belief that to truly understand Gettysburg and the nature of command in a pitch battle, you did it on horseback, the way it was first done so many generations ago. How the two had argued the finer details of that battle while riding on an autumn day so long ago. Bob claimed Lee could have won the fight, John always retorting that even if by some minutely different twist of fate he had won that fight, he nevertheless would have lost anyhow. Nearly all victories in that war came at a terrible price, and even in defeat the Union Army would have exacted a terrible price, leaving him incapable of exploiting his victory by taking Washington.

Of all the millions who had visited Gettysburg to study, to contemplate, perhaps to honor an ancestor who did give that last full measure of devotion, perhaps only one in a hundred might wonder about the strange array of antennas atop a mountain just five miles away. Perhaps only one in a thousand knew that beneath those antennas the entire mountain had been hollowed out, starting in the 1950s, to house up to five thousand military elite and government officials in the event of nuclear war. On 9/11 Vice President Cheney had been taken there in case that grim day was indeed the start of a wider war. And on the Day it became a national disgrace when in addition to some military personnel already stationed there, shelter was given to several thousand high-ranking officials who had fled there, along with families and those suddenly given a coveted pass to safety, security, and literally survival. In short, those who had the right connections to live.

When the engine started to cut, the pilot threw the switch to the booster pump. It ran smooth for thirty seconds and started to cut out again.

They were down to a couple thousand feet. When John looked out the window the ground seemed a lot closer than that, the glide slope short of the miniscule landing field at the Rock.

"Hate to put down on Route 15, embarrassing to have them haul gas out to me. I think we got enough to make the dirt strip at the Rock."

"I don't give a damn about embarrassment," John snapped. "Just put her down!"

At that instant the engine finally gave up, the propeller coming to a stop.

"Piece of cake now, we got enough glide to ease her right in. Hang on for the fun."

John wanted to scream a string of obscenities. Maybe Makala had a premonition and it was now coming to pass.

A hill seemed to be rising up in front of them, but the pilot eased the stick up and cleared it, and at that instant a horn sounded.

"Stall warning, just ignore it! We're almost there."

The pilot was at last on the radio, and banking sharply. John could see several Black Hawks and two Apache gunships next to a helipad. Just below them was a narrow grass strip that seemed impossibly short.

Deadstick, they hit hard at the very end of the runway, the pilot standing on the brakes as they slid halfway down the strip, at last coming to a stop after pulling a ground loop.

"Like I said, sir, piece of cake," he said with an arrogant grin.

John just glared at him coldly. What was the sense of calling the guy an idiot. He had always hated pilots who pulled crap like this on their passengers. He unbuckled, got out, pulled open the luggage hatch, and pulled out his flight bag. Standing up, he looked around at this place known as Raven Rock.

This whole site had a somewhat surreal look to it, like it had been taken from a Cold War movie like *Fail Safe*. Atop the mountain several hundred feet above him the vast array of antennas spiked toward the sky. Directly in front of him was one of three access points into the mountain, dominated by heavy blast doors that could be opened wide enough to allow access by an eighteen-wheeler or, if needed, a tank. Guardposts flanked the doors, a couple of MPs in front of them, old-style AR-16s at the ready. To one side was a vehicle park with half a dozen Humvees and even an old M60 tank. When John had been involved with the assault on this position a couple of years back, they had been at another opening on the far side of the mountain, and the memory of it brought back chills. This was the first time he'd been back since that fateful day when Bob Scales had led the assault on this fortress and taken it.

A battered panel truck came down to meet them, and two soldiers, both of them young women, got out.

"Billy O'Reilly, you are definitely a flaming asshole, doing a dead-stick landing again," one of them shouted, and then, seeing John standing a few feet away, she fumbled to attention.

"Ah, sorry, sir, I didn't see you, sir."

"No problem, soldier, and yes, my sentiments exactly."

"He does it every time, stretching it to the limit. Someday, rather than making it over the fence, he's going to wind up tangled in it and dead."

Billy was out of the plane now, and went up to John.

"Sorry, sir, just having some fun."

"Yeah, right," John replied, still feeling a bit unsettled from the landing.

A Humvee came out from behind the blast doors into the morning sunlight and eased to a stop by his side.

"Vice President Matherson?" the driver inquired.

It was always strange to be called that. In spite of being the president of his college, he preferred that students just call him "Doc." The honorific of "president" just didn't feel right. There was supposed to be only one president in his world, and that was his old friend and mentor, Bob Scales.

"You've got him," John replied.

With that, both women came to stiff attention and actually saluted.

"Just stand at ease, please," John announced. "I'm a civilian here."

They didn't reply.

John looked over at the driver of the open-topped Humvee. "You're my ride, I take it."

"Sergeant James Benson, sir. I'm ordered to take you straight to President Scales. Do you need to hit the head before we start, sir? It's been a long flight. There's a bathroom inside if you need it, or . . ." And he nodded toward the fence.

He definitely had to go, but a glance at the two young women stopped him.

"It's all right, sir, the men do it all the time out here, we'll wait in the truck."

More than a little embarrassed, he hesitated, then finally thought the hell with it, did as suggested, then climbed into the Humvee.

He waved to the two female soldiers, who cheerfully waved back. As he and Benson drove up the hill he saw one of them getting back out of the truck. She ran up to Billy and jumped into his welcoming arms.

"That is one crazy pilot, sir, but he's also one of the best," the sergeant told him. "Chances are he was just jerking your chain a bit and still had a few gallons left in his reserve tank."

John could only shake his head.

"Sir, you're in safe hands now, sir."

"John Matherson, just call me John, okay?"

"Yes, sir."

They inched forward a few dozen yards to the checkpoint. It was heavily manned, with half a dozen guards, most of them barely out of their teens. As he waited for the barrier gate to be pulled back, John looked around. Two well-dug-in emplacements to either side of the gate were manned, one showing the muzzle of an M60 machine gun, the other what looked like an old-style .30 caliber gun that could have been used in World War II.

One guard asked John to step out of the Humvee. His IDs were checked first by the guard, then an officer in old desert camo who eyed him carefully, holding up John's fading driver's license long out of date but serving as a photo ID. He finally nodded and then snapped off a salute.

"Sorry, Mr. Vice President, but we can't be too careful these days. Stay here until I get clearance for you to go on in. You can wait in your vehicle, but I have to caution you that your driver is not to put it in gear."

"Okay, Captain, I'm used to the drill."

Retrieving his ID and a copy of the letter from President Scales, requesting him to come as soon as possible to the Rock, John tucked them back into his wallet and got back in the Humvee.

As they were getting set to go beyond the blast doors, several small deer galloped through the compound, none of them more than a few feet tall—they weren't speckled like fawns, though, and one of them had a strangely deformed head, far too big for its body.

The officer who had just checked them turned, saw the deer, and chuckled softly as if he was watching the antics of a favored dog or happy toddler.

Sergeant Benson laughed as they passed and John looked over at him quizzically.

"What the hell are they?"

"Sir, they're kind of like pets around here, we even feed them scraps, they'll eat right out of your hand. When this place got built in the fifties, a couple thousand acres were sealed off with fencing and barbed-wire barricades. Well, a whole herd of deer got trapped inside the wire, cut off from the rest of the world.

"Anyhow, that was seventy-plus years ago, and those deer just keep inbreeding and inbreeding. They got smaller across the years, and all sorts of defects started. I seen one of them had two heads, and that's the truth."

John detected a distinct Carolina accent, and though he'd always been terrible about linking names to faces, he thought there was something vaguely familiar about the man.

"I seem to know you."

"I was with the Black Mountain militia, sir, fought in the battle with the Posse."

"Did you now?"

"Even did a semester at Montreat, just before the war. Never had you in class, though."

John extended his hand, and the young man shook it enthusiastically. He was obviously pleased that so august a personage seemed to be taking an interest.

"And then what did you do?"

"Well, college and me didn't seem to mix. Went to work with my uncle at his garage down in Old Fort. Lucky we were up in Black Mountain on the day things hit. I was helping old Jim Bartlett with a VW bus. You folks let me stay and I fought in the war with the Posse. Got hit twice but that nurse, what was her name, Makala, pulled me through. My left leg will always be kinda numb and an inch shorter. Still I owe her my life and when next you see her send my thanks and respect."

"Your family down in Old Fort, did they survive?"

"My entire family got killed by the Posse. Dad and Uncle Jim wanted to make a stand there. I went down after the battle to check on them . . ." His voice trailed off.

Damn near everyone who survived after five years had their stories to tell, few of them pleasant, most carrying scars, in a world full of scarring.

"My family, everyone, those cannibals . . ." He turned and looked the other way, unable to continue.

John knew that everyone in this world now had that struggle. Any time his thoughts turned to Jennifer, his first Jennifer, as diabetes ravaged her slender body . . .

He too fell silent.

The sergeant, embarrassed, cleared his throat and looked back at John, eyes cloudy as he forced a smile.

"It's okay," John said, putting a reassuring hand on the man's shoulder. "We all have memories like that. So, anyhow, how did you wind up here, of all places?"

"Oh, that? After everything settled down a couple of years later, you and some other men were coming back home after the first fight here at the Rock, but there was nothing to hold me back there. Took a bike and went the five hundred miles up from Black Mountain to wind up here. For a little while there, right after the general was trying to get things going, some of the roads were pretty safe and I had no problems.

"I wouldn't want to try it now, though. Things really do seem to be falling apart big time. Anyhow, being a darn good mechanic, they welcomed me here. So that's my story, I guess."

John could well understand that. As things briefly settled down after the war, many a young man took to the road to find something different. The same thing had happened after the Civil War, especially for southerners who came home to a South in ruins and despair. Thousands of them finally turned west, to build a transcontinental railroad, the mines of Nevada, the burgeoning cattle ranches of Texas—someplace to start over again.

"Well, I guess the general—" He caught himself. "I mean the president is waiting, sir, let's get a move on."

As the young soldier put the Humvee in gear, the herd of deer came running back through the parking area.

"Just a second, sir."

The sergeant leaned out the open window and whistled. A couple of the deer stopped and looked up.

"Hey, Prancer, come here, boy."

Benson fished in his jacket pocket, pulled out a cracker from an MRE, and held it up. Prancer, the deformed one with a cancerous-looking growth on the side of his neck, came up nervously, reached out, snatched the cracker, and ran off.

"I would think you guys would have hunted them out for food a long time ago."

"Yeah, I know. But, well, with all their strange growths and such, folks just figured they weren't fit to eat. Besides, since we don't have dogs down below they're like pets here. Gosh, I do miss my dog." Again, the sad pause.

How many things we mourn, John thought. He was noticing something about this place. Nearly all the personnel were young—the guards, that somewhat insane pilot—and were keeping deer as pets because they had no dogs. He had yet to see someone much older than the twenty-five or so that he estimated was the pilot's age.

The mention of dogs instantly conjured up the memory of his two goldens, Zach and Ginger. Zach had been fatally injured by two thieves breaking into his house at the start of all the troubles. And Ginger . . . To try and feed his surviving daughter, Elizabeth, he shot Ginger and . . .

He cleared his throat with a cough and tried to smile. "Let's get going," he announced; otherwise he might lose it.

As they started forward there was a bit of a shudder, and black smoke poured out of the exhaust. Like so many things in this world, the engine was in need of an overhaul and a clean tank of fuel rather than the stuff they must be burning now.

They passed through the heavy blast doors and were plunged into darkness. Precious fuel was obviously not to be wasted on lighting the mile-long corridor. Either that or they were simply running out of light bulbs. It sloped at a five-degree angle as they weaved back and forth through long curving turns, deeper and deeper into the subterranean depths.

When originally constructed, the underground command center had been designed to survive a direct nuclear hit that was estimated to leave a crater a thousand feet across and three hundred feet deep. In the 1950s, the Soviets didn't even have ICBMs, and it was confidently hoped that the Nike rocket batteries would drop any bomber that approached, therefore not much worry was given to that scenario. Even for the America side back in the '50s, a missile getting within five miles of its target was considered to be a good hit.

But by the 1980s missile accuracy was down to within a few hundred yards. Whether Raven Rock would survive a strike was now problematic. The answer was to dig even deeper, and yet deeper still.

The doomsday game became a matter of going deeper as the missiles got more accurate. They might blast a crater a thousand feet wide and three hundred feet deep, but something would survive, still function, and months later as the radiation finally abated they would dig their way up and out. At least that was the plan, unless some mad fool clad the warheads with cobalt, in which case the radiation after detonation would last for years, not days. So there was some speculation that the underground shelter would need a minimum of a five-year supply of food and medicine to allow everyone to survive before digging out.

The drive continued downward into the semidarkness, the air becoming chilly and damp. The Humvee only had one headlight working, and John asked about it.

"Spare parts, sir. We're taking to cannibalizing vehicles that finally gave up the ghost. There's a regular graveyard of them by one of the other gates. Humvees, trucks, even a couple of tanks, an entire Abrams without a transmission. Given my background as a mechanic I help out a lot there."

They turned a corner in the tunnel. Here, the walls to either side were scorched, a wreck of some vehicle was pushed to one side, what little was left of it. Several soldiers were working to fish out salvageable parts from the wreckage and pile them up to one side.

Bob slowed, gingerly going around the wreck, and muttered a curse before speeding back up.

"What the hell was that?"

"Oh, that. Another one of those suicide squads, just yesterday. Third one this month. They had a Humvee, reportedly a civilian make—where the hell they got it nobody knows. Anyhow, it all seemed right, the gate was actually opened, them claiming they were carrying urgent dispatches. Even had forged credentials that looked right. Turns out a deserter was the leader. Well, the gate was actually open when the deserter was recognized and the shooting started. They barreled into the access tunnel, I heard they were going full blast until they turned a corner where a reaction squad was setting up. So, they blew themselves up. Killed eight of our people."

"Why, who were they?"

"You know, we still don't know for sure, there were no prisoners to question afterward. Thinking is, being suicides and such, that they were from one of these Messiah groups, or the followers of some nutjob who appeared down in Virginia and claims he's both God and Satan rolled into one. Survivors out there fall for these groups that offer a few square meals, some hash to smoke, and then they're told they can get the hell out of here and reach paradise.

"Hope the bastards burn in hell," he said softly. "A couple of good friends died thanks to that scum. One of them was an old girlfriend. Anyhow, it was a hell of a mess."

John said nothing. He found the fact they got this far inside troubling.

"She was a sweet, intelligent girl," Benson said softly as he shifted gears and continued down the darkened road, "but now she's gone. That's life now."

At last the tunnel suddenly broadened out to a huge underground complex. It was indeed an incredible sight, this main cavern carved out of solid rock, stretching out for a couple of hundred yards in each direction. Dozens of 1950s-style prefab structures lined the interior, row upon row of aging trailers and Quonset huts. When John had taken part in the assault on this place, it had been filled with the chosen lucky ones. Government officials from the now extinct United States of America, their families, corporate heads with the right inside pull at the highest levels and their families as well, evacuated in the hours just before the EMP strike and brought here to sit out what was to come. On that day, as realization had set in as to just how many of the elite had been quietly whisked away while hundreds of millions died, he had been filled with a cold rage. Even now it still troubled him deeply.

PART II

Which way I fly is hell; myself am hell.

—John Milton, *Paradise Lost*

CHAPTER ONE

The rows of trailers and Quonset huts they passed as they made their way down the long underground street covered several acres. More than a few of the structures had been burned out when this place was fought over, the ruins just left in place.

Only one overhead light in ten was lit, giving all of it a dark, gloomy aura of something just sinking into a twilight as the lights of this world slowly went out.

Turning a corner complete with a street sign—Washington and Main—they drove another few hundred yards to yet another checkpoint, this one as heavily manned as the one by the entry gate with another .30 caliber machine gun, a team of three sitting behind it. Another checking of papers as thorough as outside the gate before they were let through.

Benson drove the last few hundred yards to a squat bunker facility, near as big as a city block, with no outside windows. Again, it had that Cold War, hardened look to it. The only opening in the concrete structure was a heavy steel door on one side. The entire structure was mounted on steel springs that were thicker than John's wrist. If topside was indeed cratered hundreds of feet deep, this building could absorb the shock and keep on functioning as a command center.

Finally cleared through security, John climbed out of the Humvee and ascended the half dozen steps to the steel door, which Benson opened for him. As he stepped inside he felt an outrushing of air and realized that the building was over-pressurized, to keep any outside air from leaking in, in case there was any breach with radiation, chemical, or biological agents.

Inside, the place actually looked like typical government offices, walls painted the ubiquitous industrial green. The paint, however, was faded, dingy with age, perhaps not being repainted once in all the long years after it was first constructed. The overhead lighting was typical fluorescents, but more than a few of the long cylinder bulbs were darkened. On first impression, it was a worn-out place, like a tired old man who no longer bothered to wash and shave.

As he continued down the long corridor, John noticed that some of the side doors had small porthole windows with wire mesh imbedded in them against an electronic penetration. They passed doors every dozen feet or so, most with nameplates marking the rooms as offices for senators, all of them closed and darkened, and then offices of military personnel. The door to one office, marked COMMANDER USN, was half open.

John remembered his time in the Pentagon, the endless corridors and the jokes that some poor soul could wander in one day as a private and by the time he finally found his way back out he'd be a general ready to retire.

The admiral within the miniscule office caught John looking in, but rather than acting as if a very private domain was being pried into he smiled and stood from behind his desk. He started to shake hands but then changed his mind and saluted instead.

"You're the vice president, aren't you?" He was a man well into his late fifties or early sixties, with graying temples, deep-set blue eyes, and a face deeply wrinkled into a near squint. John instantly suspected here was a man who had stood many a watch at sea.

"Just John, please," he responded, and shook the man's hand.

"Vincent Youngblood."

John was taken aback. He would never forget that name. This man, who was now in command of what was left of the fleets that once dominated the world, had profoundly affected his own life.

John had talked to him only once before, a conversation that still haunted him. The navy had been in retreat throughout the world. It was coming home to a shattered America, and as ships docked, the once-mighty force simply bled away as men and women who'd formerly served without question now walked away, eager to find their families and protect them.

In that vast shakedown after the Day, Youngblood, in command of the proud aircraft carrier *Theodore Roosevelt*—the *TRex* as it was affectionately called by her sailors—had docked in Charleston, South Carolina, berthing at Patriots Point next to another legend, the *Yorktown* of World War II. He had received orders from the Pentagon to put back out to sea, but mutinied at that order, believing his duty now was to the survivors of Charleston. The carrier's nuclear generators could provide power to a quarter of a million people for a decade or more; its hospital still functioned, its workshops could still repair.

So there he had stayed, and as command structure collapsed, the four nuclear ballistic launch submarines based at Kings Bay, Georgia, fell into his command as well.

With the ballistic launch sites in the Dakotas and Montana eventually going offline, and the air force crumbling as well, the navy's nuclear deterrent, the "Force in Being," became that final line, and to Youngblood came the responsibility of keeping those four boomers operational.

As John stood before him, though, the one thing he most clearly recalled was the day he'd managed to get a call through to

Youngblood when he commanded what was still a viable hospital, and begged for insulin for his daughter.

The admiral had refused, and weeks later Jennifer died.

That was over four years ago. So much in the world had changed; he had been forced to accept so much. He understood why the admiral had said no, but still . . .

"The president and I are looking forward to seeing you, Mr. Matherson, so we better get in there."

Stepping out of the office, the admiral closed the door to that tiny office that now revealed how far the power of what was once America had fallen.

He led the way to a simple, bare conference room with a long table dominating. This room was brightly lit after the darkened corridor, and John blinked, adjusting to the light.

"John, just how the hell are you!"

He of course knew that voice. A commander of his long ago, that formal relationship blossoming into a friendship of more than two decades. General Robert E. Scales had been the one to stand by John's side when he married Mary, and it was Bob who again was by his side when she was buried, ten years later, such a young victim of breast cancer. Bob had, in a way, taken on the role of benign uncle for John's two children, and it was Bob's voice that was the last one he'd heard from the outside world on the Day that world ended.

Bob came around from his seat at the end of the table and embraced John warmly, slapping him on the back and shoulders, which had always been his way. It was an embrace of genuine warmth and not just for show.

"I see that you and the admiral have already met and no formal introductions are necessary, so let's sit down."

As John took a seat at the small table across from Bob, the initial flush of seeing a beloved old friend gave way to concern.

John had not seen Bob for over two years. When he left him then, Bob was still the hail-fellow-well-met type of leader. A man that radiated a genuine warmth and understanding for others. He was the type of leader who regularly got up at five in the morning, not to go out for a sunrise round of golf but to go to a mess hall and sit down over coffee and breakfast with some of his enlisted personnel. Not to lecture them, but instead to let them tell him like it truly was. He would go armed with a notepad, listen, and on more than one occasion by 0800 some officer was in his office for one hell of a dressing-down, to either set things right or have a new career plan because he was out of Bob's outfit. He was an officer that could be hell on those directly beneath him, and the best of them loved him for it.

But now, as John looked across at Scales, he knew something was wrong.

In the last few years Bob had aged a decade or more. His closely cropped full head of gray hair, formerly still streaked with some of his youthful blond, had gone nearly bald.

After his initial warm greeting he now sat with shoulders slightly hunched. His former healthy tan had given way to an almost sallow look.

In that instant John realized . . . the president was dying.

"Bob? You're sick, aren't you?" he asked gently.

"Why?" Bob asked. "Can you tell?"

That answer, of course, was typical General Scales bravado, but then he simply nodded his head. "Lung cancer."

"How bad?"

"I've got some time left."

John felt a sudden tightness in his throat but fought it down.

Bob forced a smile. "Well, now that we got that out of the way . . ."

"That's why you wanted me to come up here?" John wondered.

"Yes, John. You therefore know what I'm going to ask."

Christ, not that, John thought. Until this moment he'd assumed there were to be some rounds of meetings, that as usual he would be driven to near distraction by those meetings, there would then be some sort of resolution and announcement, and then he'd go back home.

"Don't ask it of me, Bob, I don't want it."

"Do you think I wanted this? Before the Day I was looking to move up to the mountains near you with Margaret, take up fly-fishing, basket weaving, hell I don't know, but I was planning to get out. And now this?" He chuckled sadly. "I'm asking you to take over as president, John."

As he spoke, Bob looked over at Admiral Youngblood and nodded.

"John, there's really no other choice," the admiral said.

"Why do you say that?" John replied. "You hardly know me."

"Let's get coldly real. Here's a situation report, if you like. I represent the sole barrier left between what was the eastern United States and the rest of the world. You see, I control four boomers—four fully armed ships loaded with submarine-launched ballistic missiles. Each of those ships has twenty-six missiles on board. Each missile has eight independent variable warheads that can be dialed up to deliver a three-hundred-kiloton explosion on land, at sea, and yes, in near space, providing an EMP burst. That's close to eight hundred warheads, John. That's what I'm sitting on."

"Why are you telling me this?"

"Because, John, I cannot be, I don't want to be, the one who has the sole authority to use them."

"Use them where, for God's sake?"

"Scenario one? China. They currently occupy the West Coast of the former United States. You know that. Someday they just might want the rest of the pie. I'm the deterrent.

"Scenario two. There are still other warheads—dozens, perhaps a hundred or more—loose in this crazed world we now live in. Then there is this new Soviet Union, inheriting the old Russian stockpile. India and Pakistan have what's left in their reserves, then Israel, the list goes on. Another strike, perhaps this time ground bursting some weapons on what little we have left? We and Israel certainly blasted a good part of the Middle East to dust in retaliation for the Day, but who knows what entity might still have a few nukes left and want to use them? Don't even need a missile, just float a tramp steamer into Charleston, for example, and blow it up. They have to know we will make the rubble bounce if they do that."

John sat in silence, feeling overwhelmed by this sudden turn of events.

"This new Soviet Union, of course, east of the Urals. They've been quiet; what rumors we have tell us that in the old style of Russians, they are busy revolting and rebelling on each other. Suppose the wrong person, another Stalin or Lenin, finally comes out on top and decides, 'What the hell, I'm going for it.' Again, we are the only deterrent.

"Is that enough for starters, John?"

"Christ in heaven." It came out a whisper.

"We have at least the semblance of a legitimate government," Bob said. "I might hang on a bit longer, the good Lord willing, but I need your agreement that when the time comes, you will take over for me."

Bob and Vincent both fell silent and now just stared at John, making him feel like a bug being examined under a magnifying glass . . . held by a boy who was now going to focus the beam to fry him.

"I need to think," he finally said. He reached over to a carafe filled with tepid black coffee, poured a cup, and drank it in several deep gulps. The caffeine that hit him a moment later made him feel a bit shaky.

The prospect of what was being asked of him horrified John. Although he was vice president, like most vice presidents he felt it to be a do-nothing job . . . but now? He recalled the shock expressed by

Teddy Roosevelt upon the assassination of McKinley, or Truman's comment that he felt as if a ton of bricks had suddenly been dumped on him with his new responsibility.

Bob chuckled softly in sympathy. "John, I wouldn't wish this burden on my worst enemy, let alone one of the few friends I seem to have left in this world.

"Nothing like being president to find out your true friends, John. Abe Lincoln had many a story; Harry Truman came to hate the job. At least he proved his honorability by going back to the house he owned in Independence, Missouri, and didn't see the presidency as a way to go for the cash cow afterward. You can tell a lot about a man or woman who serves the public then goes back to a former private life, unlike the last ones we had, with their thirty-million-dollar book deals and mansions in the Hamptons."

Bob grinned. "Well, when I retire at least give me a lifetime supply of good scotch and I'll be content."

John was still having trouble taking everything in. "I need a break to think about this long and hard," he finally said.

"Fair enough," Bob agreed.

John knew there was something more going on. He could sense it. Was it that they wanted him to say he would do it, so they could then spring an "oh by the way"?

"Damn, I could use a cigarette just about now," he whispered.

To his utter amazement Bob reached into his breast pocket and pulled out a pack of Marlboros, actual Marlboros, tossed them over, and slid a Zippo lighter across the table.

"Damn you," John gasped. "I thought you quit years ago, before . . ."

"Yeah, I did, and they're now killing me years later. I remember you as a heavy smoker, actually it was a check mark against you on fitness reports. Had a feeling, though, that when a ton of bricks gets dumped on a man, to hell with not indulging in old vices. There's scotch inside that cabinet over there as well."

Admiral Youngblood smiled, opened the cabinet, and pulled the bottle out. It was a good twelve-year single malt. He poured three glasses and slid one over to Bob, another to John. He sat down and held his glass up.

"I won't toast to you yet, John. We might as well lay out the rest. But damn me, I will take one of those cigarettes if you do."

John, still a bit shaky from the coffee, not to mention what he'd just been told, opened the pack, drew one out for himself and one for Vincent. He lit his and drew the smoke in, and oh how glorious it felt for a few seconds. As every smoker knew, you could be quit of them for years but then in an instant of weakness be drawn straight back in by their seductive power.

Bob took only the scotch.

"I'll pass on the cancer stick," he said, "though I wish I could join you. Maybe I will before I die, but not yet."

A moment of silence followed, the three lost in their own thoughts. Finally it was Vincent who spoke.

"All right, Bob, let the cards fall. What is bothering you? What the hell is happening here?"

"Like I said, I fear the Republic is collapsing, you know that. We're putting up a false front."

"What the hell?" John said. "You're asking me to be the next president of a republic that is failing? Why?"

"That's the other aspect of this equation," Bob announced.

"Perhaps the most pressing of them all," Vincent chimed in.

Bob looked over at Vincent as if there was hesitation on his part.

"There's a new entity in play now," Bob finally said.

"What, aliens from space?" He wouldn't be half surprised at this point if that was indeed the case.

"In a way you might very well be right," Bob replied. "His name is General Joshua V. Lawrence, and you're about to meet him face-to-face in a few hours. He's the other reason I want you to stay and become president."

Bob tossed a briefing packet over to John, who opened it and studied the few pages of notes contained within.

Astonished, he looked at the two other men.

"You're kidding."

There was no reply.

CHAPTER TWO

They had given him a few hours to, in Vincent's words, think it over and try to take a nap. After being led to a small private space, barely more than a cubicle with a bed, he actually did try to sleep, but too much was happening. At some point he must have dozed off, though, because he was awakened by an insistent knock on the door.

He stood up, feeling groggy, and stretched.

The room smelled dank, even moldy, thanks to the same damp, stale air he'd been breathing since coming into the depths of Raven Rock. Other things had caught his eye after meeting with Bob and getting a meal of a hamburger, fries, and a glass of water. He noticed that everything around him felt used and worn-out. The simple burger was the best the lone cook could make for him. The few personnel around him in the café seemed to have a universally tired look to them, huddled in a corner and talking in low whispers. They obviously didn't know who he was, and he sensed they looked at him with suspicion. Gone was a media age where every day even a vice president would have his picture plastered all over the news.

This was his first visit back to the Rock since they took it years ago. He had spent all that time in Black Mountain, running a college, and he knew he'd just been stashed away for use if the unthinkable ever happened.

He was realizing that although this place was capable of housing up to five thousand people for several months, and though it hosted far fewer than that now, it was never intended for usage that might go on for years without relief and resupply from the outside world.

What was the state of the air-supply systems? He assumed they must be supported by complex filtration units that could screen out everything including fallout, bioweapons, and chemicals.

For humidity control, the pumps needed to bring water from the outside, filter it, and then filter it again before it was pumped into massive cisterns. What state were they in after five years of continual use, with most likely no logistical support from the wider world?

It was obvious, as well, that they were on severe electrical use. These were things he'd never inquired about or even really thought of in his brief time here previously; he just figured the electricity came from the usual diesel-fed generators.

As he lay in the small cubicle after his meal, he'd realized that of course they would have put a nuke reactor in here, most likely the standard military type used in subs and carriers. At reduced power, that would be good for a decade to come, but then again, what about the personnel who ran it, and what about the constant oversight and repairs needed?

That and a dozen other questions had plagued his weary mind about this place until he'd drifted off into a deep, exhausted sleep.

Now, having been woken from his nap, he splashed water on his face in the closet-size bathroom attached to his cubicle and looked for a paper towel to dry his hands. There were none to be had. Such little things often could say much. He used a shirt sleeve instead and stepped back out into the corridor, where Admiral Youngblood waited.

"Lead on," John told him.

They weaved down the corridor and stopped at a single elevator.

Youngblood used a key to get in, and then another key to activate the elevator. The panel marked four floors. John did remember that—the complex was laid out on four levels of nearly half a million square feet per floor. As they descended, the lights in the elevator flickered in an unnerving fashion.

The elevator stopped at the bottom but the door didn't open.

Christ, John thought, *is it broken?*

But Youngblood opened the control panel, revealing a slot within for a single key. He took a plastic card from under his shirt, slipped it into the slot, and punched a sequence into the keypad.

The elevator lurched and then dropped. Not precipitously, but enough to surprise John. It stopped again after what he figured was a few hundred feet or more, and the door slid open.

He wondered what he would see—would it be some Strangeloveian set with a '60s retro feel, flashing computers whirling and clicking?

There was nothing ahead but a darkened corridor with a single steel door at the far end.

"I'm leaving you here, John."

"What?"

"I'll explain it all sometime. I have no need to see Lawrence at this time, and prefer he didn't know I was here. Good luck to you, John, you'll need it. By the time you get back I'll be gone. I'll actually be smuggled out of here, for your information, and plan to be back in Charleston in time for a shrimp and she-crab soup dinner. We're having a good season for that, you'll have to bring your wife down to try some."

They shook hands.

"One final thing, John. This meeting was you and Bob Scales only. Nothing about me. Do we understand each other?"

"I think so."

"You're gonna find this interesting, John. And by the way, Bob

Scales has always thought the world of you. In a way, he views you as a younger brother. He's a good man, John, but his days, to be blunt, are just about finished. It's your turn, like it or not, to step up to the plate. Just go through that door, you'll find it to be very interesting indeed."

He stepped back into the elevator, the doors closed, and John was alone.

CHAPTER THREE

Opening the door in front of him, John stepped into a brightly lit hallway—spartan, like everything else here. General Scales was waiting for him on the other side, sitting in, of all things, an electric golf cart.

"Get in, John, we're going for a little ride." They started down the corridor at a walking pace. "John, we're on a level here that none of us knew about on the day we took over this place three years ago. It wasn't on any of the maps or diagrams of this place—it was an anomaly. I thought I had a damn high level of security clearance, but the military, as you know, sure likes to compartmentalize.

"In the months after we took Raven Rock, as you know we kicked out just about everyone, except for some of the families on the top level, who we gave compassionate housing to. Sending the bureaucrats out into the cold cruel world, that was easy—let the bastards see the world they left behind.

"You might remember there were several hundred military personnel in here as well, and some high-rankers from the Pentagon came too, just before the shit hit the fan. A lot of folks were just junior-rankers, older NCOs, the usual captains and majors who were deskbound climbers. Only a handful from the top.

"As we tried to get a handle on this place, my big concern was just the day-to-day running of the place. Remember, it was a full-size military base. How did things run, when you flushed the toilets where did it go, how's the air filtration, how often do you change the filters. Many of the personnel normally stationed here wanted to just leave. I couldn't hold them by force, so replacements had to be recruited and trained. That explains why we now have so many kids in their twenties. Idealists, many of them, who in the world after the Day wanted something to believe in again. So they got trained; the ones who had been computer nerds before our war even upgraded some things. We found some good mechanics to fix cars and such, but where in hell could we recruit an air conditioning specialist? So every day down in this hole became a challenge of keeping it up and running, even on the dullest, most peaceful day.

"But still we hemorrhaged personnel, especially the older ones with families. Most of those folks asked to go out of here, promising to return with their families if they found them still alive. Hell, wouldn't you, wouldn't anyone?"

John could only nodded his head in agreement.

"I gave all of them leave, said if they wanted they could go outside and hopefully find loved ones and, if so, bring them back. Quite a few hundred finally left. I think, to date, less than twenty have come back, kids and parents in tow, and we used the old vacated Quonset huts to house them, though the strain on our resources was beginning to tell.

"We still had a few residents left over from before, frankly because we needed their expertise if we had any hope of rebuilding. We were also sheltering a few top wigs, some who were in on what really happened that day and got evacuated to this place before everything happened, and the few that managed to get here afterward."

Bob shook his head. "I wanted to shoot all of them, I really did," he said angrily, "but of course I couldn't. I thought I wanted to tell them to get the hell out and fend for themselves like the rest of the world was doing."

They finally rolled to a stop in front of a steel door. Bob sat back and let out an exhausted sigh. "It was a mistake, at least with some of them."

"How so? I know I was tempted to shoot them myself, after all the suffering we saw while they luxuriated here in a safe, cozy bunker."

"John, this place, Site R, is like one of those Russian dolls. You know, open up the big one, there's one inside it, open that, another one, and so on down."

"Meaning what?"

"Well, to start, after we took the place over we figured out the oil-fired heating and cooling of this place was just a front. We found that a further level down there was a nuclear reactor. It's aging, identical to the ones Rickover started putting into our subs back in the fifties. We figured that out almost at the start, and thank God for it, otherwise this site would have been abandoned long ago.

"We found more food supplies than we first thought. Hell, they were feeding several thousand people two meals a day for two years, but there was a warehouse level below the main one that was stocked to Doomsday.

"You know the military when it gets something right. You got enough to do X so why not make it two X, why not ten X. So some things we were good on. Hell, at the time I figured this place would function for a while, several months till we got the new government up and running, then we'd go topside. Even talked, as you know, about making Frederick the new capital. But those dreams faded."

Bob paused for a moment and shook his head.

"So many damn dreams. Thirteen states again, but in reality, it sure has proven to be a half-ass dream."

John didn't reply. It was a dream he still wanted to believe in.

"It proved impossible, as you know, to get even a quorum of delegates together in one place to ratify our reincorporation. Hell, it was easier to travel from Massachusetts to here back in 1787 than it is now. So we at least hooked up via what computers were coming back online to link us that way, and then . . ." His voice trailed off as he realized who he was talking to. "I'm rambling, you already know all that. Let's focus on what is on the other side of that door. Okay?"

Bob got out of the golf cart, then reached into his pocket to pull out a flask and handed it to John. "The last of my stash. Save it for later." He fished into his other pocket for a pack of cigarettes, handed them over, hesitated, and then handed over his Zippo as well. Bob then went up to the blast door, punched in an elaborate code of at least eight digits, and slid his card in. The door slowly opened.

It was a monster of a blast door of reinforced steel, three feet thick, anchored by six sliding bolts as thick as his arm. Beyond the door it was brightly lit, almost like day. Two fully armed sentries waited inside, M4s at their side, equipped with flak vests and sidearms, immovable as sphinxes.

Another vehicle was parked behind them, this one a Humvee, two officers in uniform standing to either side.

"A moment, John." Bob looked up at the two officers, who nodded but said nothing.

"I asked you here to do this for us, John. There is a whole other world on the far side of this blast door. Surprisingly, Admiral Youngblood knew about it, but never said a word until three days ago.

"John, in our ramblings around in this stygian relic of a base we were most puzzled by this lowest level, the three airlock doors we ran across here, and one more over in another corridor wide enough to drive a tank through. The doors would not budge, absolutely computer encoded to the hilt. A couple of those kids I mentioned who were computer nerds finally broke the code. They opened the door and this realm was found on the other side.

"Anyhow, it was then that Youngblood, who knew about it, passed the message that a meeting was desired between myself and those on the other side. They insisted it had to be me or no one."

John looked over at his old friend, ready to ask, *Then why me, and what the hell is this?*

Bob seemed to read his mind. "I know, why you rather than me. It's simple, John, I'm dying. My head is clear for the moment, though I did drop the painkillers five days ago while thinking about this and then deciding you were the only one who can go. When I go back upstairs there's a doctor there with a needle. No, I'm not committing suicide or anything like that, too much of a Catholic here, but I will certainly be dosed up within the hour and get the first decent sleep I've had in days.

"You remember FDR and your history, of course. Ten months before he died, the doctors knew he was terminal, that congestive heart failure or a stroke would kill him. But he refused to step down. When he went to Yalta in January 1945, he was a hollow shell of what he had once been. And there he met Stalin, and more than a few believe he settled for a peace of weakness rather than facing the Russian down and insisting on what would have been justice for Poland and Eastern Europe and the millions of refugees from those nations that he condemned to the gulag for fleeing to our side. It was a crime that he agreed to force those millions to be handed back over into the clutches of Stalin. Churchill was appalled but could do nothing to stop him, and two and a half months later he was dead, and two months after that Churchill was out of office.

"John, there is an establishment we never knew about on the other side of this door. They survived the Day, and they've survived the five years since. I don't know if they are a new Dark Age, or if they can be reasoned with, perhaps even allied to.

"I refuse to be FDR. Thus, you will act in my stead. Maybe if we had more time I could have briefed you on so many things in my final weeks, then peacefully resigned. That's not an option now. We know about them, therefore they insist on meeting. We finally agreed that you will meet with them instead of me."

"Well, that is a whole hell of a lot to take in."

"Way it's gotta be, John. Your safety is guaranteed, they're not stupid enough to hold you or kill you, at least I think they're not. They agreed to have you back in two days, tops. So anyhow . . ." His voice faltered, and without another word he turned and went back through the door. After climbing back into the cart, he reversed it, then drove off into the dark.

"Mr. Vice President?"

The officer on the passenger side was holding the door open. John got in, and the door was closed behind him. Silently the vehicle started forward.

"May I ask where we are going at least?"

The captain who was driving looked back and offered a smile. "Camp David."

"Camp David? That's ten miles away."

"Underground is shorter, only six miles."

"What?" John was stunned.

"There's been a tunnel from Camp David to Site Raven Rock for years. But, then again, I guess you didn't know that, did you, sir?"

What could John say, as the shock of that set in. They'd held Site R for three years, and never realized there was another passage in from six long miles away. As they drove on, John realized the engine was silent.

"Is this thing electric?" he asked.

"Yes. Most of our underground transportation fleet is electrified, no carbon monoxide exhaust to worry about."

If they used electric vehicles, they must have a darn good power source for charging. He considered endless possibilities as they drove on at a silent thirty-mile-per-hour clip.

Doors flashed past, all of them armored, several with sentries standing in alcoves. A convoy of several Humvees had pulled to one side to let them pass. As they passed one brightly lit alcove, the armored door opened, revealing a flash for a second of what was on the far side, but he couldn't make it out.

"Just what the hell is this place?" he asked.

No one answered.

CHAPTER FOUR

After ten minutes of driving, the electric Humvee finally started to slow down. John estimated that they had traveled at least five miles. It was hard to judge distance on a two-lane corridor in the darkness that seemed to go on forever. They passed through an open armored door with sentries to either side. The guards, like all the others, were smartly turned out in spotless uniforms, M4s at their sides. They snapped to attention and saluted as the vehicle passed.

Was that salute meant for the officers up front or for me? he wondered. And were they there as showpieces of a world that looked precise, neat, clean, and efficient—unlike Raven Rock?

They continued for another fifty yards beyond the steel door and then the cavern opened into a broad concourse, a half acre or more in size. The general surroundings looked similar to Raven Rock: rough-hewn walls, ceiling soaring up twenty feet or more. Several pillars of rock marched down the center of the concourse like giant sentries supporting the ceiling overhead. It was hard to judge but it seemed as if the underground road they had traveled was pitched downward the entire way, so this cavern must indeed be far deeper than the Rock. *How deep underground are we?* he wondered. He knew the chambers of Raven Rock were carved well over a thousand feet deep—were they now even deeper? Fifteen hundred, maybe two thousand feet, or more?

He remembered how when he was a kid Camp David was billed as the weekend mountain home of presidents going back to FDR, who first called it Shangri-La. The name changed when Eisenhower renamed it after his grandson. The new name lent it a bit of a folksy charm, the retreat up in the beautiful Catoctin Mountains where the president could relax, fish, invite foreign dignitaries to visit, and knock off for a pleasant mountain weekend. It never had a Cold War, or even hot war feel to it. Just a few dozen cabins, a small conference center, and the ubiquitous helicopter pad on the surface. At least, that's what was visible to the public and the media.

Rumor, pretty well confirmed, had it that Vice President Cheney had been whisked to Raven Rock on 9/11. Not Camp David. But was he? Raven Rock was often called the best-kept secret that was not a secret, so had they actually whisked him to Camp David instead?

It was under our noses all along, John now realized, *and no one thought different.*

The concourse was squared off, no visible blast barricades, just a dozen or so corridors running off into the dark. He spotted what looked like a canteen just inside one walkway: a long table, a few chairs and tables out front. From the angle he was sitting at it even looked like there was a lit-up menu board with a fast-food look to it, offering coffee, breakfast sandwiches, and such.

Once the vehicle stopped the captain in the driver's seat got out and opened John's door.

"If you'll follow me, sir."

"Wait just a minute, will you."

John looked around the concourse. He had a sense that this was some sort of hub—the canteen, another sitting area at the far side with tables and chairs, a bar even, with liquor bottles lined up.

But no one was there. On the opposite wall he saw more tables and chairs, another bar that was shuttered. It was even decorated with some posters—the usual for a military institution: oversized prints of pastoral settings, a sunset, a mountain covered with snow. One whole row of prints depicted the Catoctin Mountains: streams, fir-clad hills, a back-country road lined by split-rail fences. It felt like an attempt to bring into this cave a feel for what was on the outside.

The artificiality of it gave John the creeps.

"This way, sir?" the captain pressed, this time somewhat officiously.

"Just a minute, Captain, maybe I need a few answers right here before we go further."

"Everything will be explained, sir."

In a minute. He reached into his pocket, produced the pack of cigarettes and lighter.

"Sir, no smoking is permitted within the facilities," a pause, "sir." The second *sir* had a sharp emphasis.

"Indulge me then," John replied, wanting to take a moment more to gather in what information he could. He defiantly lit the cigarette anyhow, damn they were stale, and stood in silence, trying to get a sense of this concourse. At first glance it had the look of some sort of off-duty place for personnel to relax, have a cold beer and a sandwich. But it was so damn sterile as well. Of course there were places like this at Raven Rock. After years of use they had acquired a dingy, run-down look, like you'd find at all those remote military outposts in half-forgotten locations. But here, the light was bright, almost too bright.

He only took a couple of puffs, not inhaling, then went to flick it out and stopped, unsure what to do with it. Throw it on the ground, pinch it off?

"Just throw it on the ground," a pause, "sir. Someone will pick it up."

There was a real note of reproach in his voice. John was starting to develop a real dislike for this captain.

"All right, let's go."

As they walked toward a set of double doors at the far end of the concourse, they were pulled open from the inside by two crisply dressed NCOs in standard fatigues, who flanked the doorway and came to attention.

A lone officer came out to greet them, wearing the old World War II–style uniform. The uniform looked as if it had come straight from the tailor, the standard trousers known as "pinks"; shoes polished to a mirror finish; an old-style Eisenhower jacket, belted at the waist; just two of the standard "spaghetti" ribbons over the left breast, topped by the blue of a combat infantry badge with paratrooper wings above that.

John, practiced from his own years in the military, noted that unit insignias were missing on the shoulder and, interesting as well, he wore no insignia of rank.

He judged the man approaching him to be in his early to mid-fifties. He was what he would call "soldier lean," a man who obviously worked out religiously every day. His hair was cut military short, gone mostly now to gray. He was tanned, and that caught John's attention. Personnel who had been working under Raven Rock, some of them for several years, had a pale, almost ghostly look to them regardless of ethnicity.

His features were chiseled, eyes an almost translucent blue-gray. He looked like he could have stepped out of a recruiting poster from the Second World War. He came up close, then extended his hand.

"John Matherson, I presume?" He shook hands with a powerful grip, almost too powerful, which John tried to match with barely equal strength.

The way he phrased this greeting instantly reminded John of the famous meeting between Henry Morton Stanley and Dr. Henry

Livingstone, and he was convinced this man had chosen his words on purpose.

"I'm General Joshua Lawrence."

There was a pause of several seconds as they stared intently at each other. This man seemed to radiate a confident something, that indefinable quality that in seconds defined him as out of the ordinary. It was far too early to say this man had charisma, the way a rare few do from the moment you first meet them, but John instinctively sensed it was there.

"I was not informed until just minutes ago that you were replacing General Scales. Barely enough time to get a quick briefing on you, but I have heard of you before."

"If you mean President Scales, sir, he's indisposed."

Lawrence did not respond to that. John suspected he had referred to Bob as General Scales for a reason.

The general forced a smile. "So then, Mr. Vice President, may I convey my respects and the hope that he has a speedy recovery. We have excellent medical facilities here if the president should need further treatment."

Did this man know that Bob was dying of cancer?

"Let's go to an office where we can sit down, have a drink and a good heart-to-heart talk."

Without waiting for a reply, General Lawrence took John by the elbow to guide the way, a move that John always hated as being far too personal. He wanted to shake it off but decided it was best not to.

They passed two more sets of doors, these flanked by guards as well, then came to a heavy steel door which slid open to reveal a conference room, decorated in what John would have called "Big Brass office": thick leather chairs; a solid oak desk; bookshelves lined with actual books, some of them ancient-looking with ornate leather bindings; and a sideboard, topped by a couple of cut-glass decanters filled with what John assumed was some well-seasoned scotch or bourbon.

The desk was bare except for a small stack of official reports and a couple of those richly bound volumes, thick with book markers. Lawrence went to the decanter on the sideboard, poured some of the contents into a glass, then looked over at John.

"Do you want yours with a splash of soda and ice?"

John accepted, and Lawrence handed him the glass. It was one of those standard military ones, emblazoned with the emblem of the Eighty-Second Airborne. Lawrence poured his own drink, ceremonially held up his glass, smiled, and then took a sip and sat down.

"Were you with the Eighty-Second?" John asked.

"Yes, it was my first combat assignment as a company commander. I've had affection for it ever since. If memory serves me, you were in Iraq."

"I was, a long time ago."

There was an extended pause as Lawrence studied him over his drink. Finally John broke the silence.

"I'll open, then. Just why am I here?"

"I had wanted to finally have a talk with Scales, but you are here instead, so let's get down to it. I will say again that if President Scales needs medical help, it's here for him."

"He's doing just fine."

"Cancer, that's what it is, isn't it?"

John said nothing.

"There have been rumors, John, no sense in hiding it."

John found himself wondering indeed how this man knew such a well-kept secret. He remained silent.

"Okay, John, let's drop the beating around the bush. Ask me anything and I'll talk. Okay?"

John put his glass down, having barely touched the drink, and leaned forward. "All right then, just what the hell is this place, for starters."

"Good opening, straight to the point. Obviously you didn't know, in fact your little government inside Raven Rock definitely didn't know, that we even existed."

Lawrence stood up, took his time pouring a bit more scotch, then took a sip and remained standing as he continued.

"A little history first. We all know that it was President Eisenhower who mandated the excavation of Raven Rock back in the early fifties as a fallback position for the Pentagon's top command structure to evacuate to in time of war.

"He of course got his inspiration from what we discovered in the final months of World War Two. Eisenhower saw firsthand the vast underground facilities excavated by the Nazis as they lost the above-ground war for the air. Caves large enough for factories—hell, they were building entire V2 rockets inside them, with tens of thousands of slave laborers. Under Berlin there were shelters to house tens of thousands, places like the Führer's bunker. In fact, some of them wouldn't be discovered until years afterward.

"With the Soviet threat becoming a nuclear threat, with their first low-yield nukes starting in 1949, and then city-busting thermonuclear weapons by 1953, it was obvious to anyone that Washington would eventually be hit. So Eisenhower started to dig, to put us underground.

"I'm not telling you anything you don't already know, of course. Raven Rock wasn't the only one, either. There was so-called Mount Weather just outside of Winchester, Virginia, Greenbrier up in West Virginia for the civilian government. They went so far afield as even little Asheville, North Carolina, building a small complex that would be run by NASA and could serve as a place for the Supreme Court to hide as well. And of course the big one, started in the late fifties, out in Colorado at Cheyenne Mountain.

"So there you have it." He fell silent and gave John a smile as if satisfied by this vast creation around him. His delivery was that of an officer, a man in charge and confident of himself. He leaned against the side table and looked into his glass and chuckled.

"I remember an old movie, some years ago. Do you like old movies, John?"

"When we used to get them, sure. Old political thrillers mainly, but it's been several years since I've seen one."

Lawrence chuckled. "You and me both. Always was partial to *Seven Days in May* with Burt Lancaster."

Surprised, John looked at his host more carefully. He'd just referred to a political thriller from the early 1960s about a plot to overthrow the government. John wondered if there was deeper meaning to that casual remark.

"Speaking of movies, you might remember the film about alien contact, the usual run-of-the-mill story. Billions are spent for a spaceship to reach out to the aliens, and just as they're ready to get the thing launched it's blown up by a terrorist. It seems like the whole project is lost until the main character intervenes and an identical spaceship is revealed, built in secret on the far side of the earth, with the line 'Why build one, when you can always build two.'"

John waited for him to get to the point.

"Camp David was six miles from Raven Rock. Allegedly a presidential vacation retreat built by FDR. It seemed to be just that—a place to go on weekends for some mountain air and relaxation. Eisenhower comes along and he was a helluva lot smarter than some people gave him credit for, and I think it became obvious. Why build one when you can build two.

"Let Raven Rock be the fallback for the military in the Pentagon. It's always been a secret that is really not all that secret, at least on the outside of the mountain."

"So a second site was built here, right under Camp David," John said.

Lawrence smiled. "But of course, John. By the way, may I call you John?"

He shrugged noncommittedly.

"Let's just go first names in private, John; Joshua is fine. With a last name of Lawrence, my father was something of a Civil War historian, so Joshua, for Joshua Lawrence Chamberlain was an obvious choice.

"Anyhow, back to our little narrative. How do you build a huge underground bunker fifteen hundred feet deep, capable of most likely surviving a nuclear strike, and no one ever suspects?"

"Build it here?"

"Exactly. It's really an obvious choice when you realize it. Why build one when you can build two, the second one right under the nose of the world, especially the Soviets, back then. Six miles from Raven Rock they blasted out millions of tons of rock and hauled it away by truck, mixing it in with the millions of tons of debris from the making of Raven Rock, and no one was the wiser. Maybe some bright boys will finally just do the calculations of x number of tons, by y number of trucks, and maybe one day it won't add up. But no one's done that yet.

"So John, thus we have a whole other facility at Camp David. Next job, dig another tunnel six miles long, from here to just outside Raven Rock. "Hauling all that rock from here to there, sooner or later somebody might have finally put two and two together. So what is the alternative?

"You most likely never noticed, but literally just across the road from Raven Rock there's a rather large quarry, called Aggregate Mountain. They even had a nice web page back in the day. Ever notice it?"

"Come to think of it, no."

Joshua smiled. "The beauty of it all. Just hide in plain sight and no one will ever notice. Site R, or Raven Rock, for all the secrecy, most people never understood the true secret nature about it. Did you ever try to drive up there?"

"Once. As we evacuated the civilians after we took the place. Yeah, it did strike me then."

"What, pray tell, struck you?"

"There are no real roads in and out. Some two-lane country roads in ill repair, but yeah, I thought even then that there was something wrong with the thought that they could evacuate thousands from the Pentagon to this location. The nearest four-lane highway, which was built back in the fifties, stopped south of Gettysburg, I think it was Emmitsburg, where that Catholic college is located. I didn't give it that much thought, though, at the time."

"Precisely!" Joshua poured himself another ounce of scotch, then offered the decanter to John, whose glass was now empty, and he nodded a thanks. He actually started to reach into his pocket for a cigarette, the old habits already back, but hesitated.

"Hooked on the weed again, are we?"

"Yeah, it happens."

"Go ahead, we have a good filtration system here, as you might have noticed. It's over-pressurized for defense against the usual hazards. Wait, John, don't smoke that shit. It's bad for you."

John was taken aback—was Lawrence messing with him, or insulting the fact that he smoked? But then the general leaned back, smiled, and opened a drawer.

"I think we have some far better tobacco. British, in fact." He produced a carton of Dunhill cigarettes and tossed them across the table.

John looked at the carton with open surprise. *How the hell?* He opened the carton up, drew out a pack, and lit one up. It was fresh, and tasted wonderful. There was also a giveaway here that whatever was going on with Lawrence and this place, they were getting outside supplies—from England, no less.

"Anyhow, back to the access and that quarry. You're right, the roads are secondary at best, and that was for a reason. But the aggregate quarry, that might have been a giveaway, so they had a perfect cover story.

"Nice well-paved three-lane road just a few miles away from Raven Rock, straight to the quarry, forty-ton loads of crushed rock going out every hour, twenty-four seven . . . for years. Even had the perfect dummy front that supplied over half of all the aggregate in the lower forty-eight for roofing shingles. Millions and millions of shingles, with a limitless supply of rock. Maybe something of a giveaway to an astute observer—just try to go up there, you know, a chamber of commerce or a Boy Scout troop tour of the place. They had a nice front office, the usual PR type flak. Actually he was usually a major or one of our lieutenant colonels being sidelined but given a nice way to set out his last years to retirement.

"Needless to say, even as Raven Rock was finished we were of course still digging away. We worried for quite some time that some investigative type would start asking questions. The quarry had a few anomalies, like a high fence topped by concertina wire, and security cameras, actually a bit too like Raven Rock. There were signs stating no public access, but you could inquire about visits at an eight hundred number and hardly anyone called. The few that did, there'd be a background check, of course.

"So people just ignored the fact that this so-called quarry was still digging away, and never guessed what it was really digging. And there you have it. The tunnel was dug from Raven Rock to Camp David, eventually two lanes wide as you saw on your way here. On the surface with Raven Rock, though, there's just that narrow two-lane country road full of twists and turns. In fact, in case the curious did drive up we always had a guy out on the road just short of the gate. Looked like an overfed construction type who would get out of his folding chair and actually put out a barrier sign, 'Road temporarily closed,' then sit back down.

"A few conspiracy types wrote about that, even postulated that

Raven Rock held some darker secrets, a fluff-up just before the Day, claiming it was a base for aliens. Fine with us, because it worked for what was wanted—no one even suspected that there was something buried even deeper six miles away at Camp David.

"So, call that the short history of Raven Rock and here."

Joshua motioned over to the decanter of scotch. John shook his head.

"You've told me a lot," John said, "but then again you've told me nothing."

"What else do you want to know?"

"Why are you here? What are you doing here? How many personnel do you have and what exactly is your mission?"

General Lawrence sat down behind his desk and smiled. "Speculate."

"What?"

"Indulge me."

"And if I don't?"

"Then there really isn't much more to say for now. We'll chat about Raven Rock, how things there are increasingly winding down. Lack of spare parts, machines after all these years starting to give out. I understand your humidifier system has given up the ghost. Except for individual small units in key places like computer and telecommunications areas, the rest is starting to feel like a damp cave."

How would he know such details, sitting here six miles away?

John sat quietly, using his empty glass as an ashtray as he lit another cigarette. That triggered from Lawrence a flicker of emotion, a flash of hardening in the eyes, a slight tilting of the head. Was it the smoking itself that bothered him, or the use of a glass emblazoned with the insignia of the Eighty-Second as an ashtray?

John had to develop a profile of this guy, or for that matter the real reason they were even meeting, to report back to Bob. He sensed already this man was the type of leader that was not manufactured at West Point or the Naval Academy but was one who was naturally born to lead. John did notice that the only jewelry General Lawrence wore was an academy ring.

In the time he had served overseas, a very long time ago when John was a captain, Bob a lieutenant colonel, Bob had that quality that no amount of training could ever create. The one percent of true leaders at the top were quite simply born with it, and John saw it in Lawrence too.

The spotless, starched-to-razor-sharp crease to his uniform— was that simply the mark of a commander who looked the part? Still, there was something understated about the man. John was reminded about leaders like General Grant who wore the simple four-button jacket of a private when in the field, compared with Omar Bradley's simple battle dress or, at the other extreme, the legendary sartorial splendor of General Montgomery. He realized the adage was true not to judge someone by their clothing. In fact, Lawrence disdained all the spaghetti of Good Conduct Medals and such, with only two small ribbons beneath the Combat Infantry Badge and paratrooper pin, the two being a Distinguished Service Cross and a Purple Heart with a single star denoting a second wound.

John assumed that was the reason for the slight limp he detected on the walk to this office, and, scanning the room for any other details, his gaze fixed on a cane of polished hickory in the corner.

He looked back at Joshua, cast a flicker of a gaze over to the cane, and then back.

"Some time back, John, I'll tell you about it sometime."

Again silence for a moment, Lawrence's demeanor giving away nothing, as he waited for John to make the next move. John decided to go for broke and see what happened.

"Well, General, it's nice to know we are neighbors. We've existed side by side for three years without that knowledge, though I assume you definitely knew about us. You're a mystery to me, to be sure, as to why you exist and did not make your presence known until we cracked that door. You haven't caused us any harm, at least none that I know of.

"From what little I could see, your base here is comfortable, well run, but since you are not forthcoming with answers to my obvious questions, perhaps we shall call it a day. I'm not in the mood for walking, so if I could get a ride back to my facility I'd appreciate it."

John stood up. He could see his sudden decision to simply leave caught Lawrence off guard, but the general said nothing. Snuffing out his cigarette and putting the glass on the table, he watched to see how General Lawrence would react.

For several seconds he was met with a sphinxlike, impenetrable gaze, then an ever so subtle hint of a small smile, which for the first time John read as being almost sinister, as if he'd expected John to be fumbling over himself with questions.

"Fine then, let's call it a day. One of my men will drive you back to your base."

Lawrence stood up, again that handshake with a little too much pressure.

"Before you leave," Lawrence announced, taking a plain, light green envelope from his desk and handing it over to John. "For your president. I had a feeling he would not be the one to come. We know how sick he is. I've always heard he is one hell of a leader. He has to be, to pull off what he did, and given his condition now, he had no desire to come here like another Roosevelt. So please convey this to him."

As John took the envelope, for a split second his own decades of military service came to the fore and he instinctively came to attention, but he stopped himself, of course, from saluting. There was indeed something about this man that triggered such a response.

"When your side is ready to meet for real and deal with the issues that are upon us, just send word through. If not, well," and his features creased into a penetrating gaze, "I don't have much time left for what needs to be done, so I do expect you'll get back to me soon, very soon, to discuss what has to be done next."

The way he said it bespoke a challenge, perhaps even a threat.

John opened the door and started to leave.

"John, take the cigarettes with you as a gift." He slid them across the table.

John hesitated, but then what the hell, he picked the carton up, nodded his thanks, and was out the door and back into the brightly lit corridor. The arrogant captain who had driven him to this meeting was waiting for him.

Not a word was exchanged as they went out to the concourse, got into the Humvee that was again all so quiet, with its electric motor. Again the concourse that looked like an off-duty gathering area was totally empty.

Just why is this place in operation now? John wondered as they continued on in silence back to Raven Rock.

PART III

John, you should know these things take on a life of their own.

—General Joshua C. Lawrence

CHAPTER ONE

"Hope you don't mind if I just read it here, do you?"

They were in the small suite inside bunker five, the command center for the Rock. It was a spartan affair serving as Bob's personal space, just feet away from his office. The bedroom was slightly larger than the other cubicles, at ten by twelve feet. At least the institutional green that covered most of the walls of this place was absent here, replaced with some faux wood paneling, as was the large adjoining official conference room where they had met upon John's return late in the day.

When his old digital watch had died a couple of years ago, John's students had honored the end of his first year as president of Montreat College by presenting him with an old-style pocket watch, complete with a gold chain. He loved it, wound it carefully every morning, its weight a comfortable feeling tucked into his pants pocket with the chain attached to his belt. Snapping it open had become a bit of an affectation, which he did now, gazing for a few seconds at the miniature painting of Makala that Paul Hawkinson's artistic wife had created for him. He saw that it was approaching midnight. *This time yesterday I was asleep in my own bed without a care in the world, damn it.* He closed the watch, and absently wound the stem before putting it back in his pocket.

Bob had asked for a few hours' rest as the evening wore on, as well as some alone time to think, but now had summoned John back to continue the conversation. He was still in bed, obviously in some pain by the strained look on his face. He reached to the nightstand beside his bed, to an opened pack of cigarettes.

"You really think you should be using those damn things?"

Bob lit up in spite of John's protest and started coughing violently for several minutes. Putting the cigarette out after a single puff, he took up the letter John had carried back from Lawrence.

"I know who this General Lawrence is. He had something of the warrior poet in him for starters. Guest lectured at the War College just after I took over. If memory serves me it was about the Anabasis of Xenophon and the art of withdrawal and surviving in the face of overwhelming odds. Familiar with it?"

"Read it in grad school. But then again I read several hundred books in grad school."

"I remember he was in the Pentagon, office of strategic planning, lot of controversy. Sorry, but I'm kinda hazy tonight, John. I'll remember more when I'm fresh again."

Bob shifted uncomfortably then swore softly, reached again to the nightstand, selected one of half a dozen pill bottles, shook out two, and washed them down with a glass of water that John could tell from the smell was mixed liberally with some of his home-brew whiskey.

"He was definitely an up-and-comer, you know the type. That officer who you know is gonna rise like a comet through the ranks if he doesn't get killed first, or finally runs across some higher-up whose tail he twisted and is lying in wait for a dose of takedown vengeance.

"He went Special Forces, got that Distinguished Service Cross and a limp for the rest of his life after some sort of op in Afghanistan back before nine-eleven. Stuff that of course will never make the press and was stamped 'Secret.'

"At least that's the way I remember him. Yeah, he was a fast-moving star on the rise, and frankly, I never liked him."

"How come?"

"I don't know, an instinct, call it. Just something about him that didn't gel right. Anyhow, that's just my personal prejudice."

"You have pretty good instincts, sir."

"Don't ass-kiss me, John," Bob said with a smile. "So he got his star, moved into some deep stuff, deep classified, and that was the last I heard of him until now."

John sat silent at the end of the bed as Scales opened the envelope, unfolded the single sheet of paper, adjusted his glasses, and began to read.

He grimaced slightly, uttering a soft curse, then let the paper fall and finally picked it back up.

"Well, that's short and sweet," Bob said, handing the paper over to John.

There was the usual memo opening: from General Joshua C. Lawrence, to General Robert E. Scales.

> This is to inform you, sir, that the location known as
> Site R, or Raven Rock, must surrender within forty-eight
> hours of this notification to a force duly appointed by
> General Joshua Lawrence and said site shall be turned
> over intact.
>
> —General Joshua C. Lawrence

"I will be damned." Bob carefully got out of bed, wrapping himself in a worn, threadbare bathrobe.

"By what authority can he even do that," John snapped. "You, sir, are the president of this republic."

John took up the letter and walked the few feet to the conference room that overlooked the war room on the next floor down. From his plate-glass view of the amphitheater he saw just half a dozen personnel below, the night crew monitoring the shortwave links for any activity. The desk was set up as the China Watch center, with a bank of several old-style monitors from a decade or more ago lit up, an alcove linking them to the naval command at Charleston, along with one other monitor revealing the location of the nuclear-carrying boomers out in the North Atlantic and North Pacific, displayed on an oversized project screen. Below the screen was the infamous DEFCON display, which had been frozen for years at DEFCON 3.

Bob came into the room, still in his bathrobe, eyes glaring as he took the letter from John and read it again. There was a moment of silence, and then, of all things, Bob laughed softly.

"The nerve of this guy? Just who the hell is he, what is he, and by what authority does he think he can act against what is our government, no matter how tenuous our hold is at the moment?"

John was silent.

"In command of what," Bob mused. "In command of what." After a moment, he spoke again. "John, I want you to get some sleep, you look absolutely beat, then go back there tomorrow. But before you do so, I want to do a little digging, so let's meet back here in the morning. Six hours, no, make it five."

John just nodded wearily in reply and left the room. Bob walked over to the window and looked down at the war room board, obviously already lost in thought.

CHAPTER TWO

To his surprise, when John entered the small mess area a few short hours later, breakfast was waiting for him. The cook, seeing him come in, smiled broadly.

"Good morning, Mr. Vice President. General Scales ordered something special for you, sir."

As John sat down the cook came over, carrying a tray heaped with pancakes drenched in maple syrup, with what smelled like real bacon on the side, and a large mug of real coffee as well. John gratefully took the cup and sipped on it—it really was the real thing.

"How did you get this?" John asked.

The cook, wearing a faded fatigue blouse with the stripes of a staff sergeant and at least thirty years of service hash marks, chuckled softly.

"We have a few things left here and there. I'll send some of the younger kids out to trade with locals down the mountain. Eggs—real eggs, not the powdered kind. Even got a side of bacon a while back, this here is almost the last of it. You know how it is."

John wondered if this was how they got some of that white lightning. Going back to George Washington's time, it was inevitable:

where there were troops stationed, someone nearby was brewing moonshine for the thirsty.

"By the way, the general told me to spend a little time with you."

"What do you mean?"

"Get the inside dope on what's going on for real, you know the drill, sir. Officer country might think all is well, but if you want to really feel the pulse, talk off the record to the men and women really doing the job."

"You've known the general, I mean president, for a while?"

"Why, General Scales, excuse me, the president and I go way back, sir. I was his chef when he was at the War College, then just after the Day, he ran across me in all that chaos at Fort Meade and told me to fall in by his side and stay close. Kind of his orderly since then, but do my turn in the mess hall when needed." He fell silent for a moment. "Enjoy your breakfast, sir, I got to get back to work."

"Do me a favor, Sergeant, get a mug of real coffee for yourself and join me."

"Sir?"

"Drop the sir, I was an officer but I work for a living now. Okay?"

The man was a bit taken aback and hesitated.

"Come on, I need the company."

The cook went to the far side of the counter, poured some coffee from an old-style percolator into a mug, then came back and sat across from John.

"That's better, okay with you?"

"Yes, sir . . . ah, Mr. Vice President."

"I prefer John, and your first name?"

"James."

John reached across the table and shook his hand.

"Now, formalities settled, mind if I ask you a few questions? Let's say strictly off the record."

James smiled. "Go ahead."

John had a feeling this man was the "go-to" that any good officer had among his enlisted personnel. The ability to sit down for a one-on-one, rank forgotten, to get some straight talk and a better feel for what was really going on in his command, be it a fresh lieutenant turning to the sergeant of his platoon, or a top-ranking general who needs to know what the real feeling and issues are with his army. A good officer cultivated that; an incompetent officer or martinet did not, to the peril of his command.

"A few questions?"

"Sure, sir . . . John."

"What's your take on what is really going on here? Don't give me the usual platitudes, just say it straight."

"You want the long or the short version?"

A pause. John simply waited until the sergeant came to his own decision.

"I know the general wants you in about thirty minutes, so we'll keep it short for now, but there's a hell of a lot to say, most of it bad, and questions I'd like to know about." He blew out noisily. "Things are going to hell, sir."

"How so?"

"Look at your rations there this morning. I hope you appreciate it. We're getting to the bottom of the barrel here, as I told you earlier. Except for local bartering outside the doors, nothing more is coming in. Sure, it's after the Day, I know that, it's the same everywhere, but I heard that before we took over, at least some supplies were being quietly brought in. Spare parts, foodstuffs, things like that. Once our government took over, it stopped. Stopped cold.

"Go down to the motor park, ninety percent of what we have now is junk, cannibalized for the few things still running. Curious, but when we took this place, fuel tanks for gas, diesel, on occasion, they'd be topped off. Not a drop since then. I understand they actually flew you up here."

"I wondered the same thing," John agreed. "Where did the fuel come from?"

"The sixty or so gallons to get you here, I think that was busting the budget. And things are starting to break, crucial things. You know just by sitting here, the humidifiers went down months ago. The few small units we have are used in key rooms with computers and telecommunications, that's all that's left. Speaking of computers? One by one they are winking off. Again, we've been cannibalizing to at least keep a few crucial links up and running."

"Is it just that this is the natural progression?" John asked. "Things wear out and that's it."

James leaned closer, his voice dropping. "More than a few of us think it's sabotage."

John leaned back, not letting anything show. "Scales knows this, of course."

"Of course he does, God save him."

John suddenly saw a connection. "Sergeant, are you really a cook?"

"Oh, of course I am." A pause. "Sir."

John suddenly could see through it. He found himself recalling a small class when Scales was the commandant at Carlisle, a late-night informal discussion on leadership. Scales talked about finding and keeping a top sergeant, that in private he would be the one for real discussions and not just the usual BS of command. That it was important to embed him, to never let anyone realize that he was an inside source. Because, first of all, his own personnel might reject him if they found out. He or she had to be a straight talker, not a snitch carrying tales for self-aggrandizement. He had to, above all else, be honest in all things. He had to be intelligent, very intelligent, able to separate the wheat from the chaff and just tell it like it is. He was also to be a sounding board for things one might never share with his own staff, especially those junior officers who far too often were on the prowl for a step up on the promotion ladder or, worse, happy to knock another off that ladder.

"Go on," John said.

"After we took over this place, and kicked the civilians out, several hundred personnel stayed on, mainly enlisted. Mostly tech types for running the databases, communications, stuff like that. You know it was kind of a strange place, with some technology right out of the 1960s, others fairly current. People were needed to keep all that running.

"When the general declared the Republic, and was elected president, he decided, I think rightly so, that it was best for the time being to keep Raven Rock as the acting capital. It had good communications, and was secure.

"The word was circulated that we needed personnel, usual run-of-the-mill paper-pushers—Lord knows more than one was banging at the door to get in—and everything else. Fully manned, this place needed just under a thousand personnel, from security outside the doors, to janitors, and yeah, cooks, or at least someone who can cook." He chuckled softly.

"But you believe sabotage is at play?" John pressed.

"Don't think it, I know it."

"Have people been caught, held accountable?"

"Whoever they are, they're good. Just things like a few months back our link to the navy in Charleston went down cold. Tech heads went to work on the unit and found a single component in the main receiver had shorted out. They cobbled it back together and finally got it running three days later. But that component, all I heard was it was tampered with.

"More and more things of late, tampered, shorted, jammed. You hear quiet talk in here, late-hour stuff when the staff in the war room are taking a break and whispering among themselves. I'm bringing them some coffee, they clam up, I walk away and the whispering starts again.

"You can smell that thing out. I have a couple of them pegged— one of them was here long before the Day, another joining in the recruiting afterward. I'd bet ten to one, they know more than they're letting on."

"You tell the general, I mean president that?"

"What do you think, sir? The dehumidifiers, that was completely ridiculous. One of the cooling coils was smashed. Oh, it was written up as an accident, someone dropping a heavy wrench."

At this point they were interrupted, the sergeant falling back into his cook role when three women asked for cups of coffee. They exclaimed joyfully when they realized it was the real thing; the sergeant acted like it was a special favor for them and told them to keep it quiet. After trading a few jokes about the twelve-hour shifts, he turned back to John as they left.

"Only got a few minutes more, sir. We'll talk more later but the general wanted me to give you a rundown on a few more things."

That was obvious; Scales was tipping a hand that John could turn to this cook in any situation.

"One final question for now."

"Shoot."

"Morale."

The sergeant shook his head. "The inner core are generally those people the general brought in, the idealists who believed in what this new government was about. But maybe that's the place to put somebody, they look and sound like true believers."

"Who?"

"From what I'm hearing, background chatter, that might be your job, sir."

With that the sergeant stood up, finishing the last of his coffee.

"I'll take the tray, sir, I think you have an appointment to catch."

CHAPTER THREE

Minutes later John was stepping out of the elevator, same routine as before, going up to the blast door with Bob by his side.

"The answer to this Lawrence is no and go to hell."

"Figured that," John said with a smile.

"Not that it'll make any real difference," Bob continued. "They undoubtedly have the firepower to kill everyone topside in short order. I assume they have the codes to get in, the barriers are breached, and that's it.

"Oh, we could put up a helluva fight for a few hours, and there's enough idealist kids down here who would fight. But fight whom? They'll be wearing the same uniforms. End result, several hundred damn good young men and women killed, conclusion the same. No, John, we'll surrender when the time runs out but at least put up a good bluff for now, and see what happens. Okay?"

"Give me a few minutes," John said. He reached into his pocket, pulled out a Dunhill, and lit it up.

"Oh hell, give me one too."

John helped him light it, Bob taking a few puffs before the coughing started and he dropped the smoke and snuffed it out.

"Good luck, John, and take care."

His own smoke finished, John nodded to the lone MP to open the barrier, and then walked through.

To his absolute amazement, General Lawrence was on the other side, smiling slightly at obviously having caught them off guard.

"If my old sense of protocol is still correct, I owe the first salute, General Scales."

Bob was silent, stiffening a bit, but not returning the salute.

"Bob, may I call you that?"

"You may not," Bob softly replied, "until you make it a lot clearer who the hell you are, why you are here, and what it is you really want."

"Since John is with you, I assume you are not the one to visit me today."

"That is correct. The vice president will be my proxy until we get some clear answers."

"Actually a wise move, sir. You do not wish to be another FDR, sir, that is obvious."

That obviously touched a nerve.

"My health for the present is fine."

"Not what we've heard, but be that as it may, I'll welcome John. As I told him, we have a good oncology staff over here, some of the best, if you should decide to get the treatment you deserve."

"That won't be necessary."

Bob stepped closer to John, took his hand—there was still strength—then turned around and without another word from either Bob or Lawrence, the steel door was shut.

A Humvee was waiting, already turned around. No driver this time, just the two of them.

"Coffee? I brought along a couple of thermoses, one black and the other with cream and sugar."

"Thanks." John poured a cup of the black and tentatively took a sip.

"Let's get started." And they were off, the electric Humvee silently accelerating.

They continued in silence down the tunnel John had traversed yesterday. Lawrence was dressed in the same uniform, all of it crisp, and he suspected this was the type of officer that didn't take a step outside without a newly starched uniform every single day.

They reached the main concourse they had entered yesterday, but this time it was full of life. Dozens of personnel, sitting at tables, enjoying burgers and Cokes, more than a few couples walking about, a couple of female soldiers off to one side playing catch, a few others gathered around two women playing chess. It looked so calm, relaxed, just like the hundreds of PXs and shopping plazas that once dotted the American landscape at every military base: army, navy, air force, and marine.

All of the personnel were dressed in standard army fatigues. A sudden ripple went through the assembly as the Humvee arrived, and within seconds every last one of them was facing them at stiff attention, those closer to the vehicle saluting.

Lawrence had the side window open, and saluted back. "Stand easy, all of you."

But they didn't. Those in the background shouted a greeting. He heard someone say, "My God, that's the general."

It was all very formal as Lawrence suddenly stopped and got out, troops again snapping to attention.

"Okay, stand easy." He walked up to a group and extended his hand. Several took turns shaking it nervously.

"Everything going okay here?" he asked them.

"Yes, sir," several answered.

"No complaints?"

No one spoke until an older sergeant stepped up.

"Everything is A-okay here, sir." The way he said it caught John, who had remained in the vehicle. It was a very stiff reply. No one else spoke.

"Fine then, fine. I could use a Coke, Sergeant."

"Coming right up, sir." The sergeant actually ran to the nearest counter, everyone else standing nervously quiet. Within seconds the sergeant was back, surprisingly with an actual bottle of Coke—not the plastic kind, but the old-fashioned glass bottle.

Lawrence took the drink from him and then mingled a bit, shook some more hands, asking the same question: "Everything going okay here?"

The replies were almost universally "Fine, sir," "A-okay," "Never better, sir."

He walked back to the Humvee then turned and snapped off a formal salute, which was returned by everyone in the concourse. Then he got in and drove toward an open tunnel, two lanes wide, only dimly illuminated, and they left the concourse behind.

John looked back over his shoulder. The gathering had now turned into knots of men and women, coming together and talking excitedly, gazing at the vehicle receding from view.

"Would you care for that Coke, John? Personally I can't stand the stuff, it's not healthy."

"No, thank you, sir, lost the taste for it years ago, not much of it around after the Day."

Lawrence drained the bottle out the open window and tossed the empty into the back seat.

John had set himself the task of profiling this enigmatic man. What caught him was the way the troops in the concourse reacted. Stiff, formal, even a bit awed, as if an august persona had come into their presence. The bottle of Coke was a nice touch but tossed aside once he was out of sight.

A good general, and Patton was of course one of them, had a stunning combination of rigid no nonsense that could leave any man, from private to colonel, quaking in his boots, but at the same time he had those moments of mingling with his men, laughing and swearing, the troops delighted by his presence.

John had heard a story told by a battalion commander from the war in the weeks after the famed "slapping incident," when Patton had actually hit a private he accused of malingering in a hospital area. Patton had been ordered to go before every one of his commands and apologize for hitting a GI. The colonel related that Patton arrived, old "Blood and Guts" himself, complete with his pearl-handled pistol at his side. He got up front, and had barely said a few words when some soldier in the back shouted out, "You should have shot the bastard, sir. We're on your side, General." The battalion broke ranks, gathering around their general and cheering him as tears came to his eyes.

It was the persona of leadership, the old veteran told him, and one he remembered. In that brief encounter in the concourse John had sensed that same respect, even awe, or absolute obedience. But, John wondered, what else did it say about him?

CHAPTER FOUR

They drove on for several long minutes, the tunnel seeming to go into eternity, until the general finally pulled into a wide garage, half a football field in size and dimly lit.

Several rows of Humvees were parked inside, but not just the usual transport vehicles like they were using. The first row of a dozen were expanded scout cars, mounting a Kevlar curtain that protected a turret with twin M60 machine guns. Another row sported tow missile launchers for antitank and antiaircraft rounds. Another row held what looked like standard Humvees, but John glimpsed field modifications that would allow them to carry either extra personnel or weapons. There was a small row of half a dozen Humvee ambulances, and then the unusual sight of two vehicles sporting high-gain dish antennas, currently folded down. Backed against the far wall of the cavern were four Bradley troop carriers, even several of the older M113s, which had supposedly gone out of service a decade and a half ago, though he assumed there had been National Guard units that still had been using them before the Day.

They came to a stop beside a double door, and Lawrence got out. Guards, yet again armed with M4s, snapped to attention as the general led the way through the doors. On the far side was a bank of four elevators, almost typical of the kind in old parking garages. Lawrence went to the one that was separated from the others by a heavy wall. When he pressed his ID to the door it soundlessly slipped open. Inside was a simple Up button and a keypad. He punched in a code, produced a blank red piece of plastic the size of a credit card, pressed it to a scanner, and at a rather startling rate of speed, the elevator took off.

"We're nearly two thousand feet under Camp David now, so this will take a minute."

The elevator finally slowed, stopped, and the doors opened. John wasn't sure what the hell to expect, but in front of him was a conference room, much like the one they'd first met in. Desks, some leather chairs, bookshelves, the far wall glassed in.

"Take a look around for a minute. I got a call to make, if you'll excuse me." Without waiting for a reply Lawrence went out a side door and closed it behind him.

John walked up to the bookshelf and scanned it. He found the usual row upon row of bound reports, but also several volumes of the official history of World War II, and a selection of faded history books, a copy of Xenophon and Plutarch, the next row the writings of Nietzsche. That caught his attention and he looked closer. *Beyond Good and Evil.* He drew it out for a closer look. It wasn't a show copy as you used to find in many a professor's collection, as if he actually read such volumes but in truth never touched them. This one had numerous place markers from beginning to end. A volume of *Thus Spoke Zarathustra* was also well marked, as was yet another, *On the Genealogy of Morality.*

This was indeed a cause for reflection. To be honest with himself, he had struggled through a graduate class on the moral philosophy of war. These works were part of that course, along with the writings of Sun Tzu, Thomas Aquinas, Thomas Hobbes, and others. Some students took to it, the ones who might not one day rise to the top but after retirement from the military would wind up as a colonel or one-star general in a D.C. think tank or one of the better universities, there to turn out papers that few would ever take notice of, let alone read; the kind of person who liked to quote a line or two at cocktail parties to sound intellectual.

But Nietzsche? He wished that the old internet was still alive, with Wikipedia, so he could check on some of the underlined sections.

There were more on the next shelf. Several thick works by Ayn Rand, then a number of works on the Ukrainian famine—that was curious, and triggered flashes of their own great famine in the year after the Day. He also found the works of Orwell and a book he did remember reading, a scathing indictment of Duranty, one of the American intellectuals of the 1930s who knew the extent of Stalin's horrors but covered up for it. The Duranty quote that came to his mind was that you need to break a few eggs if you want to make an omelet, his rationalized excuse for tens of millions dying so the revolution would survive.

There were books by Solzhenitsyn, but also Albert Speer, and even a copy of *Mein Kampf*. And it was obvious by their condition that these books were not window dressing but had been read thoroughly and absorbed.

Absorbed for what? That was the question.

As if in answer, the side door opened and Lawrence stepped out.

"So, you went straight to my bookshelf. I was just like you with that. If a man or woman had a stocked shelf that's what I wanted to look at first in a room. Was he a dilettante and the volumes were there for show, or was there something to be learned. So, before we move on to why we are here, I'll ask, what have you learned about me?"

John hesitated. A cursory look without knowing the reader might indicate something worrisome about some of the selections, especially if they'd been read and absorbed. But then again he might be a true intellectual, wanting simply to learn, and for that, the selections were indeed good ones.

"I'll wait until I know you better," John replied cautiously.

"Good, I like that. Like the old saying, 'Don't judge a book by its cover.'" And he gave a short laugh at his little joke.

"All right, let's go into the next room, shall we?"

He led John into yet another office, similar to the one they were leaving, but this one had a panoramic window that went from wall to wall. One floor down was the layout of a war room, similar in some ways to the war room at Raven Rock.

But there were differences, big differences. Although the basic design still had a '60s Cold War feel to it, with several banks of desks, each with its own monitor or bank of phones, these computers, unlike Raven Rock's, were obviously up to date. Half a dozen workstations were staffed with enlisted personnel, and a couple of officers moved about between stations.

John tried to see what was on the screens and, squinting, he studied them.

"I'll explain," Lawrence offered, coming up to his side. "The central consoles are the global threat board. We can project any of them up onto the main screen up front."

Lawrence sat down in the single chair in the center of the room. The desktop in front of him had a monitor and keyboard. He punched a few keys and the large display down below lit up with a computer projection of China. When icons filled the screen, he ran a cursor over to one and the display zeroed in for a close-up.

"ICBM base in Inner Mongolia, we've been watching that a lot of late. Four silos, four missiles, each with six warheads, in the low five hundred K to one megaton range. We can see pretty well anywhere on the globe where we still have a concern. Name a place."

"North Korea."

Lawrence swung the cursor to the left, and North Korea outlined on the large board and his monitor. It was dark, the entire country.

"When we finished with them after the Day, as Phil Sheridan once said about the Shenandoah Valley, 'A crow will have to pack his own rations if he tries to fly over.' With the half-life of radiation, I guess in a few more years the few survivors left will finally come out of their two-thousand-foot-deep bunkers. We still have satellite surveillance, quite a few have survived. I can get real-time visuals on all the usual places right down to the license plate on a car."

He paused and again gave that soft chuckle.

"Except for a hundred-mile radius from Washington out to here. We jammed and scrambled those a long time ago, some of it even before the Day, sending up false images—pretty damn sophisticated if someone hacked into the system and wanted to look around. We could go on but you get the general idea. One entity in America still functions and is running a global defense system."

There was nothing John could say but "Why, and how?"

"Let's tackle the why first, John. Remember yesterday, that quote I gave from the movie, 'Why build one when you can have two'?

"From the beginning Raven Rock was supposedly secret, but it was a secret that was known. If it was known, if we ever did go to war, it would be a target. Not a major worry in 1952, but by the 1980s with missile pinpoint accuracy, it was doomed. Anyone who was realistic knew that. Thus the far more secret command center six miles away at Camp David, with Raven Rock as the convenient red herring. But we've already gone over that, John, and your question of why is rather moot."

"Okay then, how? How did you do this? Surely there was civilian oversight, and we both know what a sieve that can be."

Lawrence's features were now dead serious. "That is the bottom line, John. There was no civilian oversight."

"What? Even with Manhattan in the world war, a few dozen

senators and congressmen at least had some knowledge. At Los Alamos, quite a few dozen knew the full extent."

"And as you know, it leaked. Los Alamos became an open link
to the Soviets. Without those leaks it'd have taken another ten years
for them to make a bomb, if they ever did. You know of Rickenbacker, don't you?"

"World War One ace. Of course, I know of him."

"During the Second World War he was sent to the Pacific to
evaluate things, and it was also a morale tour. Actually he crashed
in the Pacific and survived something like twenty days on a raft. It
was around 1944, I think he was on a base in North Dakota, or it
might have been Alaska. The base was being used to fly planes to
the Soviet Union, part of our brilliant lend lease to our so-called
friends.

"At the base, Rickenbacker was taken aside by the base commander, who started to raise hell about the Soviets. Though in the
United States they openly had their security personnel, the NKVD
thugs on transport planes supposedly shipping war material, in
sealed cases. This base commander finally got fed up with the Russians. He hatched a plan to just get the Russians good and drunk,
which our people gladly did, then drugged them. Then he sent our
people into that plane and tore open several tons of cases, mostly
filled with documents.

"The question the base commander had for Rickenbacker: 'Sir,
just what in the hell is Manhattan?' They had found a whole box-
load of stuff that looked like diagrams for some secret project and it
was stamped 'Manhattan.'

"John, the Soviets were shipping packing cases full of top-secret
stuff while we stood by, or some of our people, openly helping them
to sell out our security. Come on, John, we all know those stories."

As he was talking, Lawrence left the viewing room, leading
John back to the adjoining office. He poured both of them a drink,
which John took, feeling that he did indeed need one.

"Before our people, Pentagon people mostly embarked on this venture, and on any budget it was sealed up tight. For a while it was called Bright Star—cover story, advance hypersonic nukes. Other cover names were used, money was set aside, and those who did work on it did so in darkness. Hell, I think they did better than Area 51 when it came to cover stories, shifted budgets, necessary equipment disappearing."

"Did anyone at the top know?"

"What do you think? The White House is an open book for any-one who has the know-how to open it. When asked they just simply pointed to Raven Rock."

"And all that time across several decades they kept the secret."

"The only fly in the ointment I'd have done better would be to drive a four-lane highway right up to Raven Rock's door. As I took command that was the one big thing that bothered me."

"Why was that?"

"Come on, we talked on it a bit yesterday. Raven Rock, three huge steel door entrances that a hundred yards down the mountain face out on what . . . a two-lane road? To anyone who sat back and did some thinking, a little bit of math, the evac plan for five thou-sand just wasn't there. There had to be a realistic way to move thou-sands of personnel on short notice, a way to move personnel even if Washington was about to be vaporized.

"So, John, I'll pose to you the old million-dollar question. Take five thousand people, which the plans called for back in the 1950s, five thousand military personnel who in those final moments are scram-bling to stay alive. You're not going to get hundreds of helicopters in the area, besides, any blast would knock down the few choppers that did make it. What is the fundamental flaw to the whole damn place and how would you solve it? Go ahead and take your time."

An answer was already forming, and John found he was actually smiling as it became crystal clear. He felt that he should have real-ized all along.

"A tunnel to Washington, D.C."

It was so stunningly simple. Sure, he had heard a few rumors, the sort of thing that cropped up on crazy conspiracy sites, a theory that one might look at, think for a few minutes it was interesting, then wander off to something else.

"Exactly right, John! Amazingly simple, isn't it. For years they were quietly boring away a thousand or more feet deep. Take the New York City water system. It starts up in the Catskills, and goes all the way to the city, a hundred miles. The biggest update was mammoth, thirty feet or more in diameter, costing billions of dollars. The first bore-through was done by the late fifties, and was expanding out ever since, until the Day."

"Incredible," John whispered.

"Yeah, it really is. Just as incredible that it was pulled off without Congress or the president ever getting wind. Just sign off on more bills for Star Bright, or Vigilant, or Valkyrie—I liked that one, by the way.

"It started far below the Pentagon, sold to the few that needed to know some details about massive shelters being dug. First stop, then, CIA. They were wholeheartedly into it and plenty of help if someone got too nosy. Fifty miles of it, John. And of course add in the storage areas, reserves for equipment that was sent down there over the years, and just let it grow.

"It wasn't convenient to haul out old equipment that was obsolete, so they'd just stash it somewhere, build an extra cavern, and mothball it. Some amazing stuff in those mothball tunnels. Cars and trucks from the 1950s that a collector would have died for. All sorts of equipment, old mainframe computers . . . it really does look a bit like that warehouse in *Indiana Jones*.

"I think you've guessed from my bookshelf that I have a healthy interest in history and philosophy. Maybe you'll take a tour with me once things between us are settled. Hundreds of jeeps from the fifties and sixties, thousands of weapons going back to M1s—the computer equipment down in some of those caverns could be used for a museum of technology. We've mothballed old IBMs with 4 Meg capacity that are the size of a truck. Again, it was simply easier to just store it away rather than haul it topside and quietly try to dispose of it.

"So there it is. A tunnel from the Pentagon—and no, there are no links to the Capitol or White House—out to McLean, straight up to Frederick, to Fort Detrick, then on to here."

He hesitated for a few seconds, looking over at John and then his drink.

"And around five thousand carefully selected personnel, very carefully selected."

"How's that?"

"If we had more than rifle carriers, not just rifle carriers, but all the tech fields, construction people, all the myriad people needed to run and maintain a base, and more importantly its mission, and just rotated them out after the year or two of an assignment, that would add up to tens of thousands of personnel who had served here in the years leading up to the Day. Of course we had them compartmentalized. We used to actually bring them in at Raven Rock. They're thinking maybe the entire time they are actually in Raven Rock. We'd then move them around over a few weeks, never more than a few miles, nearly all of them assuming that they were still inside that rock even though they'd end up maybe thirty miles away.

"They'd be assigned to a mile or so of tunnel, or digging a new concourse under the rock. We were always telling them that Raven Rock had to go deeper. When it came time to leave they would think they were coming up just outside of Gettysburg. We even built a few miles of tunnel that was one continual curving loop, going up and down, to throw people off the real location. Anyhow, that's trivial stuff now."

"You've told me why all this." John vaguely waved his hand

around. "But you haven't told me the *real* why. I can see the logic of long before the Day," John said. "But this? This whole subterfuge is a relic of the Cold War. Can see the deception, the money, and it must have cost billions. I still don't get it."

"Hell, who hasn't seen a military contract that didn't have overruns of few billion here, a few billion there," Lawrence replied.

John stood up, and without asking poured some more scotch, remaining silent, Lawrence patiently waiting. And at last the thought he had been groping for came to him with crystal clarity as he sat back down with his drink and took a deep swallow.

"Just before he left office in 1960, Eisenhower gave a remarkable speech," John said. "I've read the history of him same as you. The speech was a warning. That America was falling into the hands of 'the military industrial complex.' In fact I think his speechwriters invented the phrase.

"He embraced all that had to be done in the early to mid-fifties to face and hopefully overwhelm the Soviets, said that war with us was impossible for them to win, and maybe thus open up rapprochement. But at the end of his terms, he was felt to be having serious doubt about what was happening to America as a result.

"I wonder if this was one of the things he was warning us about, that maybe this vast complex could be used for something beyond just surviving a nuclear war, something far deeper, and he knew from experience the direction it might be heading."

Lawrence's gaze was fixed on John. "You are far more perceptive than I first gave you credit for, Mr. Vice President."

"The why, General, the why. Though I am starting to suspect the answer."

"John, look at what both of us have been through the last five years. I know more of your story now from information I've gathered since yesterday. You saved your village of Black Mountain, and your college, of which you are president. You even became vice president of the Republic, but at what cost? Such a horrible cost. We've all paid that cost, haven't we?"

He fell silent for a moment and John had a sense that this man had lost something dear as well. A daughter like he lost, a wife, friends, what?

"We watched a civilian government that failed on its watch, the signs were there weeks, months before the Day, we both see that now. We knew the deluge was coming, that terrorist cells had obtained the missiles to send a nuke aloft, three of them actually. They knew the dirty secret of EMP. You didn't need hundreds of precision ICBMs, you just needed three warheads, detonated up there," he waved toward the ceiling, "then sit back and let chaos take its course. In the end who benefited, answer me that."

"China, of course," John replied. "They own the West Coast now, they're the top dog, after the next two were burst over Eastern Europe to include Moscow, and the last east of Japan, to take out Japan but not high enough to hit China as well."

"It was a well-thought-out plan, John, we have to admit that."

"So here we are five years later, five very long years as the world reordered itself. So I ask who will be the winner five years hence? India and Pakistan blew each other apart, who else is left?"

"Siberia, the so-called reconstituted Soviets, and China, we both know that."

"Suppose they blow each other away. Then what? Your new Republic, which has about as much power as what? We both know that government is a fantasy. Maybe in thirty years if nothing else intervenes. Not another war, even another EMP strike. What else, a plague, maybe? You're barely containing the old enemies of typhoid, malaria, yellow fever, cholera. But how about a new strain of flu, an airborne disease no amount of sanitation can contain if it gets loose in an already weakened populace? We both know your population is barely surviving above starvation level even now.

John, your Republic is a like a balloon: one prick of a pin, and it will burst."

John said nothing. He felt a cold chill, though, that this man was hinting at something.

Lawrence poured another drink for both of them. John was watching how much Lawrence was taking in, but he was still calm, measured in delivery.

"We do still have the boomers, the four nuke subs in the northern Atlantic and Pacific. They're our guarantor against China," John replied. Lawrence chuckled dryly, and downed the ounce of scotch in one gulp, then sighed and fell silent.

"John, we control the boomers, not you. Oh, there might be an admiral out there, what's his name, it escapes me at the moment, who thinks he's the finger on the trigger. John, he isn't, in the end we down here can control those as well."

My God, what is he saying? John wondered.

"We've controlled them all along, though the force did diminish over the last three years. Bound to happen, given lack of bases and repairs, and the damned personnel problems. But yes, we just let you think you controlled them. Even the Chinese believed you controlled them."

"What the hell are you trying to pull here?"

"Think about it, John. Do that for a few minutes. Process it out, I'll be quiet while you do."

John downed his drink as well, then shook his head as Lawrence gestured whether he wanted another. He didn't bother to ask out of politeness but simply reached into his shirt pocket, pulled out a Dunhill, and lit up.

"Glad you like the Dunhills, John."

John said nothing, but thought Lawrence's act that he had forgotten the admiral's name was most likely true. He took another drag, exhaling slowly, savoring the sensation.

This man is telling me that what we thought was the one element in

*our control that could counterforce the Chinese and keep them at bay
has been compromised all along.*

Then what about the few naval assets that answered to the president, or at least still answered? What about the three carriers? For
that matter, anything of weight.

He smoked the cigarette down, then dropped it in his almost
empty glass of scotch with a sizzling sound. Like their first meeting, the glassware and decanter here bore the Eighty-Second emblem, and he sensed that at least with this gesture he could needle
Lawrence just a little.

He immediately lit a second one, then finally focused back on
Lawrence.

"So again, why? What are you, are you in command of everything, or just here at Camp David, if what you said is true about
some giant fifty-mile-long tunnel to D.C."

His mind reeled with the questions bubbling up. Was there still
an actual government of the old United States of America, biding
their time, waiting until things calmed down to announce themselves and return? Was there still an actual president? John did
know that before the Day, the military crew knew about the doomsday plane, the heavily modified 747 that flew out of Omaha, that in
case of nuclear war and a decapitation strike against Washington,
there was an active list of who would succeed to that exalted office
if the president was killed. It went down the whole list, starting
with the VP, to secretary of state, and so on, down through the various cabinets and senators. On the Day, did that actually happen? If
so, was there really a legitimate president, and if so, why didn't they
just reveal whoever they were?

Scenarios and questions welled up. John had always prided himself on his ability to think quickly in a time of crisis when seconds
counted. But this time? Now? He felt overwhelmed.

"With all that has happened these last five years, why the hell did
you sit in the hiding hole and remain silent? Damn it all, Lawrence,

just where we parked I counted dozens of Humvees, ambulances. Just one of those Humvees mounted with M60 machine guns could have wiped out those barbarians who attacked us, or more likely scared them away without a fight. So why, damn it?"

"Yesterday you played a bit of a game with me, of asking no questions. I'm glad to see I really have your interest now," Lawrence said with a bit of a smirk.

"Don't patronize me," John snapped. "I'm here as a representative of my government, which is now in legitimate control of most of the original states."

"How did you get to be the government?" Lawrence replied. "That legitimate government you now call yourself. You held a so-called election, in scattered locations around the East Coast, and declared that to be the will of the people?"

"At least it's something, an attempt to start things back again."

Lawrence chuckled. "Have you actually convened this Congress, formed the usual committees, passed laws, held a few of those investigations Congress used to love so well? The largest city left in all of your thirteen so-called states is maybe ten thousand people down in Roanoke, and the only reason that exists is because there's something of a military base there. And Charleston, of course, thanks again to the military and a carrier there. Some coastal towns, but the rest, just scattered remnants of what once was."

"So what are you saying?"

"You exist only as a fantasy of what you might one day be, not what you really are now."

"Therefore . . ." John sighed, voice trailing out to silence. He suddenly felt tired, so extremely tired, because in his heart he knew this man was right. Maybe, if left to themselves, as a backwash region in a post-EMP world they might gradually reconstitute themselves into at least a semblance of what had once been. If left alone . . .

"I think it is now time for us to take over, John."

"A military takeover, is that what you're saying?"

Lawrence smiled. "John, power was lying in the gutter, in spite of all your efforts. Someone was bound to pick it up. Look at the chaos out in the Plains states. There is no center of power. Well, maybe one, but we'll talk about that some other time. It's like the frontier of the nineteenth century out on the prairie. Half a dozen places, you got some Texas rangers, riding around like in the old days, most of those little better than bandits themselves. Be that as it may, though, we're talking about here and now. Someone has to bring back control, real control. It's that or just drift on in a twilight world of chaos."

"And that entity who is going to bring back control is you."

"Why not?"

"For one thing, what legitimacy do you have? President Scales has labored these last three years to bring back some semblance of order."

"Has he been effective, John?"

Again a moment of silence followed.

"Has he?" This time Lawrence raised his voice to one of cold command. "You made a noble effort, John, you really did, but it was doomed from the start."

"So that's it?"

"Don't make it sound so harsh. This will not be some bloody communist-style coup, with the first act to line up those opposed to us in front of a firing squad."

"Really?"

"Yes, really, and don't insult me by implying differently. It'll just be the quiet replacement of inefficiency with efficiency."

"And you'll be at the head, I assume."

"We can talk about that later."

"Why not now?"

"Later, John, later."

"Let me ask this, then. This is our second meeting. So far what you've showed me, at least the physical presence of all of it, has been,

I'll admit, a shock. The fact that our military built a whole other complex here under Camp David, using Raven Rock as a red herring, was masterful, I'll admit that. To fear a decapitation strike from the Soviets and build this as the real alternative, and keep it secret then, was masterful. How hardly a rumor leaked out about it for decades, masterful as well. But why now?"

"Before or after the Day?"

"Let's start with before."

Lawrence poured another finger of scotch for himself and motioned to John, who shook his head. He'd had more than enough, and wanted to keep his mind clear.

"John, you should know these things take on a life of their own. It was kept so ultra secret . . . well, it was just kept that way. If smarter minds had prevailed during the Second World War, I think they should have kept even FDR out of the loop. They didn't, and you saw what happened. We are on the inside, and I've been in on this secret for fifteen years—we were almost like some secret Masonic group. Maybe a couple of hundred knew the truth of this facility. The CIA, at this point, were partners in it, and Lord knows they can keep a secret. They were doing stuff throughout that the various presidents barely had a hint of. In some ways it was almost a joking matter. Just because the Cold War ended didn't mean that it would just be shut down. But I think the real question for you was why after the Day we just didn't show our hand."

"Precisely."

"Because we could, that's why. John, I'll let you in on a cold truth, a very cold truth. You just scratched the tip of it when your people first seized the Rock. John, we knew it was coming weeks in advance."

John was silent. Finding all those civilians hidden under the mountain, most of whom had fled there in the hours before the Day, had been bad enough.

"All the chatter that the CIA was receiving told us it was coming."

"Could you have stopped it?" John snapped, suddenly filled with a dark anger.

"Yes and no, if you'll accept that. The particular incident of that day, maybe yes, but John, they had layers too, right down to more than a few warheads. Stop the first attack, there would have been another, maybe even a third until they got through. In short, America was doomed in those final weeks, someone was bound to get through. I'm sorry, John, but that's the way of it. We were doomed, and therefore those in on this site, and others, felt it was time to activate our plan."

John reached down to the pack of Dunhills and lit another one. "Go on."

"So we did. There was an outer layer, to be sure, like people you found at the Rock. But beyond them, more came here, mostly military in various branches, but some civilians as well, who had been in on it for years, even helped plan for it. Oh, for days beforehand they'd show up at the CIA, some with families in tow, take a deep elevator. So that's it."

"So what is this damn takeover?"

"Now we get to the brass tacks," Lawrence replied with a smile. Those airlocks between Camp David and the Rock will be open tomorrow at twelve hundred hours. Nothing dramatic, John, just opened up. Some of our personnel will then move into certain positions and take up the running of the place.

"Your government will continue for a while. President Scales will still be president for a while. There'll be some troop movements, like Roanoke, your town, others. There'll be aid to those who need it. Even medical personnel. It's that simple, John, painless even."

"For what reason, damn it? You'd need tens of thousands to seize the various state governments."

"Come on, John," he said with a short laugh. "We show up: 'People who want ten days' rations please form on the right, if you or your family needs medical attention, please form on the left.' Do you think most people will ask questions, John? It's hard to argue on a full stomach, I mean really full, and your kids are getting inoculations. Call it our new 'hearts and minds' program."

"I seem to recall something about grabbing a populace hard in the right place and hearts and minds will follow."

"No need for that, John. It will be quiet, painless. Things will seem the same as before. We take over, reorder things, and everyone will come out happy."

In a way it seemed so seductively easy, and he feared to think maybe it was bound to happen.

"To what end does all this lead, Lawrence?"

"A new order, John, for the future."

That chilled John to the core. It had echoes of "new orders" from throughout history.

There was something about the way Lawrence stood there at that moment, hands on hips, features set, a trace of a smile, but what was behind it? Should he now stand up and say "Yes, my Leader"? Or . . . "Sieg Heil"?

"So," he finally replied, snubbing out his cigarette and putting the glass filled with ashes back on the table. "Tomorrow at noon, the door opens and you walk in. Is that it, no if, ands, or buts?"

"Precisely."

"And if we refuse?"

"To do what, John?"

"What if we barricade the door, for starters."

"John, don't you think we have the codes to open it?"

"We could smash it, scramble the code."

"Delay us a few hours."

"Suppose our people then shoot."

"For God's sake, you're not going to do that, John. End result, you kill some of ours, we kill some of yours. You can't stop us and you know it."

"There's one other point, Lawrence. You could be bluffing."

"A bit beneath me, but you don't really believe me, do you?"

"Frankly, no."

Lawrence stood back up. "Let's go, then."

"What?"

"Just that. Let's go for a ride if you need that to convince you."

"To where?"

"The Pentagon."

"It's abandoned."

"Aboveground, yes. But belowground?"

John had to admit curiosity was getting to him. This whole thing Lawrence had been spinning out these last two days had stretched his credibility to the limit.

In the weeks after the Day, according to Bob Scales, who was stationed at the Pentagon when things hit, the headquarters had become a nest of the upper echelons of command with nothing to command as the country descended into the post-EMP chaos. Thousands of personnel had just simply walked off the job within a few days of that attack and never come back. It had been the same at every base, or for that matter any civilian corporate infrastructure. Communications were gone; the executive who had lorded over it in his corner office on the top floor of some fifth-story headquarters was suddenly blind and deaf. No computers, no phones, no one to give orders to or receive them from. What could be done?

There was no lunch, dinner, or breakfast to be had in the executive dining room, no coffee and donut to be fetched, no water to flush a toilet, let alone wash your hands and face. What was to be done after a day, two days, a week? Meanwhile out in the streets below there was no traffic, the only sounds those of a growing chaos as people searched for a coffee, a bottle of water, a cheap burger for a meal, when nothing worked and it appeared would never work again.

So they left their desks, closed the door to the office, not even bothering to lock it, and walked out the door. John suddenly recalled a woman who still haunted him. A corporate exec type who had walked to Black Mountain from Winston-Salem. Her neat, crisp business-style dress and hair disheveled, the heels of her shoes broken off, a walking tragedy who had offered herself to John in exchange for a bowl of soup. He of course had refused, instead allowing her to have a drink of water before she was forced to move on, away from Black Mountain. She was most likely long dead now, most likely a suicide within a few more days after they had met, lost in a world filled with the lost.

The Pentagon was no different than the corporate towers of a fallen America. What stake did the tens of thousands of enlisted personnel who manned the thousands of offices have in a post-EMP world when their families were "out there," and increasingly subject to the breakdown of any social order?

Then there were the officers of middle rank, the captains, majors, and colonels, men and women who were assistant to the assistant for procurement of something or other. The day after the Day, they would not be far behind in the exodus out of that building. No cars, of course, no Metro to whisk them twenty miles outside the city to their little split-level beyond McLean or Centreville. Abandon the family, or try and walk home, and the choice was obvious.

At the start there was some military order at least, for after all it was the Pentagon, but how long did that last? According to what Bob Scales had told him, not long at all. How did you go to a meeting when your last meal was an MRE two days ago and shared with three others, and the water was just about gone?

Until this general came into sudden appearance, John had assumed that the command structure had just melted away. But now?

"Let's go take a look, Matherson. Come on, you'll find it edifying."

CHAPTER FIVE

John followed Lawrence out of the office and back down to the parking lot, where the Humvee was waiting. Guards to either side stepped back from the vehicle as they approached; this time Lawrence got into the back seat and a driver climbed up front.

"I assume we have enough power to get to the Pentagon and back?" Lawrence asked.

"Yes, sir, fully charged as ordered."

"Let's go, then."

The Humvee silently started off, accelerating up to forty as they turned onto a wide two-lane road, lit every few hundred yards to edge back the darkness.

"We're leaving the Camp David complex," Lawrence told John. "Kind of hard to get oriented at times in these tunnels. After sixty years of digging it can be quite a maze at times, with side turn-offs, depots, storage areas, and such. Sergeant Lucas knows the way, though." He called up to the driver. "How long have you been with us now, Sergeant?"

"Six years, sir."

"Sergeant, if you don't mind a question?" John asked.

"Go ahead, sir."

"You've been here six years, you say."

"Yes, sir."

"How'd you wind up down here? How were you chosen? I guess I mean to ask."

"You know the army, sir. Standardized test for starts, army is great for that kind of thing, you know what I mean. Told I was in the running for a promotion assignment, top secret, if I went for it, absolute secrecy. And finally was assigned here to what we call the Deep Hole."

"You have family, Sergeant?"

A hesitation for a second. "Not that I know of, sir, at least anymore. Divorced, no children, no attachments topside. Most of the men and women here, same thing, actually. Kind of a requirement to get in and then stay here."

"What the sergeant is saying, Matherson, is that to get assigned to what we call level five, there's no outside, above-world direct family. All of it is classified top secret, with a minimum three-year hitch."

"Minimum of three years down here?" John asked, a bit surprised.

"The personnel at Raven Rock, once the place had been secured from the civilian government, could go outside any time they had leave, or just even for a day topside to see some blue sky, the change of seasons, take a walk in the snow."

"So you haven't been outside for how long?"

"Five years," Sergeant Lucas told him. "It was just before the Day. We called it the Deep Dive."

"Don't you miss it?" John asked.

"Sure, we all do at times. But then again, what's left up there? If it had been a full-out nuclear exchange, sir, we would have been down here for years anyhow. With what we do know about up there, I prefer here. We got some recreational areas, even some R and R places for weekends, even tanning rooms for those who like that look, some swimming pools, a lot of diversions to relax. After a while, you kinda forget what it was."

"Form new attachments as well, Sergeant?"

The sergeant chuckled. "Well, sir, of course. I mean there's no one else really, is there? Some of us even eventually get married."

"I'm from up there, as you say, Sergeant, and there's a lot still out there."

"Excuse me a minute, John," Lawrence interrupted, a bit too quickly. "We are coming up to the first exit, the road up to Emmitsburg. That was all the original design work in the early fifties, when you had to drive aboveground from Washington to Emmitsburg."

The road went from two wide lanes to an open concourse half an acre in size, with a vehicle park to one side filled with yet more Humvees even some standard military-style road signs, the one to top side at Emmitsburg three lanes wide blocked off by a security gate manned by a couple of MPs who snapped to attention and saluted as their general passed.

"We're fifteen hundred feet deep here as a precaution. The road now is basically a straight bore from here to Frederick, Maryland, then on to the Washington area. I think we can pick up the pace here, Sergeant Lucas."

Seconds later they were tearing down the tunnel at breakneck speed. The endless dark tunnel ahead was illuminated only by the Humvee's headlights and a dim overhead light every few hundred yards. There was no deviation to right or left; if there were ups and downs in the road they were barely noticeable. The concrete surface, protected for all these years from rain and snow, heat and cold, was almost as new as when it was laid decades ago. Just a seemingly endless ribbon, hundreds of feet underground.

As John sat quietly in the back seat of the Humvee, the monotony of the drive almost lulled him to sleep. He was still trying to make sense of all he'd learned recently. This was either some sort of monument to geniuses who had conceived it, built it, and then kept it hidden for sixty years, or a monument to a nation seized by paranoia.

There had always been rumors, most likely true, that the Soviets had done the same thing during the Cold War. Secret tunnels that ran for dozens of kilometers to underground bunkers, command centers, and even missile defense systems that ringed Moscow. That in the event of Armageddon, the Kremlin would go underground and survive, if need be, for years.

Then it was paranoia, John thought. If the Soviets had one, then so should we. And as they continued to race down the endless tunnel, John realized that it all was indeed true. That all along they had built a system, the red herring of Raven Rock—a place civilians and government plutocrats could run to, but eventually be found— and then this underneath it all, where those who created all that the world had become could survive after all.

They slowed when a warning sign appeared, announcing the egress to the town of Frederick and Fort Detrick.

Another concourse, but this one was different in some ways. More security, for one. But why have security at all when they were a thousand feet down, the outside world sealed off? The turnoff to Fort Detrick was marked with yet more gates, a sign requiring all personnel to get out of their vehicles, and then something of interest: the guards at the second gate were wearing hazmat suits.

"Why the hazmats?" John asked.

"Oh, that? I think it's just some sort of training exercises, routine actually," Lawrence replied as they continued past the exit gates.

John filed that one away—Lawrence had seemed a little quick with that response, and yet again, why the extra security?

Opening a thermos between them, Lawrence offered John some coffee, which he accepted. The miles clicked off, back to top speed. Lawrence said nothing other than offering a brief comment as they passed yet more storage depots, another for side tunnels that went off heaven knows where. It was, if anything, monotonous in its uniformity.

And then at last they slowed as the tunnel went deeper by several hundred feet, Lawrence mentioning they were going under the Potomac, and then they stayed deep. After a while they slowed at last as the road widened from two lanes to four. John saw a regular traffic intersection ahead, complete with flashing red lights. Signs advised personnel to leave their vehicles and to have IDs and passes ready for inspection.

They cleared the first gate, security guards coming to attention and saluting, and drove a short distance but then stopped before the second gate. Lawrence leaned forward to the driver to tell him to turn around.

"Sorry, John, but this is as far as the tour goes today. Maybe someday I'll take you the last few miles."

"Where are we now?"

"McLean. The CIA is about two thousand feet straight up."

John said nothing.

"Being the CIA, they're kind of their own world in there. Same bunks and stuff. They were of course eager to get into this as well, back in the early fifties. They're kind of a sealed-off area, you understand that. Some other time I'll arrange a tour if you want."

"Yeah, sure."

Lawrence laughed softly. "Before we do though, John, we'll have to make sure, I mean really sure whose side you are on. You understand."

John looked over at Lawrence and forced a smile. "At least let me get out to stretch my legs and have a smoke."

A second of hesitation and then he nodded in agreement.

"Just don't do anything stupid like trying to go beyond the next gate. Their people have some pretty strict orders regarding that."

"Like shoot to kill?"

Lawrence didn't reply to that.

John got out of the Humvee, pulled out one of the Dunhills Lawrence had given him, and lit up.

The guards at the second gate stood silent, but they were staring straight at him as if he had two heads. John nodded a greeting to them, but none was given in return.

Lawrence got out beside him. "Though military personnel guard the entrance, this is CIA territory."

"What does that mean?"

"Just that. They control this part of the tunnel. Takes some very special passes to go to either side of that gate, to the access ways up to their underground headquarters."

"Underground."

"Of course, John. Hell, by 1949 they were already digging deep, even before the Soviets got their first bomb. Since the Day, we've gotten more cooperative with them, and they with us, I guess because we're the only games in town now, with everything else falling apart."

"That's comforting."

"I know."

He said nothing more and stood silent as John finished his cigarette under the watchful eyes of the guards. Not sure what to do with the butt he just dropped it to the ground and stamped it out while staring back defiantly at the guard watching him, then got back into the Humvee.

"Let's go for home, Lucas."

"Yes, sir." And they were back through the security gate and picking up speed.

"So that's it?" John asked. "That's the tour?"

"As I said, if we know firmly that you are on our side, there's more to see. John, you are, for right now, the opposition. A government we had no hand in conceiving. So that's all you can see for now. But it proves the point. The tunnel is real. Believe me when

I say we are a viable force, and either your so-called government allows the inevitable to happen or . . ."

When his voice trailed off, John finished the thought. "Or you take it by force, Lawrence."

"Not that crude. You're almost nonexistent to start with, John, more a figment of your fantasies that somehow you can create, peacefully, this New Republic, but come on, John, it is never going to happen. The world topside is in shambles, it will never happen, at least in our lifetimes."

"I'll disagree. And another thing that's been bothering me. Why did you stay hidden? The world topside could have really used your help, for God's sake. You could have at the least offered medical support and food."

"To how many? Fifteen or so million in the greater Washington area. We've stockpiled all of this, for what end? Sure, we could have fed, provided shelter and medical support to fifteen million. We weren't some cornucopia, John. Do a little math. In a short time, a matter of months, and we'd have been like the rest of the world out there. Drained dry and starving. It was a calculation, Matherson, and the calculation said stay in place, and hidden."

"Damn it, Lawrence, so you're telling me you just sealed the bunkers and let everyone else starve. Do you even have a remote idea of how many suffered, or are you too cold for that?"

There was a moment of silence. Without waiting for permission, John took another cigarette out and lit it, in part because he wanted some kind of reaction. Any kind of reaction.

"Maybe you remember the old *Twilight Zone* series. There was a lot of wisdom in those episodes. Like the bomb shelter one. A family is having dinner with friends when the alert comes in, a nuclear attack is imminent. The family hosting the dinner had prepared long before, so they go to their shelter in the basement and lock the door. In a short teleplay of just twenty minutes or so, the neighbors are smashing the door down to get in. The feared nuclear attack turns out to be a false alarm and in that final scene those once friendly neighbors look at each other knowing they had turned into savages to get into the shelter."

Lawrence fell silent for a moment.

"If we had revealed ourselves," he whispered, "for what you would call the greater need of humanity we would have perished with the rest of what had been our nation."

Again a moment of silence.

"That was the decision we down here had to face. Perhaps we do need God to forgive us our sins, but what alternative was there John?

"Think about it. In the end, would it have made one iota of difference whether we opened up our stockpiles or not? Sure, we'd maybe have extended the life of some for a week longer, maybe a month, but the result would be the same: mass starvation."

He was silent for a moment as John continued to smoke angrily.

"Don't you think some of us thought of helping? But the moment that door was cracked open, chaos would follow. We were a lifeboat on a sinking ship, a *Titanic,* if you will. You offer a lifesaving operation for one person on the outside, but then a hundred, five hundred more now want theirs as well. That was the paradigm, John, and in a quiet dispassionate moment later, think on that."

"Did you have any insulin down here?" John asked bitterly, unable to stop the anger welling up inside him.

"Why, there are no diabetics down here." Then he paused. "Right, you had a daughter, didn't you?"

"You're damn straight I did, you son of a bitch. You can talk triage, save the few because you can't save all, but have your child on the side that can't be saved and see how you feel about it, damn you."

John threw his cigarette out the window and glowered in raging silence.

"You're too close to it," Lawrence said, no emotion in his voice. "I learned to let that go years ago. If not, it would have driven me mad. More than a few did, some even of the highest ranks down here. They reached a breaking point and went beyond it. Call it survivor guilt if you will. With what they knew, we couldn't just open the door and let them out. So they came to terms with it, or just chose a way out."

"You mean suicide."

Lawrence said nothing and John wondered if for some, it was a very assisted suicide.

"Then what about the scum that hid out in Raven Rock? Why not at least end that travesty and kick them out?"

"They served a purpose. You and Bob Scales at last figured out they were there, and who they were. Convenient for us, actually. Call it a transference of rage, you focused on that pathetic hideout, cleaning it out, taking over, none the wiser about a hidden truth just a few miles away."

Lawrence actually sighed and shook his head. "They really were pathetic in a way, a shambles of a Washington bureaucracy, surviving down at the Rock, too weak to do anything major, a not-so-secret secret that would be found out sooner or later, and you then figuring you had wiped it out and now could rebuild for your so-called New Republic. It was very convenient then to just let you continue on."

"To what end for you?"

"I love the analogies of old movies and such. Ever see that great PBS series *I, Claudius*? You know the one. About Rome and the Emperor Claudius."

"Yeah, I've seen it," John replied, his voice filled with sadness for all that this man was now confronting him with.

"There was an underlying theme there at the end of the series when Claudius realizes he can no longer fight the corruption eating at the heart of Rome and he would soon be assassinated. He said, 'Let all the poison come out, let it all come out.'

"That's why we stayed in the dark, John. The Day was bound to happen sooner or later. America was simply too ripe a target for the myriad of enemies, overt and hidden. Ironic, isn't it? We actually did save the world back 1945. Even if we didn't necessarily fight the wrong enemy the way we should have."

"What are you saying?"

"Don't get me wrong up front, John. Hitler needed to be taken down. His racism and meglaomania alone was cause enough to fight. But fight where and when? Churchill hinted at it often enough. When it came to Stalin and the entire Soviet Union, he said he'd enlist the aid of the devil himself to fight Hitler. But marry him?

"If Churchill had been the dominant power in the alliance, rather than Roosevelt, he'd have given just enough aid, enough promises and platitudes to keep the Soviets barely alive. If need be, let the war drag out, rather than let it take the turn towards our inevitable victory by 1945. I've studied it a lot, John, he would have kept the Soviets on a short leash, giving just barely enough aid and no more, thus preventing them from advancing into Europe until we finally had the bomb, finished off Hitler, and then told an emasculated Russia to go to hell. Or better yet, see it collapse, Stalin eliminated, and finally there would have been real peace in the world." Lawrence sighed and shook his head.

"But it didn't turn out that way," John said.

"That's right. It didn't. Imagine the world without the Soviet Union? Without the Soviets. Providing, of course, China never goes communist. It becomes a true American century. No fear of the bomb, perhaps not even digging these monolithic underground fortresses, a true century or more of peace."

"But again, it wasn't. We cannot change the history we got. But you're avoiding the question," John protested.

"No, I'm not, I'm answering it, Matherson. Down in this labyrinth, which you've only seen part of, we are the real government now. Just not yet revealed. We have close to a light division of mobile infantry and Special Forces here, more than enough equipment, even some air assets, all stored away. We have additional assets in a couple of other locations. You can guess Cheyenne Mountain is one of them, but there are others. John, we now have had more than sixty years to get ready," he paused, "and, my friend, we are ready."

"To do what? Take over? If so, take over what? Perhaps you haven't seen the world I've seen. It's little more than wreckage out there. I'll admit the New Republic was mostly a pipe dream, but at least it's something."

"John, from what I've seen it was just that, a pipe dream. Has the life of the average person out there changed, whether you exist or don't exist? Has it really?"

John knew the answer to that. Except for an ideal that there was something better building, he was right. New York City was still an abandoned hellhole, as were Boston, Philadelphia, D.C., and so on down the eastern coast. Florida was just simply gone, a realm of small coastal fortresses, some benign, others just pirate states feeding off each other.

West of the Mississippi he couldn't speak of. The cities, he knew, were gone. The West Coast, maybe there was some semblance of order there, thanks to the Chinese occupation. Reports they'd received from the Plains states talked of some semblance of a return to a sort of frontier justice, but then the frontier was lawless as well, with horse-mounted posses ruling.

"Let's get to the core of it, Lawrence. We've been talking for hours, we'll soon be back to Raven Rock, let's cut to the chase here. What do you propose to do?"

"We finally come out. We come out bringing—oh God, I almost hate to say it—we bring Peace, Bread, and Land. We suppress the banditry that is still out there. You've done a good job of it from Black Mountain to nearly all of western North Carolina and into Tennessee, but you are the exception.

"We wave the old flag and it will resonate. We set up a modern medical facility, eradicate all the diseases that we had once eradicated a hundred years ago, and we put people back to constructive work, stringing electricity again, for example. They really won't give a damn if we are elected or not.

"You know that to be true, John. The people who are left will trade a vote for your New Republic for security any day. A full stomach, knowing their kids are safe, will trump anything you can ever offer."

"And who elected you, then?"

Lawrence actually laughed out loud at that.

"Don't be naïve, John. The fact that I have the only modern fighting force east of the Mississippi is my vote for power."

John knew that to argue further was useless. "So why court me like this?"

"How 'like this'?"

"What you've been doing the last few days. You could have just as easily breached the barrier between Raven Rock and Camp David, stormed in. Maybe we would have fought, but I know the president. In the face of such odds a lot of kids would have to be killed for a cause that can't win. He would have surrendered the Rock. So why not just kick us out, or for that matter shoot us and be done with it?"

"Because I want you on our side. That's why."

John looked over at him in surprise, then fished into his pocket and pulled out another cigarette and lit it.

"You know those things will kill you."

"They haven't yet," John said coldly. "So you'll be proposing this to President Scales."

"I know his answer," Lawrence said, and there was actual sadness in his voice.

"So do I. Go to hell."

"Cruel as it is, Bob is dying and we both know it. I fully intend to leave him in place at Raven Rock, though we will occupy it starting tomorrow. But it's you, John, that I really want."

"Why?"

"Oh, the usual platitudes. I'll skip them all for now."

"I refuse to be your token. If it's to leave me as head after Bob is gone, again, you can go to hell."

"Nothing so base as that, John. You're a proven quantity that we need. An interface between what was, and what will be."

"Again, go to hell. I'll not be your token, and that's final."

"We'll see," Lawrence replied.

John tossed his smoke out the window and lit another. Their driver finally came back to the egress to Frederick. They slowed to a stop for the security barrier, again the personnel snapping to attention at the sight of Lawrence. As they slowly started up, John again spotted the guards in hazmats by the entry to Fort Detrick.

And again he wondered. Fort Detrick. It just didn't ring a bell for him what its purpose was. It was just another of the hundreds of military bases once scattered around the country.

He looked over at Lawrence. "What is Fort Detrick?"

"Just a logistical nod now, downgraded long before the Day."

"Really?"

Lawrence had no reply.

The rest of the journey passed swiftly, and twenty minutes later they were at the barrier between Camp David on one side, and on the other side Raven Rock. The massive thirty-ton blast doors were open and as they came to a stop and John got out, several security guards from his side of the door approached, weapons drawn.

"Are you okay, sir?" they asked General Lawrence.

"Just fine."

"Little tense here, sir. I don't know who these jokers are on the other side but it was getting tense."

"It's all right, Sergeant. Everything will be fine." Lawrence was standing by the open door of his Humvee and actually gave John a casual salute.

"Until tomorrow." He hesitated and then smiled. "When you come to your senses, John, you'll see there's no alternative. We actually do need some form of a government, even if it's only to convince people that it's real. I've taken the time with you because I know that once past your anger, you see there is no other alternative. John, I'm convinced you could be an essential component in helping us. Bob will pass soon, we both know that and you are the obvious, the so obvious choice to fill his shoes. I'll say goodbye for now and see you tomorrow . . . Mr. President."

He got back into the vehicle, the driver pulling U-turn, and set off into the darkness.

"The president is waiting to see you, sir."

"Let's go," John answered, "and by the way, I'm starving, think you can whip something up for us?"

"Already have, sir, last of the bacon and eggs. If what those guys said is true about tomorrow, guess I'll be out of a job."

CHAPTER SIX

Bob was sitting up in his office, and had changed to a fresh shirt and slacks. He looked rested, though his features were still sallow and worn.

"He said he wanted me to stay on," John announced, sitting down across from Bob. "Actually told me I would be president. I told him to go to hell and that was it."

"Interesting tour you had, John," Bob replied, sipping a cup of coffee. "I'd like to have seen it myself. You know, there always had been rumors about it. Seemed too fantastical to believe, and anyone who casually speculated, well, it was dismissed. Though I do remember a staffer, a light colonel some years back, who was a little too vocal and insistent about it. Well, he got arrested. Oh, not over that—caught drunk with a general's daughter, at least we were told it was a general's daughter, and he was gone. Report later said he hung himself in the brig. Several others like that through the years, caught with drugs, that type of thing, and then they're gone. Anyhow, now it all adds up. Amazing in a way, isn't it?"

John did not reply.

"We'll let them in at twelve hundred hours tomorrow."

"Sir?" John asked in astonishment.

"What am I going to do, John. Resist? Let's be realistic. We're running out of supplies as is. Systems are breaking down increasingly of late, to the point that I suspect sabotage, but just can't put a finger on who's behind it. We resist and a lot of innocent people get hurt. Hurt for what?"

"For the Republic," John whispered.

"Nice dream, my friend, but I see the handwriting on the wall. Short of a miracle, some sort of popular uprising of sentiment, most will flock to Lawrence's new order of things without a second thought."

"I can't help but feel that there's something behind the mask though," John protested. "Something sinister."

"Isn't there always?"

"What's that supposed to mean?"

"There's always something behind the mask. Peace, Bread, Land, but what did it bring? A new Reich. Maybe the greatest miracle of modern times was that we once set out to create a republic but we were blessed to have George Washington at the helm and somehow it actually worked. But remember, there was an Aaron Burr ready to subvert it. Even Jefferson had his doubts it would last."

"I don't trust Lawrence as far as I can spit."

"How come?"

"I think his library was a giveaway. It was the collection of a warrior intellectual to be sure, but there was something of a dark side in those volumes as well. I always felt that if you walk into a man's house, and he has a library, in fifteen minutes you can tell a whole helluva lot about him.

"I remember the first time you had me into your home as commandant of the War College. You had a damn good mix, sir, for a military man. Strong emphasis on the Civil War, which was your personal interest, but also a good smattering going back to Plutarch and Xenophon."

Bob laughed softly. "Can't say I actually read them. But they looked good on the shelf."

"Be that as it may, that emphasis on Nietzsche, the whole man and superman—the 'overman,' I think Nietzsche called him. It troubled me."

"Maybe he's just got a healthy curiosity."

"We shall see. But there's one other thing. What exactly is Fort Detrick?"

"You mean in Frederick?"

"The same. The guards in the shadows at the approach were wearing hazmat suits."

Scales blew out noisily. "You sure?"

"Definitely."

A moment of silence followed.

"Detrick was the center for biowarfare research for forty years, John. It's a dark place. A very dark place."

"Shit."

They both took a moment to let that sink in.

"It was supposedly deactivated from that role shortly before the Day, but then again . . ."

"So what do we do?"

"What can we do for now?"

"Nothing."

"That's right, nothing."

"Bob, what do I do?"

"I take it you're not interested in being part of this New World Order."

John couldn't respond to that. At the moment he was just so damn tired of it all.

"Go home, John."

"Are you serious?"

"Dead serious, my friend."

"How?"

"I thought this might be your answer. That Bonanza is gassed up and ready to go if that's what you want. Go home, sit it out, and see what develops."

"The Bonanza, crap, same kid piloting it?"

"Why?"

John tried to smile. "What about you, Bob?"

"Come on, John, my day's done. They won't hurt me even though I won't cooperate. They'll make the usual announcement, most likely that I'm terminal, they've stepped in to help. The Republic won't go out with a bang, just barely a whisper. Go home, pick up your life, move on. You got a nice little enclave down there, maybe they'll let it alone for now, maybe not, but only the future will tell."

John looked over at Bob and in the harsh light of his office he saw just how much his friend had aged in the last three years. From a general intent on a fundamental reorder of everything, imbued with the ideal that a new republic could actually take root in the ashes, he'd withered into the defeated man sitting before him now, resigned to the realities of fate.

"Okay then, sir. I'll go."

"Yes, go back, be that college president again, and just wait, sooner or later you'll be back in the fray."

As John stood up he felt a sudden tightness in his throat. He had served with this man, on and off, for three decades, and knew this really was farewell.

He snapped to attention and gave a crisp salute. Bob, forcing himself to stand firmly erect, returned it.

"Old friend, let's not get sentimental about it. Okay?"

"Yes, sir." John cleared his throat, having a hard time with the words. "I'll see you at sundown, sir."

He turned and left the room.

General Bob Scales sat back down. He had not taken any pain meds; he wanted his head clear for this. He'd had a thought, a hope, that in the end Matherson would maybe, just maybe find a way to set things right.

But he wouldn't have a part in it, definitely not.

He reached into his desk drawer, pulled out the old style Colt 1911, and thought of his long-lost wife, dead on that Day, along with so many other dreams.

It would be a relief at last.

PART IV

[S]everal sources indicate that the disease is spreading with unprece-dented speed. . . .

—BBC broadcast

CHAPTER ONE

John awoke to the smell of eggs cooking, and slipped into his old, rumpled bathrobe. He was barely out of the bedroom before three things happened at once: the call of his wife, "I think Daddy's awake"; his terrorist puppy, bounding around the corner to greet him; and two-year-old Genevieve running right behind the dog and leaping into his outstretched arms.

Chloe, their six-month-old puppy that looked to be some sort of mix of golden retriever and heaven knows what else, now had her paws up on his chest, begging for attention as well.

Makala came out of the kitchen, dressed in her usual bathrobe, brushing a wisp of graying blond hair out of her eyes. She stood on tiptoe to kiss him good morning. He turned a cheek to her, not wanting to subject her to his morning mouth, or the fact that before turning in last night he had gone outside for a Dunhill. She had argued passionately about it, but finally just conceded he was an addict, as long as his addiction was kept outside, not in front of others, late at night, and one only—though this time he had cheated and smoked two.

He had made his usual resolve to quit. In the four months since

Lawrence had given him the carton of imported smokes he had finally rationed them out to one, at most two a day. He would quit, of course, when the last one was smoked, but now there was a wrinkle with that plan. His friend Forrest up in Burnsville had planted a crop of tobacco back in the spring. Forrest had announced last time he had visited that he'd return with some fine Virginia pipe tobacco and cigars. Makala had more than half seriously announced that she would take Genevieve and leave him if he succumbed.

"Daddy smoked, Daddy smoked," Genevieve chirped, always glad to inform on her father.

"Guilty as charged, kiddo, but come on, can't I have a little indulgence?"

"John, I really am tempted to have Genevieve tear them up, if we could find them," Makala announced, ruefully shaking her head as she took the toddler from his arms and motioned for John to sit down for breakfast.

John didn't reply to that; they were of course fully justified in imposing martial law on him. A nurse who had seen too many dying of cancer had every right to protest.

He resolved to find a better hiding place.

There was a knock on the screen door. Today it was Barbara Grierson, a charming blue-eyed woman in her early twenties. After losing her husband, a maintenance man at the college who had been killed in the Posse fight, and their precious daughter during the starving time, she had come near to suicide.

Makala had poured countless hours of just listening and understanding into Barbara, and convinced her to open a nursery school for toddlers. She was a godsend now to the community, allowing Makala and others to work.

"Ready, sweetheart?" she called, stepping into the kitchen.

Genevieve ran to her embrace, while Makala handed over a lunch box with a jelly sandwich and several dried apples.

"It's such a beautiful day, so we're going for a picnic up on Flat Creek," she announced.

Makala gave them both hugs and watched them head down the drive with three other toddlers in tow.

"I nearly go crazy at times, just chasing Genie," she sighed. "How she handles four is almost beyond me."

Chloe pushed the screen door open and followed the chattering group down to Montreat Road, barking up a storm, then trotted back and begged to be let inside again. Makala opened the door, and after jumping on her a few times, the puppy settled down by John's feet with a sigh.

John watched the children until they were around the bend in the road. The morning fog was starting to burn off, a diffused light glowing through the trees. All was silent. Gone was the world of mechanical noises, of cars passing, a school bus stopping at just about every house to transport students a half mile or so.

Half a dozen older kids ran down the road, playing a game of tag as they passed. Schools were now strictly a local affair of walking or riding your bike, no matter what the weather. For some of the kids it was a hike of a couple of miles, and of course grandparents were always glad to talk about "back in their day," when you had to walk uphill both ways in a blinding snowstorm.

John actually preferred what was happening to schools and teaching. Gone were the days of factory-like complexes housing a thousand or more children who were bussed in from miles away to those somewhat soulless buildings planted in a field far from town, only to go inside and stare at a monitor for hours, rushing out afterward to be driven to some sports event miles away. To John it had become soulless.

Schools had again become one-room schoolhouses. Perhaps it was nostalgia for a simpler world, but he definitely approved of what was evolving. In the morning and late afternoon the streets were again filled with the sounds of children running, shouting, playing, until, of course, they returned to do the myriad chores that now awaited them.

Still looking out the window, he spotted Old Man Winston, going in the opposite direction, heading for the town of Black Mountain two miles away. He must be close to ninety, a Vietnam vet who always wore his baseball cap adorned with a Big Red One insignia. He'd walk to town to sit by the fire station in one of the rocking chairs set out front. He'd gossip with other elderly folks who had made this their daily ritual, catch up on any news, stop by the secondhand shop on Cherry Street run by the Gilfords.

Gilfords' store had turned into a rather flourishing swap-and-trade place. It was now two floors piled high with junk that once ran on electricity. It housed cast-off televisions, from eighty-inch flatscreens to old black-and-white portables; radios of all kinds; window air conditioners; electric stoves; light bulbs, hundreds of those; water heaters; electric knives and can openers; and of course monitors that had shorted out on the Day and could not be resurrected by Paul Hawkinson or Ernie and Linda Franklin.

For those who knew how to fix things, to recycle or repurpose something into something else, the place could be a gold mine. So there was always a lively scene of bargaining and dickering to be found there.

John saw it as another indicator that their town was crawling back from the abyss. As he watched Winston slowly continue down the road, Scottie Peterson came into view, riding his bicycle, pumping hard against the slope. Attached behind the bike was an old red wagon with a dozen or so bottles of milk. Turning into their driveway, he came to a stop and grabbed one of the old-fashioned bottles.

"Scottie, how are you this morning?" John asked, coming out to greet him.

"Doing great, Doc, glad college started."

"Don't be late for class."

"I'll make it, sir." They traded the empty bottle John was holding for a full quart of fresh whole milk.

"Anything new this morning?"

"No, sir, just the usual. Hot day yesterday, a real scorcher working in the field. Harvest is looking mighty good, looks like a real bumper crop for apples this year."

"Excellent news. See you later," John said as Scottie turned and got back on his bike. He coasted back down the driveway, wagon rattling, then continued up the hill.

Now, to make this Norman Rockwell moment complete, John thought, *we need another kid coming past, tossing the morning paper, and Lord what I'd give for an old-fashioned bread and pastry delivery. And an ice truck, now that would be something,* he mused, going back inside to finish his breakfast. Scottie's milk delivery from his mother's farm up on the North Fork was a pleasing kind of thing to have back in their lives.

As he walked into the kitchen he popped off the paper cap to the one-quart bottle and sniffed. It was raw milk and cream, as pasteurization had yet to come back, and Makala refused to drink it. She didn't like it, said it tasted funny, and besides she claimed it was a good way for any number of illnesses to spread. She remembered from a history class in high school how Lincoln's mother died from "milk sickness" after drinking milk from cows that ate white snakeroot plants. Her fear was made worse when she learned that pasteurization didn't affect its toxic qualities. Checking old issues of *Foxfire* survival books and *Mother Earth* magazines at the library, she found out that the toxic snakeroot plant did grow mostly in the Midwest but also well into North Carolina; therefore, she declared, there'd be no milk for her or Genevieve.

When Scottie's family started their business, having raised up four cows, she had announced her research, wanting to ban the product. She sent students, armed with photos of the deadly snakeroot, to inspect the Peterson farm, almost like the county agricultural agents of old. Scottie and his widowed mom of course cooperated, and the farm was found to be clean of the root, but that still didn't completely change Makala's mind on the subject of whole, unpasteurized milk. She did eventually come to tolerate it, however, as long as it was same-day fresh, which the Petersons guaranteed.

"Eggs are getting cold, John," she called as she pulled up her chair at the kitchen table. John joined her on the other side, pouring out some cream for what passed as coffee, made from grounds that had already been used twice.

John studied his wife, as he did every morning. Twelve years younger than he was, Makala still had youthful features. She was thin—as everyone was these days—but still appealing. Her strawberry-blond hair, to her dismay, was streaked with gray. At least the playful gray-green eyes would never change, the slightly pouty lips, and a voice that tended to still be a bit whispery and low. He would laughingly tell her that she sounded like Lauren Bacall or Kathleen Turner.

They made small talk over breakfast. They talked about the pumpkin harvest at the Crampton Farm, and that the students had been rehearsing for the fall play, *Our Town,* having found a copy of the script in the library. It would premiere in two weeks.

With breakfast done, John helped with the dishes and kissed Makala several times until she laughingly pulled away, announcing there wasn't time for that now, or he'd be late for school himself.

After dressing casually in a pair of faded jeans and equally faded blue button-down shirt, he picked up his book bag and headed for the door. Makala had finally convinced him that his beard just made him look too old and it was time to get rid of it. He had yet to shave this week; actually it was Makala who shaved him with an old-fashioned straight razor, something that he had never mastered, slicing himself nearly every time he attempted to do it alone. She, on the other hand, deftly handled it with ease and barely a nick each Saturday night.

It was a short walk up to the college. As he turned the corner to the campus he passed over the Mill Dam Bridge. To his left the waterwheels that powered the generators inside the powerhouse splashed away with a good head of water from the dam.

The campus bell sounded, signaling the start of the first class, and he quickened his pace. There was still that old custom that gave tremendous leeway to professors being late for class—or, for that matter, presidents of the college—but he hated to abuse it.

Climbing the walkway behind Belk Hall he did his usual ritual of stepping first into a small six-sided chapel, not more than eight feet across, with three sides open to the elements and the bubbling creek, crowned with a maze of rhododendrons.

Known as the Prayer Porch, it was a place where anyone could wander in for a few minutes, listen to the creek whispering by. A few open Bibles were left on the side table, and students could write a little note, be it a prayer, a thanks to God or whomever, and tuck the paper into a crack in the shingles. Next to one of the Bibles was his old, old friend . . . Rabs the Rabbit. On the day Jennifer had come into the world a loving grandmother had tucked that rabbit into her crib. It had become her always best friend forever, until she held him, worn a faded patched green with love and a hundred thousand kisses, as she slipped away forever.

He no longer cried when he looked at it—well, almost never. He just smiled wistfully at what once was, leaned over, and kissed Rabs, the way he had once kissed his sleeping daughter before heading to class. As he walked in, the eight students enrolled for a new course he was offering titled "The Age of Totalitarianism" stopped talking, smiled, and offered their good mornings.

He sat down in a creaky old office chair and leaned back. "Where did we leave off?" he asked, offering his usual opening to any class he had taught across the years. "Oh, yes. I remember. We all finished *Animal Farm,* of course."

It was amusing to observe his students, who fell into several categories: those who'd read the assignment and looked calm and relaxed, the ones who avoided eye contact because they didn't want to be called on, and those who tried to bluff him by indeed looking calm and relaxed but of course were not.

John took a deep breath and looked out over the class. He was terrible at remembering names. He looked at the girl in the front of the room and thought to himself for a second, *Is her name Alisha?*

The petite brunette with thick glasses smiled, intuiting his problem. She told him, "I'm Alisha, sir."

"Thanks," John said with a shy smile, "I'm getting absentminded in my old age."

The class laughed politely. How different they now looked compared to the kids who had occupied this room five years ago. All were dressed now in jeans or work clothes, mostly bib overalls, a T-shirt underneath, for the day promised to be warm; all of them were slender. Makala said it was the aftereffects of the starving time in the two years after the Day. It had stunted their growth, and they would always have that look, the way their great-grandparents who'd survived the Great Depression too often did, thin and drawn from a time when malnutrition was the norm. He remembered learning that when the draft started in 1940, something like a quarter of all draftees were categorized 4F, or unfit to serve, because of rickets, vitamin deficiencies, being underweight, or just not being healthy enough due to the sad aftereffects of years of poor diet.

These were good students, though. Gone were the days of before, when so many went through college just because that was the thing expected of them. Gone was the world of diversions, of phones, of internet, of TikTok and Facebook, and endless mind-numbing shoot-'em-up fantasy games. There really wasn't much to life again, except for work, often backbreaking, or reading and studying.

The two hours went quickly, with talk of Stalin, the Terror, the complacency of the West thanks to the likes of Duranty and other leftist apologists of the day, and back to just how easy it was for the pigs in the story to mislead the others, the mindless following of the sheep and geese, the tragedy of those who were blindly loyal to the end, only to be killed by the very party they worshiped.

John found himself wishing yet again that he had a good working television, and if not a set of DVDs, at least old VHS tapes of classics such as *1984, Schindler's List,* or the frightening tapes of *The Killing Fields,* the Cultural Revolution of Mao in the movie *The Red Violin,* and especially *Triumph of the Will.*

He remembered a professor he'd had as an undergrad, who would use the campus theater for a showing of a 35mm print of *Triumph.*

"To see it on a television screen does not covey the power of it," the professor had announced before showing the film. "I want you to see Hitler filling the entire screen, twenty feet tall, to see the thousands upon thousands of troops, all faceless, all identical, marching in the torchlight parades the way your grandparents saw them in all their frightening murderous power, the way all of Germany did."

John had gone to see the elderly professor the following day. He was German, you could tell by his accent, but until that moment he had not said anything about his country or heritage.

Troubled by the film, John finally got to the point. The film had hypnotized him. He had been caught up in the power of the pageantry, the sheer power, and the old man smiled.

"I was in that army in the last year of the war," the old man replied, staring out his office window. "They called us the Deutsch Yugen division. Sixteen-, eighteen-year-olds, thousands of us, and we marched to that power and believed in it, and believed there was no finer fate than to sacrifice one's self, body and soul, to their Führer."

He paused.

"We all died at Normandy that summer of 1944, if not killed physically, then in our souls. It was when I finally wandered back to Germany after deserting a few weeks before the war ended that

I realized the poison I had drunk. Of those of us who deserted, most were caught and strung up on telephone poles as traitors to our beloved leader. I was caught, and was about to face that judgment when some British soldiers surprised the unit, killed them, and rescued me. Funny in a way, in the end rescued by my enemies.

"That was our final reward, our reckoning with the Führer. You sensed it, Mr. Matherson. Always remember it for the rest of your life. It is a heady brew, but in the end . . . there is nothing but bitter loss and regret that you did not stand up and somehow say no, I won't, and I will always carry my share of guilt for all that was done by Germans who once were considered the most civilized."

Funny, that memory coming to him now as class let out—and next week they had a lesson on Nietzsche. Something he had learned for Lawrence and he chose that topic because maybe it could help him as well in unraveling what was behind that man. With no longer an internet he again had to rely on the old-fashioned method of going to the college library where he did find copies of more than few of Nietzsche's works. He thanked God for whatever philosophy professor it was who had ordered them, and required their reading decades ago. He increasingly sensed that the mystery of Lawrence was within the words of Nietzsche.

CHAPTER TWO

After class, John walked over to the Graham chapel and offices. Looking in and seeing no one was there, he entered and sat down to think in the silence.

For the last four months he had been telling himself that the world beyond Black Mountain and Montreat was no longer of his concern. There was more than enough for him to do right here. Paul Hawkinson, now something of the head engineer, had multiple projects running. They were putting in a new electrical generating system at the old North Fork Dam that would again light up the entire valley with energy to spare.

The old curmudgeon, Ernie Franklin, and his wife, Linda, were hard at work repairing and refitting old computers. They had never realized, until random chance drove them to a stockpile of discarded computers, that older models dating back to Apple II and Pentiums, when replaced by the near-yearly updates, had just been tossed in the basement, often into out-of-the-way corners that had not been touched by the EMP. Most of the Franklins' home down in the gap had been given over into something of a lab that drew the tech nerds, some just showing up after a hike of days, even weeks, toting a few late-model machines that had not been plugged in on the Day. They could be gone over, repaired, and set into the hard-wired network. Wi-Fi was still way beyond their capacity, but Ernie promised in a year at most he'd have that back as well.

Makala's clinic was a school now as well, turning out the equivalent of skilled nurses and physician assistants, who not too far into the past would have qualified as actual doctors.

Food was stable; they were even looking at something of a surplus even after seed was set aside for next year's planting. The farm herds that had nearly been wiped out in the starving time, when people were slaughtering anything they could eat, were starting to see a resurgence, especially pigs and the few dairy cows whose owners, like the Petersons, were actually expanding their herds.

So what was there to worry about?

Instinct just said that too much was brewing. The Camp David situation, for starters—and what was Lawrence's game? He had not heard a word about him since leaving the Rock.

Three students came into the chapel, slowing a bit when they saw John sitting alone, deep in thought.

"Ah, hi, Professor, everything okay?"

"Sure, Sarah, sure, just thinking, it's a good place to do that."

"Ah, we were going to use the stage for practice for the play, do you mind?"

"Far from it," he said with a smile. He got up and walked to the back of the chapel, and for a moment stood in the shadows by the door to watch. Sarah had been chosen to be Emily in *Our Town*. A good choice; she was seen as the most gifted student on campus now that Tori had graduated. In another world Sarah might have gone to the stage in New York or even Hollywood after graduating. But just last month she announced she was happily pregnant; she and her husband were married a week later in this same chapel and they were planning to go back to the family farm after graduating to raise a family. Who was to say that staying here, working another of the small farms that had been starting up in the area, and settling down was all that bad a future. That was what John thought as he smilingly watched her perform, the whole meaning of that song "Simple Gifts." If life was again to take hold in this small town, that is how it was always done, for countless generations, especially after a time of war, as if it was a primal instinct to "increase and multiply."

After a while he took the few steps to his office, where suddenly the whole world came crashing back in on John Matherson.

Makala was waiting in his office, a look of anxiety causing her features to look drawn with worry.

"Hon, what's up?"

"The BBC. John, did you hear it just now?"

In spite of his habit of trying to step away from news from the outside since he left Raven Rock, he still did listen in once a day to the one global news source that he still trusted.

"Turn it on, it's time for their evening London report."

He clicked on the shortwave radio behind his desk. It was one that Ernie had brought back to life, an old tube model from decades ago, and took half a minute to warm up.

He carefully adjusted the dials, finding the usual static—at times the station could barely be heard, but atmospherics were good today and the station came in clear.

There was the classic sound of Big Ben tolling six o'clock, and by old instinct he looked at his pocket watch, a few minutes off one o'clock local time, then the ever-calm, classical-sounding voice of a BBC announcer came in clear.

It is six P.M., London time, and this is the BBC Home News for today.

There have been a number of reports coming in today from mainland China of near simultaneous outbreaks of disease in Shanghai, Beijing, and several other coastal cities. As reported

three days ago, the Chinese government has made no official an-
nouncement, but several sources indicate that the disease is spread-
ing with unprecedented speed, and today the government has
declared a citywide quarantine on Shanghai, and a dusk-to-dawn
curfew in Beijing.

In its first report today, the Chinese government said the illness
appeared to be a rapid-onset lung infection, and the usual precau-
tions are now being taken.

China's health minister, in a statement released two hours ago,
has stated China has the situation well in hand and they expect
the state of emergency to be short-lived.

The government on the island nation of Taiwan has declared a
full blockade and sealed their nation off from all outside contact.

In the five years since the Day, China has gradually resumed
international flights, including to the West Coast of the United
States, Australia, New Zealand, and Indonesia, and there is ques-
tion this evening if those flights might be temporarily suspended,
either by China itself or by nations having arrivals from that
country.

Our own health ministry has stated that it is watching the sit-
uation with "acute interest," but as yet have not indicated any
precautions.

A further analysis of this situation after the other news of
the day.

The renewed government of Kandahar today announced . . .

John turned the radio down. "Why the concern, sweetheart?"

Makala sat down across from his desk and slowly shook her
head. "First of all, you and I both know that if they are isolating an
entire city, it's bad."

"Maybe so . . ."

"I know so. Remember the global panic with that last contagion before the Day? It pales to insignificance compared to what we have been through since, but a million people died here, and our country damn near went crazy with restrictions, wearing masks that actually weren't much good, promoting inoculations we came to mistrust. And then it passed.

"One million out of a nation of three hundred and thirty million, grim as it sounds, that's less than one-third of one percent who died from it, and we survived. China's half a world away, Makala. Could just be some damn bat crapping into a pigsty thing."

"John, I'm not sure. Call it a bad hunch. After my first class this morning I went to see Paul Hawkinson over in the library. He was listening to the same thing on his shortwave. He pulled in some ham operator in Northern California. One of those small independent states out there that are refusing Chinese aid. He said he heard a report of people in San Francisco getting sick these last few days, with plague-like symptoms, and several people have already died from it."

John wasn't sure how to respond. It was Makala's job to worry about public health. She'd had a similar reaction to an outbreak of pneumonia last winter that had killed half a dozen in the community and sickened quite a few hundred, but then that had died off with the coming of spring.

The ham operator out west could simply be dealing with the almost-daily rumors that were just part of the background noise of life. If he worried about every single one, he would have gone off the deep end years ago.

"Let's wait it out a few days, see what happens. Besides, we are a helluva long way from California, let alone China. Okay?"

"I hope so," she replied softly. "We are ripe, you know."

"We're what?"

"Ripe for something big. We've crawled back part of the way from the edge of starvation, we're having a good harvest, general health is improving, but John, it's still iffy. It wouldn't take much. China claims now to be the one remaining superpower, but are they? We all heard the reports of major crop failures in their heartland for two years running.

"Before the rise of global transportation of food, basic stuff like wheat and rice, China would go into starvation mode on a regular basis and tens of millions would die." She stood up and headed for the door. "Maybe I worry too much, John, but then again, that's my job."

He would never say it but she did, indeed, worry too much.

After she was gone, he closed the door and turned the shortwave back on. For the rest of the afternoon he barely paid attention to his paperwork, the correcting of papers, or the town meeting to discuss the latest developments with the building of the new power station over on the North Fork. He had a bad feeling about this that would not go away.

CHAPTER THREE

John listened in again at midnight London time—for any updates, but there were none, other than a report out of Taiwan that Shanghai was definitely on lockdown. Gone were the days of a global network of news sources, including both official journalists and the millions of local sources on the internet, or just anyone who wanted to comment. The internet today was a skeleton of what it had been during its former glory days. America, of course, was out. The Middle East, except for Israel, was essentially gone. Europe had been devastated east of France by its own EMP extending far beyond Moscow. The new Soviet state was still in control from just west of the Urals across to the Pacific, but like the Soviets of old they were a closed state. Japan was struggling in a post-EMP world, which left China, and Indonesian links, and it seemed like that link to the last first-world state might be in trouble as well.

The following morning John woke again to the same routine. The dog running rampant through the house, Genevieve leaping into Daddy's bed to bring him blearily awake. It was another beautiful fall day, the first dabbling of autumn was coloring the trees, especially the maple in the backyard. Makala, he knew, had gotten up earlier than usual; he could hear the shortwave playing in his office, volume up loud so she could hear it in the kitchen as she made French toast. No coffee today; until someone took pity on his supply, it was back to herbal teas.

As he stepped outside for his morning indulgence of a single Dunhill cigarette out of Makala's sight, the Peterson boy came pedaling up the street, wagon rattling with bottles of milk and empty returns.

There was the usual exchange, the usual pleasantries about the weather, then John was back inside.

"If I ever could find where you hide those cigarettes, you know what I'd do," Makala announced with mock seriousness.

"What are you, my warden?"

Makala, of course, abstained, but he knew his loving wife would definitely turn a blind eye if their daughter did indeed uncover his stash behind the bookcase.

With breakfast done and Genevieve off with her nursery group, there was a momentary, peaceful lull.

"You were up early. Anything new?"

"The Chinese are saying nothing more, at least that's what the BBC says. Picked up a weird one, Radio Taiwan."

John, when playing around with the old shortwave in his office late at night, had also stumbled across it a few times.

"And?"

"They're saying it's bubonic plague."

"What?"

"You heard me, John. They claim a Chinese air force pilot defected from the city of Quanzhou, with a planeload of people."

John wondered if the information was reliable.

"Where's Quanzhou?" he asked.

"I looked it up in your old encyclopedia. It's a large city of a couple of million, I assume it's a lot more now. Major port as well. The defector claimed the plague started down at the dock area five days ago and has spread into the city. The city has gone to a full lock-down, roads blocked, rail and air service stopped, but tens of thousands had already fled before the city was closed. He said thousands are dying from it. Then I lost the station, as if it was being jammed."

John took that in. He tried to picture where Quanzhou was, his knowledge of the region hazy at best. Southeast China, across the straits from Taiwan.

"Rats have always lived in port cities, more so than elsewhere, and I think it's fair to assume a Chinese port isn't the most sanitary place in the world. John, suppose it's pneumonic bubonic plague."

"I know about plague, Makala, but what's the difference? Pneumonic?"

"I mean the plague most people are familiar with, we'll just call it the Black Death."

That term immediately conjured for John images of horror, of black boils and horrible suffering as they ruptured, the whole thing of "bring out your dead" and people dying in the streets of medieval London.

"Usually it's spread by rats and fleas. The rat is the carrier, the fleas jump from rat to human and infect him. If left untreated the fatality rate can be as high as fifty percent."

"So what's pneumonic?"

"That's the one of terror, John. In the Middle Ages the bacillus mutated to direct human-to-human contact. Remember that old nursery rhyme, 'Ring around the rosy . . .'"

He knew the lines. The last one wasn't originally "Ashes, ashes we all fall down." He whispered, "Achoo, achoo, we all fall down."

"It transmits from the lungs of someone infected through their cough, the sputum, a sneeze, even by touching a handkerchief after someone sneezed in it. If left untreated it's almost one hundred percent fatal, in as little as twelve hours from the first symptoms of cough and a rapidly rising fever. It is an absolute killer, and if a disease had a conscience this is one with no remorse. It's frightening how quickly it reproduces from first onset: an arithmetic of one cell to two, to four, to eight within minutes, and in twelve hours the body is overwhelmed."

She fell silent.

"Why are you obsessing on this, Makala?"

"It's my job, John. I'm in charge of public health, the health of this community. From the day I first came here as a refugee, and your community let me in because I knew medicine, it's been my job to keep it alive. This damn thing, if it ever hit here, it could wipe us out, turn us into a ghost town filled with corpses in little more than a week."

"Sweetheart." He reached across the table to take her hands. He suddenly realized she was on the point of tears. "You have to stop worrying."

"John, there's something sinister about this, I know it."

"Even if it's true, it's half a world away."

"Maybe not, if that report from California is true."

"All right then, three thousand miles away."

"John, when the big one hit in the fourteenth century, it started in China and Mongolia. It took ten years but eventually reached Europe through the trade routes, and within a few years, a third to a half of the population was dead. This town, this region, is barely hanging on. We are all weakened to a certain extent. I hate to think what a plague would do to us, it'd be more like fifty, even seventy-five percent dead."

"If it ever gets here, Makala. *If* it ever gets here. For right now let's pray for the best. And besides, I've got a class today on origins of the Cold War, so I better get ready for it. Okay?"

She didn't reply as he picked up his cup and dishes, rinsed them off, and got dressed. As he started out the door he looked back to see her in his office, slowly turning the dials on the shortwave radio.

CHAPTER FOUR

John absentmindedly went through his two-hour morning class. He found himself yet again talking about Stalin and Hitler, the political maneuverings of the late 1930s, and the less-than-awake West that could not see the handwriting on the wall. Afterward, still dwelling on the conversation with Makala that morning, he was tempted to drop in on the class she was teaching, but decided against it. He headed back home and got the old Edsel out of the garage.

The car was there strictly for town business now, but he justified the two gallons he would burn as a much-needed visit to his old friends, the Franklins. Driving carefully at not more than twenty-five miles an hour he nursed the car through town, waving to those he passed. He headed east to the top of the Swannanoa Gap and went up the long driveway, having to stop twice to pull limbs out of the way from the last storm, the tires far too delicate to simply run over the debris.

As he reached the last curve in their long third-of-a-mile drive-way, their dog Maggie barked a greeting. Linda was out on the porch and shouted a hello; Ernie ducked inside for a moment and then came back out with an uncorked bottle of wine.

"Just in time for the afternoon tasting," Ernie announced as John reached the porch and settled down in one of the rocking chairs. Maggie showered him with a good licking.

Ernie could easily be defined as a pain in the ass, a genuine curmudgeon of the first degree. He had been a thorn in John's side from the earliest days, always challenging anything the town committee tried to offer. But then again, he had saved John's life in that battle in Asheville, and in knowledge of computer technology he was rivaled only by Paul Hawkinson. It was Ernie who had helped Paul rebuild at least some semblance of a network using old computers scrounged from various places, some of them not being shorted out on the Day.

Linda was the mathematician of the family, long ago writing some of the algorithms that put Apollo on the moon, and then running the family business that had to do with software for large-array antennas used by the Department of Defense and a few other entities she never talked about.

"To make this a legitimate business call so I can write off the cost of the gasoline, I'll ask how things are going."

Ernie of course held forth for the next twenty minutes, after pouring John some godawful wine that he tried to sip politely. The upshot was that now they had over a hundred computers up and running, networked together, and Linda could even eavesdrop into some of the satellite data, though encrypting it was in general far too advanced for her now.

He finally slowed down enough to at last ask why John had come.

"Call it a need to just get away for a few hours, drink some of this stuff you try to pass off as wine, and ask for a few opinions."

"I always have opinions, John," said Ernie, and Linda just sighed in response.

"First off, what do you think of China?"

"I've been listening, though Linda's more of the ham radio type than me. I'm just trying to figure out how to make our system better."

Linda took John's half-full glass and tossed its contents over the railing. "Ernie, you can serve something better than that weasel piss, for heaven's sake." She went inside and came out a minute later with an actual bottle of merlot.

"For God's sake, Linda, that's private stock."

"We can afford a drink for Matherson here." It was already opened, and she refilled his glass.

"To old friends," she announced, and nodded for him to take a drink. It was good, the best he had tasted in some time.

"All right then, guess I have to return the favor." He reached into his breast pocket and pulled out two Dunhills. Ernie laughed with delight as John passed one over, got his Zippo out, and lit Ernie's smoke and then his own.

"Ah, but beware of Greeks bearing gifts, as they used to say. Something's bothering you and you don't feel like talking about it in town."

John blew out a puff of smoke and nodded his head. "China first. I've heard the usual BBC reports, nothing new there."

"That's because China is in a blackout," Linda said. "They've repeated the same news every hour, 'Everything is under control,' and then they switch over to their godawful music.

"Without your prompting, I've been curious too. Heard the report on Quanzhou on Radio Taiwan, they are definitely being jammed now. That's not good, never is."

"The Soviets, nothing new there, are not even reporting anything whatsoever on China, not even their usual propaganda about some new incursion on the Amur River. The only thing floating out there are the independents. Picked up a broadcast from someone in Thailand, in English of course, who says they had a contact in Taiwan but that the defector and his family have disappeared.

"Now California, did you hear about that contact, calls themselves Radio Free Sierra, up in the mountains. Talked with him briefly, before he said he had to shift frequencies so as not to be zeroed in on by Chinese authorities in Sacramento. He said the plague is definitely there, apparently came in on a military flight from Shanghai, both pilot and copilot dead within hours of barely landing their plane."

John took this in, silently smoking his cigarette clear down to the end.

Ernie had only smoked his halfway before pinching the flame off and putting the butt into his pocket for later.

"This guy said a friend of his who worked at the airport saw them taking the two pilots off the plane. He said they were vomiting blood, raving mad with fever. Word was they were dead a few hours later, faces turning black with their blood vessels rupturing under the skin. It sounds horrible. Everyone who came near them has been locked up in quarantine but rumor is they're down with it as well."

"Do you believe him?"

"Why shouldn't I, John?"

There was a moment of silence, as if each was lost in their thoughts.

"If it was the old days, before the EMP, with our international flights crisscrossing the world, we'd be screwed big time," Ernie finally said. Then he sighed, pulled the butt out of his pocket, and relit it.

"Think we're safe here?" Linda asked.

"We're isolated, so I'd like to think so."

"What do you think will happen in China?"

"God only knows," John replied. "A state like that, if it is what we think it is, they'll go draconian. Seal off Quanzhou airtight. Heaven help the people inside, though. According to the old encyclopedia Makala checked, two million were living there back in the 1960s. I bet it's six, maybe ten million there now."

"They have to seal it off."

"Is there any other way to stop it?" Linda asked.

"If I remember correctly I think penicillin, something like Cipro or Avelox, if given at the first symptoms can save you, though you'll still be damn sick and open to other things later like pneumonia."

"Surely there's a vaccine out there. Isn't there?"

"I guess so. I believe it's bacterial, so sure, there must be vaccines for something that virulent."

"Poor bastards," Ernie interjected. "Yeah, they're Chinese, no love lost between us, especially now, but still, you gotta pity them."

"Do you think it'll spread in California?" Linda asked, trying to sound hopeful.

"Well, California got hit just as bad as we did after the Day. Difference is, China came swooping in with their all-so-helpful aid. Still, estimates are by then maybe three-quarters of the population had died off. Place like Los Angeles with no electricity in the summer, no less?" John shook his head. "A nice pliant population left to welcome the Chinese in with open arms. Let's just hope they remembered to bring medicine with them."

"Long way from California to here, even to just on the other side of the Rockies. Folks on the eastern slope will see which way the wind is blowing and seal off and hope."

Linda actually chuckled sadly. "Ever read Poe's 'The Masque of the Red Death'?" she asked.

The two looked at her quizzically.

"Don't, but guess it sounds like something he'd write about." And she fell silent again.

"This is getting really cheerful," Ernie finally interjected, reaching over to the merlot next to Linda. He tossed out his own wine and refilled the cup with Linda's offering, pouring the last of it into John's glass.

"The old soldiers' quote then: 'Here's to a long war or a bloody plague.'"

"You can be so appropriate at times, Ernie," his wife snapped peevishly.

"Well, there ain't a damn thing we can do about it, sitting here on our porch on this beautiful afternoon, and John, you wouldn't happen to have any more of those cigarettes?"

John sighed and drew out one more. "I'd been saving this for the ride home." But he lit it, took a long puff, and handed it over to Ernie.

"The way you two are handling that thing, it's like we were back in college and had some weed."

There were a few short chuckles for memories of a better time, then John was ready to change the subject.

"I have something bugging me. I haven't talked about it since I came back from the Rock but it started nagging at me this morning."

"If you mean Raven Rock, John, you've said nothing about it to anyone since your return. Why so mum?"

"I have my reasons."

"Such as?"

Until this morning there was precious little he wanted to share with anyone who asked. His story was simply that the site went dark. John had announced that their effort to form a republic had simply slipped away. They were too spread out, too preoccupied with just staying alive, be it on the coast of Maine or as far south as Charleston, where the navy still operated.

Word had come of the death of President Scales, but not a word about John's own resignation.

And as it had proven to be with such things, there were farms to attend to and coax back to life, livestock to be raised, returning game to hunt up in the mountains, computers to fix, a new generating plant to build, and the thousand and one other things to attend to in a local community trying to come back to life.

And there was nothing whatsoever to be heard of from what had been Raven Rock, and all the rest of what was buried up there in Pennsylvania, Maryland, and Virginia.

There were times of late that he barely gave any further thought to Lawrence and all the rest hiding in the mountain. If they had some sort of grand plan for the future, he was no longer privy to it, and as long as they did not bother him and his community then quite frankly, the hell with them.

But now? These new rumors—could there be a link?

"Ernie, you had some of the frequencies that Raven Rock used to broadcast from, didn't you?"

"Yeah, why?"

"Ever check them?"

"After you came back in May, said that the place was going into collapse, yeah, I tuned in at times, got nothing but static."

"Ever get anything like data, uplinks to God knows what satellites we still have functioning up there, anything like that?"

"I don't think so. Why, should I be listening?"

"How about the navy, anything there?"

"Yeah, we get some things at times, ultra-low frequency, HARP-type transmissions. Assume our boomers are out there as a counterforce to the Soviets and China. And . . ."

He fell silent, looking at John, brows furrowed, and after taking one more drag on the cigarette he handed what was left to John, who took a final puff and then tossed it over the rail.

"Start listening more closely."

"You think something is going on?" Linda asked.

"Who knows," John replied, his features grim.

PART V

Thou shalt not be afraid for the terror by night; nor for the arrow that flieth by day; nor for the pestilence that walketh in darkness; nor for the destruction that wasteth at noonday.

—Psalm 91:5–6

CHAPTER ONE

Makala had been called out during the night to see to a new patient at the clinic, so John made breakfast for Genevieve. His attempt at two eggs over easy was blocked with "Yolks-ugh-Daddy," as Genevieve disdainfully pushed it away. That gesture triggered a flash memory of when, as a boy, having breakfast at his grandmother's, if he didn't eat everything, she'd cluck sadly and say, "Think of all those poor starving children in China." This morning it perhaps might hit too close to the mark and the runny yolk went to Chloe who eagerly wolfed it down.

His morning class had been canceled so the students could help with the fall apple and pumpkin harvest, and he looked forward to a morning of reading and listening to the shortwave.

As the tubes warmed up, he dialed in to one of several BBC frequencies, but atmospherics were iffy, and the signal faint. There was the usual back-chatter, barely heard even with volume turned high.

The news from China had essentially gone quiet. Radio Taiwan was now offline as well, due to the jamming. Essentially all of East Asia was dark.

"John?"

It was Makala, and he went out to the kitchen to greet her. Before he could say a word she held her hands out.

"Don't come near me yet," she announced, and without further comment she stripped off her overcoat, and then the denim dress and flannel shirt, and kicked the bundled clothes out the door. She had nothing on underneath and for a few seconds he thought she was starting to play one of their wonderful pastimes that frequently happened when Genevieve was gone. Smiling, he took another step toward her.

"Don't!" she snapped, edging around him and heading into the bathroom. He heard the shower turn on. Hot water was a luxury for them; there wasn't enough surplus electricity to turn the old hot water heater back on. Their custom had become weekly baths in an old-style tin tub next to the kitchen fireplace.

He heard her curse vehemently as the cold water rained down on her. After a few minutes the water shut off and she got out, still mumbling curses about wishing for a damn hot shower, then ran into the bedroom. She emerged a minute later in her frumpy bathrobe and sat down.

"I wish that had been the start of something different," he said, still smiling.

"John, I think we have a case."

"Case of what?"

"Plague."

He froze in place, not moving.

"I think I'm clean now. Scrubbed down at the infirmary before coming home too, but I didn't want to take any risks." She lowered her head and rested it on the kitchen table. "I have a K-cup of coffee hidden in the cabinet, top shelf on the left for emergencies. Would you brew it up for me?"

He found the cup and opened the plastic lid.

"It'll take a few minutes to perk."

"I don't feel like waiting, just pour some hot water on it."

The kettle of hot water was still on from the morning fire, so he did as ordered, stirred the cup, poured in a little cold water to cause the grounds to drop to the bottom of the mug and, since she liked it black, he handed it over to her.

She downed it in a couple of long gulps and then just sat there for a moment in silence.

"Damn all to hell, find me one of your cigarettes."

"Makala?"

"Just do it, damn it."

He did as ordered, fetching two cigarettes from his ever-dwindling stash, lit them both, and handed one to her.

"I never confessed that in college I smoked these damn things. Time on a cancer ward cured me until today." She took a drag, broke into a coughing fit, and then took another drag.

"God in heaven, John, I'm certain it's plague."

He sat down across from her, then tentatively reached out to take her hand. She grasped his firmly.

"I got woken up last night by the phone call to come at once to the infirmary." She paused and shook her head to clear it. "But you know that."

He waited for her to continue.

"All they told me was that it was an emergency and they needed me ASAP. I drove the Edsel down there and the minute I walked in, I knew it was bad, very bad."

"Go on."

"The night staff was the usual shift, two nurses, you know them. James and Laura Carson. Good kids, well trained. They were out in the hallway, obviously scared. The patient was Will Patrick."

"Lanky kid, wandered in after the Posse, we let him join the home-defense unit 'cause he had military experience in Afghanistan, if I remember correctly," John said. "I remember he left some time ago, said he had family up north."

"That's the one. Why he came back, I don't know. His family, wife and kid and mother, brought him in. Said he had deserted some militia unit up north, that he stole an old car and drove it back here to get help."

"Help? What help?"

"John, he was on a bed in the next room. Oh God, John." She picked the butt out of the ashtray, he held the lighter for her, and she took another puff.

"It was a nightmare in there. Vomiting blood that was nearly black, lungs filling up . . . The sound of it, John . . . I've seen my share of illness but this, it was worse than pneumonia, he was chok-ing on the phlegm, coughing it with every gasp.

"We had a kid in the next room, an appendix we operated on yesterday. I had the Carsons take her outside and wait. Suited up the best I could. John, we just don't have the equipment for this. Our hazmat suits are makeshift, we wash our masks to use them again. We just don't have the equipment, damn it.

"God forgive me, I didn't go in the room. I've been a nurse for more than twenty years and seen horrible things, but this time, I was frightened.

"And then, there in the room was his wife, mother, and infant child. What could I do with them? His mother was by his side, holding his hand, trying to clean him, his wife was in the corner of the room with the baby, scared to death as well. I ordered them out of room and then outside the building.

"I managed to keep them away from me, lied that I was sick too and avoid me. John, I felt horrible about it but knew I'd get it and frankly was terrified of them, God forgive me."

"The mother was at least coherent. Said they were up in Vir-ginia, where, I'm not sure. He was with some hard-ass militia group that held some territory and lived by raiding neighboring groups. Sounded like a bad lot. Anyhow, he stole a car and deserted, said there was disease in the group. Packed up his family and took off."

"Why come here?"

"Poor son of a bitch, told his mother they'd be safe here. So they actually drove the whole distance in an old VW. Took two days, and he started getting sick by the time they were halfway here. They got through by ditching the VW just below the I-40 pass and took a foot trail sneaking past the guards, they knew they would have been stopped cold otherwise so they snuck in, the mother dragging that sick kid the last two miles to town.

"Symptoms were classic. Rapid onset of fever. She said he felt fine a day ago, but had a bad cough. Then within hours a very high fever, delirium, vomiting." She stopped to take a deep breath. "Good Lord, that was awful, smelled like death, it did. He was dead an hour later. At the end he was fighting to get up, his mother and wife . . ."

She paused . . . then snapped out "Damn them, they crashed back into the room trying to restrain him and screaming at me to do something."

"And you?"

She sounded on the verge of tears. "I did nothing. I stood out in the hallway. John, walking into that room, that horrid mess, the stench, it was a room of death. I had to force myself to think of Genevieve and you before him."

"Go on."

"I knew it was plague. John, the floor was slick with vomit, he was covered in vomit and phlegm, all of it laden with pneumonic plague. What could I do, John? I'm supposed to help but I was frozen in place with fear. His mother begged me to help him, and there was nothing I could do. If I had gone in there, chances were I'd be down with it within forty-eight hours and dead a day later.

"I've never seen it before. We read about plague, I even remember some of our briefings at the hospital in Charlotte when Ebola broke out ten years back and for a week there was a mad panic. But that was in a modern hospital stockpiled with top-of-the-line hazmat equipment and, just as important, up to date antibiotics, even Cipro.

I stockpiled a few dozen doses years ago, it's not very effective, but for that kid it was too late anyhow. A modern hospital might have been able to do something. But here, my clinic?"

She shook her head. "So I just watched him die, what else could I do, John? He died and I just left him on the bed, sealed and locked the infirmary and came back here."

John got up and went to his office. He came back with two more cigarettes and lit both of them. Hands shaking, she took one.

"Laura Carson had helped the poor guy into the room and yes, her uniform was splattered with blood."

"Jesus," he whispered.

"I had her strip naked outside, said her husband was not to go near her, then had her get a hospital gown, and wait outside the infirmary while her husband took that girl with the appendix operation home."

"What about the sick man's family?"

"The family? What to do? I ordered them out the back door. The poor mother was hysterical with grief, but his wife was listening to sense, wanting to protect the baby. Same routine—strip, put gowns on—then I gave them directions to go down to the Days Inn down by the highway. There are plenty of abandoned rooms there. I told them to avoid any contact with anyone and wait until I figured out what to do.

"And as for the body? John, I just left it there, what else could I do? He's one mass of infection and corruption now. You tend that body and chances are you'll die too. Plague bacillus can survive for hours after the victim dies."

She lowered her head.

"John just give me a few moments to think . . ." and she stifled a sob.

John simply held her hand as she finally allowed the tears to roll quietly down her cheeks. After a few moments she began pulling herself back together.

"John, we have to think this out. Number one, Laura Carson." Her voice was quavering but John knew she was trying to find some inner strength to deal with what was a real crisis.

"Chances are Laura already has it. She admitted the guy and he was coughing on her as she helped him into the infirmary. She did have a mask on but there's not much that will do. I think for her, we keep her in isolation, her husband can tend her, suited up as best we can, and hope for the best."

"What about Will Patrick's body? You just explained that you can't go in there to get him out and clean the mess up."

"Let me think," she whispered.

In the meantime he went back to his office, where he turned off the shortwave and opened a bottom desk drawer. He pulled out his "for emergencies only" bottle of scotch. In the years that he had known Makala, he'd seen her enjoy a glass of wine, but that was it. But when he poured her a drink and set it in front of her she sniffed the glass and then just drank it down, gasping for breath after swallowing.

"That's better," she said softly. Her breathing steadier now, she went back to her planning. "One option would be to burn the infirmary to the ground, which would be my choice."

"That drastic?"

"That'll take care of it at the source. We can't do that, though, even if I'd wish to. We've spent years building that place up."

"So what's the alternative?"

CHAPTER TWO

It seemed medieval to John what they were doing. The lasso thrown by one of the town's firemen had snagged Will Patrick's feet. Standing outside the door, volunteers dressed in their homemade hazmats dragged the body off the bed. It fell with a sickening crunch onto the floor and one of the girls who had volunteered to help turned away, staggered off, and vomited.

"God this is horrid," John whispered, looking over at Makala.

The entire team, including the volunteers for hauling out the body, those waiting to throw buckets of lime and disinfectant into the room, were all dressed the same: faded hospital scrubs, rubber aprons, and gas masks in the absence of the standard-issue hospital masks and respirators.

The body was dragged out the door, into the open air, the sight of it so horrible that John turned his head away. A half dozen yards past the door a hasty grave had been dug in what had been a flower garden. The grave diggers were still working hard but seeing that the corpse was now outside they quickly got out and stepped away.

Makala looked at the hole which was only several feet deep.

"It'll do," she announced. "Now keep your distance, and drag him into it. The task took some maneuvering as if the body was reluctant to partake in this final journey but they finally managed to roll the corpse in with ropes while keeping half a dozen yards back.

Reverend Black started to approach the grave to offer last rites but Makala yelled for him to keep back and for the work crew to keep upwind as they threw shovelfuls of dirt in until the corpse was at last covered.

As ordered, everyone kept a wide berth from the trail of congealing blood and excrement the body had leaked out while being dragged. A couple of the town's firemen splashed a brew of alcohol and ammonia along the path while the grave was topped off with crushed lime.

As John watched in silence, with this procedure done for just one unfortunate soul, he wondered what they would do if the plague really did explode on them.

Reverend Black conducted a short, perfunctory service a dozen feet away and then the small gathering backed off, one of Makala's students tacking up several hand-written signs with a skull and crossbones on them and the warning to stay ten yards back from the lone grave.

John, Makala, and the others turned away in horror and disgust at what they had just done.

Makala could not say how long the body was dangerous to the living. Was it contagious after death she just wasn't sure, but any liquid coming from it she assumed would be a swamp of infection. They had nothing whatsoever in terms of modern equipment and supplies. John wondered if this indeed was the beginning of the end of all that he had strived for these last five years.

It was not even noon yet. Genevieve would be at nursery school for another three hours, oblivious of course to all the perils the outside world held. Makala had already decided that she was not coming home for at least five days, not wanting to even remotely risk their child's health. Perhaps because of his own previous loss he did not debate her decision, though he thought it excessive.

Charlie Patton, now head of the town's civil services of police, fire, and EMTs, was waiting for them.

"Ghastly sight, that," Charlie said.

John had to agree, but what was there to say? Beside Charlie was Gus Younger, the town dentist. Usually Gus had something to say to John about seeing to the molar that had been bothering him of late, but now was not the time.

"Saw that on a mission trip to Rwanda some years back. That Ebola outbreak, they were burning the bodies."

"I got some bad news for us on top of everything else," Charlie said.

"What now?" Makala asked.

"That Patrick family that were supposed to go down to the Days Inn and wait for help?"

"Yeah?"

"They're gone."

"Oh shit," John whispered.

"Yeah, oh shit. No telling where they've taken off to."

"If they're out there walking around, no telling who they are in contact with."

"Precisely," Makala snapped. "Damn it, I should have put a guard on them. Damn it, damn it, of course they'd run. The way they snuck in here, getting around the guards, of course they'd run when I wanted to quarantine them."

"Well, they're on the loose. I've got our bike patrols out looking for them with orders to not approach them, and to hold them in place till we figure out what to do with them."

"Damn, I should have thought they might try and run. Damn it!"

"If we find them, what should we do?" Charlie asked.

"Stick with your plan, freeze them in place. On the spot, we'll send some people out there in hazmats and escort them."

"Where?"

"How about what's left of the old nursing home up by exit 66. No squatters in there. Still got beds and such. Send them there."

Charlie nodded but the look on his face indicated he had more to say. After a moment, he asked, "And if they don't cooperate? I remember Will Patrick and his family. Not the brightest light bulbs in the pack. Had some drug problems, meth and such, back before. I don't think they care much for anyone other than themselves. Damn them, for that matter, for even coming back here."

"What are you saying, Charlie?"

"If they don't listen, they try to run, we should shoot them."

"Come on, Charlie, you can think better than that," Gus said.

"My opinion but what's the alternative, they just run loose and infect how many before they drop?"

"Charlie." It was Makala, her voice pitched low.

"Ma'am?"

"Shoot them."

"For heaven's sake, Makala, you think it's that bad?" Gus interjected. John felt he had nothing to say, and besides, at this moment he would defer to Makala's judgment. In the last few hours as she recovered from the initial shock, she had become hard, and he would not debate her.

"Try not to harm the baby. I don't know what the hell to do with the child. We'll cross that when we come to it."

The only halfway good news was that they had slipped past the guards so no one was exposed, but that was an issue nevertheless. John had taken thirty minutes before moving the body to drive up there and raise holy hell with the four for not keeping a closer watch.

John was surprised with how coldly Makala had said, "Shoot them," but knew she was right.

"How are things otherwise, Charlie?" he asked.

"We've gone through five years of hell, John. And we seemed finally on the road to some sort of return, at least to a semblance of

normalcy. This is throwing people for a loop. I've already posted
the notice, had my bike squad going around announcing that the
town, for the time being, is in quarantine. Like Makala suggested,
we've told everyone to stay indoors for now. People on the farms
and such, as long as they stay isolated, only people around them
their families, they can keep working their fields, but no contact
with anyone else, even neighbors."

"What about the kids at school?" Gus asked. "I got two children
there now."

"I think it best they stay in place, at least until the Patricks are
located and detained. If need be, they shelter there overnight. I don't
want a couple of hundred kids wandering back home. We have
some emergency supplies stockpiled at the schools so they'll be okay
for a day or two."

"Agreed," Makala interjected.

John could see that her mind was racing, trying to bring all the
different factors together into a coherent action plan.

In the years after the Day, they had held plenty of contingency
meetings and plans for all sorts of eventualities, from another EMP,
to an actual nuke exchange, and even outbreaks of disease. But now
the reality was exploding on them in terrible suddenness.

"All right, hunt that damn family down and hold them, no one is
to come within ten yards of them. Those out looking, at least wear
masks. Kids stay in place until we know if they've been found. And
now?" She looked at the men gathered around her.

"You're the head of medical services," Charlie replied. "What
next?"

"Can we combat the plague with what we have?" she asked.
"That's the question."

"Well, can we?"

"We have a small stockpile of penicillin-derived medications,
even some Cipro but only a few dozen out of date prescriptions.
Stuff people found in medicine cabinets and turned in for public

use. There's not much, and most of it is way out of date. We'll contact Mission Hospital in Asheville but you know how they are."

Mission was a shadow of the former powerhouse medical facility known throughout the southeast. They'd suffered the familiar hemorrhage of personnel dying off, collapse of a supply system, and the dwindling of the tenuous lifeline that had existed for a while between them, the local National Guard, and the navy down in Charleston. The suggestion was a long shot at best but John felt it was at least worth a try.

"Surely there's a vaccine for this."

"No" was her one-word reply.

"Damn it," Charlie snapped. "It's a bacteria, isn't it?"

"Yes."

"I thought we had those types of things beat."

"In Rwanda," Gus interjected, "we fought the illness and that was it. There was a vaccine out just before the Day, but manufacturing was limited and it was supplied only to the highest-risk areas. But for plague, I don't think so. You'd think they would have gone full bore with making one, considering how deadly it is, but my friends, the last big outbreak was in the Orient a hundred years ago."

"And it just wasn't a priority," Makala replied. "So no, there's no vaccine, our treatments are limited, we are going to have to fight this by containment. It'll have to be draconian. If someone is exposed, they get put in isolation. If they come down with it . . ." Her voice trailed off, but her meaning was all too clear.

"What's the fatality rate without medication?" John asked.

"Almost one hundred percent for the pneumonic variant. Same for septicemia—that's if the infection goes into the blood. There's little we can do if that takes hold of someone."

"So what do we do with the sick?" Gus asked.

"We'll have to seal them off and let them die," Charlie whispered softly. "Family can try to treat them at least to make them comfortable, but their house will have to be sealed until everyone is dead or some have miraculously survived for at least ten to fourteen days."

"I almost don't want to think about this," Gus said. "Maybe the Patrick family will be found, it spreads no farther, and that is that."

"But it is out there, Gus," Makala replied gently. "Will Patrick must have caught it from someone. They said they fled from Virginia, so it's up there, and almost inevitably it will come marching down here."

"Then we totally seal off, the way we did after the Day," Charlie replied sharply.

"A question though," Gus interjected.

"What's that?"

"Is this related to China?"

John almost answered this, but stopped himself. He had a theory he was not yet ready to share even with his wife, let alone the town council.

"If it was before the Day, I'd have said definitely yes," Gus responded. "That was always the big fear for anyone who studied these things. I'll confess I had a bit of a fascination with it. The Ebola outbreaks scared the crap out of me, especially after what I saw on that mission trip.

"There's this formula where you take any given disease, and it helps calculate on average, starting with one person, how many other people that first person will infect before they get better or die. The lower the number, the greater the probability the disease can be contained.

"I remember there was a nurse coming back from a hot zone. The authorities put her in quarantine and she raised a holy fit that her rights were being violated. I think she was a selfish bitch but it highlighted just how difficult it can be.

"Anyhow, a higher number of contagion for person number one, the more difficult it gets."

"So what policy do you want, Makala?" John asked.

"As I said before, it's got to be total isolation. For the few antibiotics we have, I suggest the town council decides on a case-by-case basis. I'd prioritize children, of course. Expectant mothers, mothers with toddlers. I hate to ask this of those personnel directly involved in emergency treatment, but in order to administer the medicine, the person has to ask for it and be approved. No one over age forty-five and that's it."

There was silence and finally just slow nods of agreement.

"God protect us. But how do we dispose of the bodies?"

"The bodies," Makala said softly. "If family members survive, I'll have to say bury the deceased in your yard. That's up to the family." She wearily shook her head. "Look, I've got a meeting of my staff at noon, then a meeting with students in the medical program this afternoon. I definitely do not want our students volunteering to help, no matter what. We have to be coldly pragmatic. Okay?"

Again, she waited for their nods of approval.

"Let's call it for now. We need to try and find that damn family, and quick. I've pulled some supplies from the infirmary and locked it. I hope I'm right but we keep it locked for a week and any airborne pathogens in there should definitely be dead."

She got up and headed off, John beside her.

"You did the right thing, best to be cautious. If you don't mind, I'll take the Edsel, I have a few things to do," he said.

"Such as?"

"Oh, usual stuff."

"You're keeping something from me. What is it?"

"You always could read me. Please, for the moment just let me deal with it. You've got too much on your plate anyhow."

"Maybe you're right," she sighed, and leaned briefly against his shoulder before heading to the meeting with her staff.

John climbed into the car and hit the starter. He cursed when it just simply clicked, the engine not turning over.

Charlie, who was just leaving, saw John climbing back out of his car in frustration. He came over and popped the hood. After a brief look, he jumped on the bumper a few times and told John to try again. This time it started up.

"Why does that work?" John asked.

"If I told you, I'm not sure you'd understand, John. Just trust me." He dropped the hood back into place and wiped his hands on his pants.

John put the car into gear and lurched off, hoping there was enough gas in her to get him to the top of the mountain and Ernie's place.

He hoped as well that there might be an answer there.

CHAPTER THREE

"So what do you have for me, Ernie?" John asked once they were seated comfortably on his friend's front porch.

"China is definitely going to hell," came the reply.

"What do you mean by that?"

"No sources inside of China; they are in a complete blackout. But I've managed to eavesdrop on other places, including South Korea, of course. They are under a complete embargo, all flights canceled, no ships allowed to dock under the threat of sinking on sight. Shortwave is out but I've been able to get some data over what's left of the internet."

Ernie looked over at Linda, who explained further.

"I had some contacts there from long before the Day, clients of our satellite uplink system. They report Korea is on a wartime footing and so far has no cases. They have a couple of links to old contacts as well, inside of China. People they are in touch with are supposed to be silenced under pain of arrest, which means execution. It's in Beijing and spreading."

She flipped through some notes she'd kept on an old notepad, the pen-and-ink kind.

"Total curfew, regions sealed off, deaths could already be in the millions. But here's the part that should concern us."

"Go on," John urged.

"China is claiming that America is the source of the contagion, that it was somehow deliberately spread by us, starting with ships docking in Guangzhou. They are blaming Taiwan as well and are talking about retaliation."

John took in that sobering news. "They could use it as the excuse to finally go to war."

"With whom?" Ernie replied. "What do we have to do with it?"

John didn't answer.

"What sense would there be in it?" Linda asked. "It just seems like the world is slipping again into insanity. We still have some semblance of a navy, those boomers out in the Atlantic and Pacific. I pick up some low-frequency stuff at times that points to sub communications. They hit us, we hit them. The old mutual assured destruction game and nobody wins. At least I hope that still is the thinking."

John did not want to show his hand. There was no sense in saying more, especially to Ernie, who could at times be a bit too talkative with what he knew. His greater concern at the moment, though, was not some international drama but what was playing out in his backyard. He felt compelled to at least do something there.

"Ernie. You still have some of the old access codes and channels to Raven Rock, don't you?"

"Yeah, why?"

"I want you to put a message out. Not encrypted, in the clear."

"You said Raven Rock was abandoned, John. I don't see what you are driving at. All the circuits there are dead, aren't they?"

"Just do me the favor. Send the following over several of the old internet lines."

Ernie took the notepad and pen from his wife and turned to a fresh page. "Okay, go ahead."

"Send the following: 'Hello, Shangri-La. Hello, Shangri-La. This is J.'"

"What does that mean?"

"Just do it for me. Okay? Call me if something comes back."

After spending a few minutes playing with Maggie, Linda's beloved dog, in a vain attempt to act as if nothing was out of the ordinary, he went back to his car. When he reached the end of their long driveway, he got out to take a short walk.

It was a lovely early-fall afternoon. The trees were beginning to turn, and a warm breeze came up from beyond the mountains, down in the lowlands to the east of Black Mountain.

We had a paradise here once upon a time, John thought to himself. Back in the beginning, though Mary was already sick, there had still been hope, and his two beautiful daughters, who were once so very young. He sat down beneath a maple tree and just closed his eyes for a moment.

Part of him wanted to just sit and forget it all. He struggled to find some hope, some answer. He'd never wanted any of this, having to take over his community, then the damn politics of deciding whether a return to a national republic was worth his whole-hearted effort.

Bob Scales was dead, the hoped-for republic was dead. Was there a new shadow government behind everything that was unfolding?

A plague upon humanity, after what it had already been through. Was it released deliberately? And if so, why? What could possibly be gained by it all?

He knew that the last time there had been a plague of this type, ultimately humanity had survived it. In the Middle Ages between one-third and one-half of Europe did survive, those people who were genetically lucky enough to have sufficient antibodies and at least took some precautions when it came to exposure. But upward of half did die, and it was a hundred or more years before the population recovered to its pre-plague level.

Fort Detrick. That was the wild card in this equation. It was indeed the center for military biowarfare research, so who knew what demon brews were frozen and locked away in their labs? But it seemed so fantastical to believe that was the origin. It went against all logic; at least his logic.

So why am I contacting Lawrence up in Camp David?

That entity had been silent after Raven Rock fell. He wanted to believe that they continued to exist because . . . well, to be honest because they were existing in some relative comfort, but he still didn't know to what end. There had to be some sort of endgame to what Lawrence represented.

Perhaps, he hoped, the location of Fort Detrick was just a coincidence, and it just happened to be nearby when the tunnel was dug in the 1950s. But he couldn't dismiss that fleeting glimpse of the guards in hazmat suits. Why?

So why am I tipping my hand to Lawrence now? he asked himself again. He had just sent a message, thinly coded, perhaps strange enough that anyone doing some unauthorized listening would not wonder about it, like the BBC broadcasts that ended with coded messages like "The chair is against the door."

He knew Lawrence would pick up on the name Shangri-La. He would be aware, like John was, that not only did it refer to a legendary place of peace lost in the Himalayas, but it was the name FDR originally gave to the retreat later known as Camp David. And he would realize, of course, that J was him.

He had nowhere else to turn, actually. Whatever the cause of the plague, it was now in Black Mountain. Only one case so far, but Makala had convinced him there would be more. Definitely that Carson girl who had helped carry a dying man into the infirmary and was splattered by his blood and vomit. The Patricks were undoubtedly carrying it, and as they became contagious and interacted with anyone they would spread it as well. The longer it took to find them, the more people they might meet.

There would be little if any help from the life-saving antibiotics in Asheville. They could reach out to the navy in Charleston, but he doubted they'd find any hope there; they too would be thinking of their own.

But Fort Detrick? If at one time they were playing with an annihilating fire, they must have had the preventive stockpile as well. Though Makala said there was no vaccine for the plague, he found it hard to believe that they wouldn't find one in a classified setting. The old adage that the elite will always take care of their own definitely applied here. Surely this scenario of a plague breaking out must have been on their horizon. With a die-off of upward of eight out of ten Americans after the EMP, there had to be thought given to the diseases that would run through a steadily weakening population, and how to protect those who would clamor loudest for that protection.

He had to place the bet that Lawrence and whatever he represented had a vaccine, or at the very least stockpiles of penicillin-based drugs. Damn, he knew such things could be manufactured for pennies a dose in the old days, no matter what would finally be paid by the time it got to middle-class consumers with their ever-increasing insurance bills.

He'd now have to just wait and see. He'd have to tell Makala at least part of it for the present.

He finally stood back up, and took a few more minutes to try and absorb a little calm from the view. He said a silent prayer, then drove the half mile to check in at the roadblock at the top of the gap. The barricade stretched across all four lanes and the truck stop. The four students from the college militia who were on guard duty, two male and two female, scrambled to their feet at the sight of John's Edsel gasping up to the top of Route 40. The guard shift had just changed, the four who had let Patrick slip through were in isolation as a precaution, but as he pulled up he felt a wave of anger taking hold.

Two of the guards were actually caught a bit by surprise and came scrambling out of the bushes, clothing disheveled and faces beet red with embarrassment. The other two were sitting atop the low barricade, doing their usually boring job of watching.

In another time and place John would have turned a blind eye to what was most likely going on with the first couple, but not now, not today, not after what had happened just hours earlier. There was a good five-minute chewing out before he let them off with a stern warning that if it happened again they'd be up before the militia tribunal.

He finally left them, the girl actually in tears of remorse, and headed for home.

PART VI

Why this is hell nor am I out of it . . .
Hell hath no limits, nor is circumscribed
In one self place; for where we are is hell,
And where hell is must we ever be.

—Christopher Marlowe, *Doctor Faustus*

CHAPTER ONE

It would have been another sleepless night for Makala, but John finally convinced her to come home at midnight and at least get a few hours' sleep.

Genevieve was staying with her preschool teacher and he knew that was the safest place she could be. Makala was still trying to insist that she keep herself removed from John. He'd finally convinced her, however, that she didn't have the plague, and even if she did, he was already exposed as well. She finally relented after thirty-six sleepless hours, came home, stripped at the door, and five minutes later was fast asleep in their bed.

He was the one that couldn't sleep. He sat up through the night, trying to coax news out of the wireless, but found precious little other than more reports from South Korea saying they were still clear of the plague, and what reports they had of China were that the country was trying to hold fast with the spread.

He could well imagine what "hold fast" meant in that regime.

At least, according to South Korea's reports, they had a ready supply of antibiotics. But, John reasoned, in a nation of over one billion, how long would that last?

There was no milk delivery the next morning because the Patricks were still somewhere out there and all deliveries were therefore shut down. He could only hope they had gone to ground somewhere, and if the disease did take hold it would render them immobile until they died.

Charlie at least came through in a small way, giving John two K-cups "for your lady, God bless her," and while she was still asleep he broke one open and put it in the percolator. He toasted a couple of pieces of stale bread and cut up an apple from the ongoing harvest. He was about to take it all into the bedroom when she came out wrapped up in her bathrobe against the morning chill.

"I smell coffee."

"That you do, sweetheart."

"Oh, God bless you," she sighed. She sat down and took a sip.

She had that "morning look" he found so appealing: no makeup (but then again no one had used makeup in ages), her hair disheveled and a bit tangled, her sleepy eyes looking over the rim of the coffee cup at him as she smiled.

He let her finish her coffee in silence. He was tempted to join her, but the coffee was her reward this morning. Still, when after several sips she offered it over to him, he took one good sip and then passed it back to her.

"Any more news?" she asked, starting on her toast.

"Nothing important. We didn't talk much on the drive back when I picked you up last night, so, how is it at your end?"

"I got the infirmary locked down. No one admitted. Still haven't found the Patricks." She paused for another sip of coffee. "Damn them. I know we should pity them, but damn it, if they had gone straight to the abandoned hotel and waited there we could have at least made them comfortable. Who knows how many others they've come in contact with by now. Damn stupid of them."

"They panicked."

"I know. The downside of it. The other bad news is that I think

Laura Carson might be coming down with it. She started with some sniffles. I immediately locked her in a room, no time to take her up to the elementary school, and besides, by moving her there, others might have been exposed." She hesitated before admitting, "I put her on the few outdated Cipros in our stockpile."

"You know our supply," John warned.

"John, I'm not going to let a member of my medical staff die from this, that's asking too much. Her husband volunteered to stay with her. I gave him a dose of antibiotics as well."

"And what's our reserve?"

"Don't ask. Let me worry about that."

The phone rang, and John quickly rose to answer it. Maybe there was a response to his coded message sent yesterday. It was Alice at the switchboard. She was normally the most phlegmatic of personages, almost like the stereotype switchboard operators of decades earlier with a crisp "number please" delivery, but this morning she was anything but.

"John, there's a call from the roadblock at the gap. There's trouble. You better get up there fast."

"Where's Charlie?"

"Over in Swannanoa, following a lead on the Patricks."

"Contact Kevin Malady, tell him to get a reaction team deployed and meet me up there."

The reaction team was comprised of a dozen of their veteran students and a couple military vets. They had a World War II jeep that was on permanent loan from his friend Maury Hurt and one of Jim Bartlett's old VW buses that could haul eight, along with an assortment of arms. But it'd take time for them to turn out. He wasn't going to wait.

"I'm on my way."

Picking up his own emergency bag from the hall, which held a Glock and a pump shotgun along with a combat first aid kit, he was out the door, Makala following.

"John?"

"Stay here," he urged. "Hopefully it's nothing. Just stay here until I come back."

This time the Edsel started easily, and he left a trail of black smoke down Montreat Road to the turnoff east of town that merged into the interstate. Just before the final turn before the crest he slammed on the brakes. They squealed in protest as he skidded to a stop.

Four students, the same four who had been posted there yesterday, were atop the barricade, weapons drawn and aimed.

As he got out of the car, pulling open his emergency bag and drawing out his weapons, he could hear one of the girls screaming at someone he couldn't see: "If you take another step I will shoot! Don't do it, don't do it!"

He started to run the last few yards to the barricade.

A shot went off.

"That's your last warning, damn it, please listen to me. Don't—"

There was another shot, hitting one of the girls. She crumpled up and fell back from the barrier, then half a dozen more shots, the other girl on the barricade grabbing her arm and falling backward as well.

John cocked his shotgun and shouldered it. "My people, get back!"

The two boys jumped off, one firing off several rounds toward the other side. The wounded girl staggered back, having dropped her gun, and the other boy reached down to try and help the girl who was sprawled out motionless on the ground.

"Leave her and fall back!" John screamed.

"Sir, she's—"

"Leave her for now. Fall back."

What in hell was this? He heard cries from unseen people on the far side of the barrier, the sound of a car revving up, tires squealing. A few seconds later it crashed into the gate, busting it open and then lurching toward him.

John couldn't see who was driving, but there was no time now to think. He pumped three shotgun rounds into the windshield, shattering it, and shattering the face of the driver. The car swerved across the truck stop and crashed into a guardrail.

He kept his gun leveled at the busted barricade, the two male students falling to either side of him, helping the girl shot in the arm.

"You on the other side, don't move, damn it," he shouted. "Stay where you are."

He spared a quick look to the girl whose arm was wounded. "How bad?"

Grimacing, she just nodded her head. "I think I'll live."

"We've got to stay here till help arrives, get behind my car!"

Just as they stepped behind the Edsel, several shots rang out, one of them shattering the windshield.

Damn all to hell, that's my Edsel was his first reaction. He could hear that at least one of the attackers had gained the barricade wall on the other side, but he couldn't pinpoint their location.

Several more shots were fired, another striking the car.

"Just stay down low," he snapped to the students, "help is coming."

The four of them huddled on the ground behind the Edsel.

"Just let us through," a voice sounded from the other side. "We don't want trouble. Please let us pass."

John came to a crouch, shotgun shouldered. "Stay where you are!"

"We need help. Just let us through!"

A girl with blond hair tied into a pigtail and dressed in coveralls and a camo jacket stepped from behind the far side of the barricade, weapon half raised, and took a few tentative steps toward John through the defensive line. She was weaving slightly as she walked.

And in that instant he knew what was wrong. She was sick, very sick.

"Freeze, damn it. Freeze or I'll shoot."

She stopped a half dozen yards away. Another girl came into view, this one without a gun, leading a toddler. Behind them were an elderly couple, the man armed with a rifle, which he pointed at John.

"Drop it! Please drop it!" John shouted.

"My son and daughter are in that car." He pointed to the vehicle that had tried to force the gate and was wrecked on the far side of the road.

"Stay where you are!" John shouted again.

The woman with the toddler collapsed into convulsions, coughing violently.

"Merciful God," John whispered.

"Doc?" the wounded girl next to him cried. "What do we do?"

"Hold here, if they come forward," he instructed, looking over at his three students, almost not believing the order he was about to give them. "Shoot them. We can't let them in, they've got the plague."

He hesitated for a few seconds. "If need be kill them, you have to kill them."

He heard another car in the distance. For a second he thought it was the reaction team, then he realized it was on the far side of the barrier. He could just see the top of the vehicle—an old jeep with a large canvas bag strapped to the roof. It was one of the cars, increasingly common, that used charcoal gas fumes for fuel.

Over time, some people had figured out how to use a charcoal fire to generate fumes that could be fed into the carburetor in order to get a vehicle moving. In town Jim Bartlett had actually rigged up several Volkswagens that way.

He could hear people getting out of that car, shouting, asking what was going on.

"We are coming through now," the elderly man shouted. "We want to get help, that's all."

"I can't let you in!"

"The hell you say." And the old man shouldered his rifle.

"God forgive me," John prayed as he took aim and fired.

The shotgun blast caught the man in the chest, knocking him over. His wife cried out and stumbled over to him.

At the same moment Maury's old jeep appeared on their side of the barricade. Riding with Maury were three students, along with Kevin Malady, the militia leader on campus, sitting in the front passenger's seat.

For a moment, the scene was a frozen tableau: the toddler screaming; her mother on her hands and knees, coughing; the blond girl holding her weapon up, but frozen with fright; several more people approaching the barricade, all armed.

Kevin didn't hesitate. He shouldered his weapon, a semiautomatic, and opened fire. When he dropped one man at the barrier, the other two backed up. The three students with Kevin piled out of his jeep, weapons raised, and started forward at a run.

"Freeze, damn it. Freeze!" John shouted.

The blonde looked confused at first, still holding her gun, then in an instant dropped the weapon and just stood there, sobbing. The first student out of the jeep sprinted forward, ignoring John. He knocked her to the ground and pointed his weapon at her.

It was, for John, almost as if it all happened in slow motion: him calling yet again for nobody to move, the other two students starting to go forward, one of them pointing his gun on the elderly man John had just shot, who was convulsing and then going still.

"God damn it, everyone freeze!" John screamed. His use of a profanity he rarely uttered somehow had the shock effect of bringing his students to a halt.

Kevin made his way to John's side, his weapon still pointed at the ruined gate. There was one man on the ground there. The other two were out of sight but still a potential danger if they climbed up on the wall and opened fire.

The old VW van of the reaction squad now approached up the

mountain, several of the militia leaping out of the open side door and running forward, ready to shoot.

"Montreat militia, freeze in place, don't move another inch!"

The command held.

John took a deep breath.

He had to gather his senses. It had all happened fast, too damn fast.

"Those on the other side. Don't shoot and we won't. Just stay where you are."

There was no response.

He looked at the blonde, who had rushed toward him. She was curled up now on the ground, crying. She looked up at him, her face contorted with the agony of her sickness. The front of her shirt was stained with blood and vomit. "Doc, remember me? Diane Vincetti. You taught me. Remember me?"

He felt frozen, recalling a bright-eyed girl from some years back, before the Day. A brilliant young lady, infectious laugh, well liked. And now this?

Everything was going to pieces before his eyes, he had to think quick. He had to contain this.

"Everyone on my side, step back to the jeep now!"

There were some looks of confusion. God save them, his students who a moment ago were soldiers, now were taken over by the instinct to help the injured, obviously not fully registering that as a blood-soaked casualty or corpse they were just as dangerous as when they were alive.

In that instant, the world had to change for John Matherson.

CHAPTER TWO

When Makala arrived at the scene, driven by Charlie and two more armed men, John had pulled his people back a good fifty yards. His wounded student was still on the ground where she'd fallen, softly sobbing.

The man hit with John's shotgun blast was mercifully still, being quietly soothed by his wife. There was silence from the other side of the barrier.

As Makala got out of the jeep that had brought her to this nightmare, she ran toward John.

"Don't!" John screamed, and she stopped.

"How close were you to them?" she called.

"Don't. Ten feet, fifteen maybe."

She drew closer anyhow. "Just pray you're all right," she whispered as she came to his side.

Charlie soon approached as well, and John explained the situation, that there were four or more people on the far side of the wall, at least one of them armed.

Charlie looked at Makala and sighed. "You better be the boss here," he said. "I'm not sure what's next."

Makala took in the confusing carnage.

"That car over there?" She pointed to the old Chevy that had crashed on the far side of the road.

"Two people inside," John informed her. "I shot one, almost certain I killed the poor bastard, the other person I don't know."

Even as she surveyed the scene, Charlie pulled out one of their homemade hazmat suits and tossed it over to Makala. She donned it, pulled the hoodie over her hair, and put on a heavy gauze mask soaked with an antiseptic mixture. She edged over to the wrecked car, looked through the shattered side window, and drew back.

"They're both dead, at least I think so. Rest of you, stay here. No one is to go near the vehicle," she announced, then slowly walked forward, stopping half a dozen feet from the girl.

"Sweetheart, can you hear me?"

"Yeah." Her voice was choked.

"What's your name, sweetheart?"

"Diane," she whispered out between convulsive sobs.

"Diane, we're going to get you taken care of but you've got to stay calm and hang on a few more minutes. Can you do that for me, sweetie?"

"I'll try, oh God it hurts . . ."

"We'll be sending an ambulance up shortly to take care of you. Okay? But you have to hang tight. For heaven's sake don't get up." She pulled a bottle of drinking water out of a side pocket and tossed it to her.

"Drink that down, it's got medicine in it, help you to get better."

She then turned back to the center of the interstate, stopping to look down at the man who John had shot. He stirred, surprising John who thought he was dead. John could not hear what his wife was saying, but Makala produced another bottle of water and tossed it to the injured man. Next she went up to the barricade and checked on the first student who was shot. An ugly pool of darkening blood beside her was starting to congeal. Makala shook her head, and edged up to the barricade. John held his breath, about to shout at her to come back. The woman with the toddler by her side was on the ground. Both were so obviously sick, the face of the child swollen dark.

Makala stood back from them, "Ma'am, your baby is very sick. We can help but you must stay still. Do you understand me?"

Her reply was a barely understood yes.

"Good, we're bringing up some medicine and blankets to wrap yourself and the baby up tight. An ambulance will take you to a hospital but you must not move till then. Understood?"

There was nothing but a whimpered yes in reply.

She shouted to whomever was on the far side of the barricade, telling them to stay in place, and that if they tried to get in they'd be shot on sight, then headed back to John.

She stopped a half dozen feet away from her husband.

"The guard is dead, poor kid," she sighed. "The others shot are dead as well."

"What do we do next?"

"Nothing."

"What?"

"Just that. I want you to pull back from here. Make it a hundred yards or so. Start making a barrier here. Reinforce it with at least fifteen to twenty volunteers, try and get some of the older folks, types who are vets, to man it. I'd prefer the students didn't see some of this."

"See what?"

"That man that was shot, the girl, the mother and baby . . ."

She paused, lowered her head, then looked back up, features suddenly hardened.

"They stay where they fell. We'll toss them blankets and bottles of water, let them think, if they still can think, that help is on the way."

Again a pause, "They'll die in a few hours. I don't want any of my people near them."

"Jesus, that's hard," Malady whispered. "What do we do if they get up and come towards us? You want us to pull back?"

"We've got to be hard if we're going to survive this. You shoot them, you got that? If not you'll die as well."

John realized a profound change had come over her in just two days. In a way it was like the reaction his students had had in the Posse fight. They had been kids playing soldier the day before the battle. The day after they had become veterans. They had grown old in war.

This was now Makala's war.

"We need someone to go up to the barrier and talk to the people on the other side."

Of course John felt it should be him. He started to open his mouth to say so, and she shut him down.

"Not you, John, definitely not you."

"I think I should do it," Kevin announced, and Makala nodded agreement.

So typical of Kevin, John thought. He'd originally been the school's librarian, his build and demeanor causing him to be nick-named "Conan the Librarian." His experiences in Afghanistan caused him to eventually take over the militia after the battle with the Posse and the death of John's trusted old friend Washington.

"Suit up then," Makala announced. She and Charlie helped him get into a hazmat suit. Before he set out, with rifle slung over his shoulder, Makala went back to the jeep she had come up in and pulled out half a dozen bottles of water.

"Tell them that we're going to send help and they have to be patient. Tell them to do the usual thing for anyone that's sick— make them comfortable. Drop the water bottles over the barricade and tell them . . ." She hesitated for a few seconds. "Tell them the water is treated with antibiotics and will help them."

He took the bottles and looked at her. "What do I do if none of them are sick?"

"They still don't come through. Sick or well, no one comes through. Tell them that if they do attempt to pass the barrier, we shoot to kill without warning. Do you have that?"

He nodded. Before walking away, he bent his head, muttered a prayer, and made the sign of the cross.

John felt a wave of guilt that he should be helping, but a look from Makala stilled any protest.

Gaining the barrier, Kevin climbed atop it. He was facing away from John and the others, so it was hard to hear what was being said. He lowered the bottles over the side and looked like he was about to get back down, when something caused him to unsling his rifle and aim it.

"Don't do it!" John heard him scream, but then a dozen shots echoed in the narrow confines of the mountain pass. Kevin took cover behind the barrier, stuck his weapon out and emptied his magazine, dropped it, put another magazine in, crouched in silence for what seemed an eternity, and then carefully aimed two more shots.

He stayed silent for another moment, then left the barrier and came back toward John, walking slowly. John could see that he was crying.

"No more problems there for now," Kevin muttered, then went off to stand alone. Makala ordered that no one was to go near him. Eventually she went over and gently told him to take off the hazmat suit and throw it aside and then scrub his hands and face.

No one spoke. He looked back at them. "They're all dead, no one else in sight."

"All right," Charlie said, a little too quickly. "Everyone pull back, establish a barrier line. We'll make a sign to hang on the barrier that it is a dead line. Cross it and we shoot. Now, let's pull back. Kevin, why don't you head back, too. We can get the new line organized."

The group pulled back as ordered.

"Kevin, ride with us," John offered. "We'll take the Edsel back."

He walked up to the old beast, as he sometimes called it, and saw that the windshield was punctured with a round bullet hole, the remaining glass fractured around it.

"Damn it all," he whispered. After brushing the broken glass off the seat, he got in. He hit the starter and it thankfully came to life. Makala got in the passenger side and Kevin in the back seat.

"What happened?" John asked him quietly.

Kevin, normally so stoic, was fighting back tears. "I'm quitting," he replied.

"You just need to take some time off. You like to hunt, go up in the woods by yourself for a few days, let it pass, Kevin. It will pass."

"I'm done with hunting, all of it, all of it . . ."

Makala turned around in her seat, the softness in her coming back. She put a hand out and touched Kevin on the cheek. "Please tell us. Whatever you had to do, it's okay."

"I killed them all . . ." His voice trailed off for a moment, and then became distant, hard. "There were five of them out there. Old woman, holding a toddler, couple of younger women, two men—the men were still armed.

"They said they were from Old Fort. They knew us, knew your name, John. They survived all this shit for five years. Three days ago a family in a battered old VW pulled up to their farm. They were kin, said they were moving back this way."

"The Patricks," Makala said softly.

"Yeah. The Patricks started getting sick, the others got scared by it and demanded they leave. Yesterday morning the sickness started with them. Damn it, they had friends drop in at some point. That was the second car that came up, with the charcoal burner. Damn all, John, damn it all." He wiped his eyes and drank a swig of water. "So that's it. They were all sick, some just starting, the toddler was already bad off. John, they just wouldn't listen to reason. They said I was lying, help wasn't going to come."

He stared out the window for a moment before continuing. "They were right, of course. We weren't and they knew it. Said, but they were coming in to get help, and they started for the barrier."

"So you shot them," John said softly.

"What else could I do, what the hell else could I do?"

"You did what you had to do, Kevin."

"Really? Really? Those last two shots," Kevin whispered, and broke into sobs. "The toddler. The adults were dead, but I had avoided the toddler, who was lying there in a pool of her mother's or grandmother's blood. That poor baby was so sick, you could hear its gurgling cries."

His voice was now a monotone.

"I took aim, I was shaking. I asked Jesus to forgive me and then squeezed the trigger twice to make sure . . ."

"He's at rest," Makala whispered. She was crying now as well.

"And I am in hell."

And then there was silence, for nothing more could be said. John put the car in gear and started back toward town, Kevin curled up in the back seat crying, Makala holding him tight like a child who needed comforting.

CHAPTER THREE

John Matherson finally walked through the door to his home. After first stripping naked, along with Makala, and helping each other to scrub, they put on their old bathrobes and sat down in the kitchen.

He didn't even bother to conceal the half-empty pack of cigarettes any longer, tossing them on the table and lighting up. It had been a long day. Makala's first task had been to place the students, who had undoubtedly been exposed, into a vacant house near the center of town. They had a supply of food to last a week, plenty of water, and more than a few prayers offered outside the door by their friends.

She'd dosed Laura Carson with a couple more of the precious Cipro, then tended to the girl who had been shot. It was a clean wound in the fleshy part of the arm. It was almost old routine; after checking her over she had handed her off to one of her assistants.

Over in the town office, meanwhile, John had met with Charlie and the rest of the town council. The Patricks had yet to be found and it was hoped they had just simply holed up someplace . . . and died there.

There was no dissent about the town and the college going on lockdown. Every single back road and foot track out of the area was to be heavily guarded, twenty-four/seven. Orders were now to warn once on a sighting, then shoot to kill and not to go near the body.

Of course other issues now came to the fore. If they were on lockdown, what about bringing in the harvest? The decision was that guards would now have to go out with any group no matter what the task, be it tending the orchards, fields of corn, pumpkins and squash, gathering wild food, or weeding. All of it.

Classes would be on hold, and students were advised not to gather in any kind of group. The dining hall was mostly closed; small groups were allowed to enter, pick up their food, then head straight back to their rooms.

The list went on till John felt as if he was numbing over with it all. He'd dealt with crisis before: the time after the Day, and the battle with the Posse, or the fight in Asheville, and he found he could handle it. But this? This was the new terrifying foe in the shadows of all their fears.

Just before sunset, as John finished at last and was heading out the door for a few hours' rest, Charlie came up to him. He reached into his pocket and pulled out a small mason jar.

"I think you need a drink, John."

Actually, he wanted to get drunk, but it was something he didn't dare to do.

Instead he had found Makala in the garden outside the infirmary, just sitting with Kevin and listening. He waited until they were done, and Makala hugged Kevin, then he pulled around front to drive them home.

Sitting in their outdoor garden with the open mason jar, Makala took a long sip, coughed, and tried to laugh.

"First cigarettes, now moonshine. I'm turning into a mess, John."

"You're doing fine."

"Kevin really does worry me. He was always the stoic, but underneath has a gentle soul." She paused. "To shoot the baby like that . . .

It was a mercy but he'll never see it that way, though it was the right decision."

"Let's just hope we've contained it," John said, taking another sip from the jar and lighting a second cigarette.

"What if we don't?" he finally asked. "I don't want to think it, but I have to."

She blew out the last puff from her cigarette, crushed it out, and leaned back, looking at the sky.

"We don't know the actual contagion rate. Meaning, if you take a hundred people and expose them to the germs, how many will go on to get it? Is it a hundred percent, seventy-five, fifty? I don't know. Some diseases, even after exposure it's actually rather hard for it to take hold. Polio, for example. The way it would seem to just strike an individual here, another there. More people were actually exposed but few caught it. Take Franklin Roosevelt. He was an isolated case, no one around him got it, but someone had to be the carrier. Maybe that person crossed paths with dozens, hundreds of people, but he was the one who got sick. But then no one else in his family did, even though he was loaded with germs.

"So on that count, I don't know. All I know for certain is that once you start to display full symptoms, you're dead in as little as twelve hours. Three days at most.

"Damn it, if only rather than a hundred doses of antibiotics we had a thousand, five thousand. We could dose people as a prophy-laxis the moment we know they're exposed, we could beat it, but we don't have the medicine for that."

John was silent. Until he was absolutely sure, there was no sense in giving her any kind of hope, if indeed there was hope.

"If it breaks through, which it almost did today with those poor people on the barricade, what do we do?"

Without asking, she took out another cigarette and lit it.

"I think starting tomorrow we take a two-tiered approach. If anyone is exposed, they go into immediate lockdown, give them a supply of water, food, and they are quarantined. If after seven days symptoms don't appear they are free to go."

"What if they don't want to go into quarantine?"

"Let's hope voluntary quarantine will answer ninety-nine percent of cases. After five years I hope we have a strong enough sense of community. Those who refuse? We expel them to the other side of the barrier and be damned."

It sounded so medieval to John, but he knew it had to be that way.

"No town meetings, no gatherings to hear the news on this. Get Charlie and his town criers out there to spread the word, and pray people see it has to be this way. So far, at least, we might be lucky and have contained this."

"What about the school? If a kid living in the dorms gets it."

"MacGregor dorm is pretty well abandoned. Set that up as the plague house." She actually chucked sadly. "Plague house, it sounds medieval."

"It is."

The shadows in the garden were lengthening as the sun set, the two of them now just sitting in silence. He thought that maybe with luck they in fact did have it contained, and by holding the perimeter of the town they could stay safe.

Just as he was about to suggest they turn in and hopefully get some sleep, the phone rang.

Wearily he stood up and went into his office to answer it. He talked only for a minute, then went to the bathroom to splash water on his face. After dressing in a faded pair of jeans and flannel shirt against the evening chill he came back out.

"You get some sleep, love. I've got to go out."

"Why? Who was on the phone?"

"Charlie. I might be late. You just stay here for now."

He gave her a brief hug, then went out to the car, which started yet again. As he pulled out, he saw the windshield was now a spiderweb of cracks around the bullet hole in the middle.

"Damn all," he cursed, and then drove off.

He wondered just how much longer the Edsel was going to last: clouds of black smoke pouring out of the exhaust, the cracks on the windshield spreading to the point that he felt it might be best to knock the broken windshield out completely. Passing through the town he drove out to the west end, pulled into the gravel parking lot of the old Methodist church close to the veterans' cemetery. Charlie was already there, along with a reaction team that stood around, obviously nervous, turning to face John.

Charlie pointed his flashlight at John, blinding him for a second before he lowered the beam.

"We found the Patricks," he announced. "They're in the church."

John said nothing but knew what that meant before Charlie told him.

"They're all dead, plague of course." Charlie raised his flashlight, pointing to four people standing beside the church entrance. One of the reaction team was a dozen feet away from them with a raised weapon.

"Yeah, it's bad, John."

"Who is that standing over there?" John asked.

"Some of the Stepp clan."

"What happened?"

"The Patricks came to them for help. Damn all, I should have thought to look closer at this end of town. They have, I mean *had* kin here. It's not good, John."

"How bad?"

"Maybe you should talk to them." He nodded to the four figures huddled by the church door. "I know them, they're good people, God help them. The grandmother, Victoria, lives with her three grandchildren. Parents died during the starving time. Talk with her."

John took Charlie's flashlight and walked toward the group, stopping a good ten yards away.

"Miss Victoria? It's John Matherson."

"John, you know me." She paused. "Are we gonna get sick now too?"

"Just tell me what happened here. Just relax, you're going to be okay."

"We've got an orchard not far from here. You know me, John," she repeated.

To tell the truth he didn't, but he'd never say that. The kids— two boys in their early teens and a girl several years older, maybe sixteen or seventeen—had that ragged look of so many living on the edge. All of them wore ill-fitting bib overall jeans, pulled tight at the waist, with that look as if they'd stepped out of a photograph taken during the Depression.

"They came to my door yesterday morning. Wanted food and a place to stay. I never did like those Patricks, a bad lot, but I'm a Christian woman. We had the apple harvest coming in, I said they could stay if they worked.

"They didn't seem right, though. The mother and daughter worked a few hours but then the daughter started coughing, the baby too. I just had a bad feeling about it all. I gave them a supper of fried apples and fritters and said they had to move on.

"They were obviously coming down with something. They were mum, didn't say a word about their boy. I remembered him—he was a bad sort, given to thieving and drinking. They said he had run off and left them stranded." She paused.

"Go on, Victoria. It's going to be okay."

"Anyhow, I said the church next door was vacant, they could stay there for the night. Gave them some blankets, some food, and sent them to the church. Anyhow, come morning we didn't see them again. I took pity on that poor baby, worried about him, any Christian would do that, so I fried up some more fritters and grits and took it over to the church."

Her voice choked up.

"Oh Lord, they were sick, awful sick. It was just horrible, it was. I was afraid, but said I'd take the baby for now and they gave him to me and I put him to bed in my house. I knew nothing of what was going on. We're kinda isolated up here, you know. We had a good surplus of apples coming in and I had my boy Harold here take a bushel down to town to see if he could trade it for something. He was out hunting while they were here so thank the Merciful Lord he wasn't near any of them Patricks."

She cleared her throat and wiped her eyes.

"He's mighty good with hunting. We thought maybe he could trade the apples for a few bullets and powder, he might get us a rabbit, even a deer, so I could make some stew for the baby."

Again she hesitated.

"The baby died around three or so, poor little angel, I was scared but held him as he died." Now she started to cry.

"My boy Harold came running back a couple of hours later, said the whole town is going crazy, said it was a plague, that the devil was loose. I'd gone over to check on the baby's mother and grand-mother"—she took a deep breath—"they were both dead as well. Oh, it was horrible how it looked in that church. I think we should just burn the building down, it was such a mess.

"I told Harold not to come near me, to get back to town, and tell Charlie."

John was silent, still holding the flashlight beam on them.

"Are we going to die?" she finally asked.

John took a deep breath. "Not if you listen to me."

"All right, John, you're a good man, I seen what you've done. I know you'll help us."

"Where are the bodies?"

"They're in the church."

"Good. And the baby?"

"I bundled the little dear up, I was bringing him down to his mother, that's when I found them. I left the baby inside the door."

"Okay. Just wait there."

John drew Charlie back behind his car.

"What do you think?" Charlie asked.

"Don't go near the church, for starters. Get some food out of your wagon, some gallon bottles of water. Leave it all in the parking lot for that poor woman and grandkids, then pull your people back."

Charlie nodded and went off as John approached Victoria again, still keeping the ten-yard distance.

"Victoria, listen carefully. I know you're a good woman and don't want to cause anyone else to get sick. Will you listen to me?"

"Anything, John, just tell us we're going to be all right."

"We're going to leave some food, and the water has medicine in it. I want you to go back to your house with the supplies and lock yourself in. Don't go into the room where the baby died, lock it. Do you understand?"

"It's bad, isn't it, John? My boy said people are fixin' to die left and right."

"Not true, Victoria. Just trust me."

She started to cry again, hugging her grandchildren close to her side.

"We'll send someone up to your place in the morning to check on you and bring more medicine, but you have to stay calm."

"I'll try."

"You sure that was your only contact?"

"Yes, I took care of the baby. He did get sick on me, the way babies do, though."

John said nothing, realizing that chances were, if she didn't start antibiotics soon, very soon, she was already walking dead, and the way she was holding her grandkids, they were dead too. Harold might not have been a carrier when he went into the town but he most likely was infected now, given how he was protectively hugging his grandmother. Makala would have to release more of their precious supply if they were to have any hope.

"Were there any other contacts?"

"You mean people coming close to us or them?"

"Yes."

She hesitated.

"Please tell me the truth."

"Out in the orchard yesterday. We had so many apples coming in, I told neighbors to feel free to join us and pick a bushel for themselves."

"Oh God." It came out as a whisper. "How many?"

"Not sure. Clara had her two children out there, my cousin Deloris came with her grandfather to pick some. I don't know, John, people were wandering in and out."

"How many?" he insisted. He was afraid the rising panic in his voice could be heard.

"I don't know, John. Maybe a dozen or so." She paused. "Good Lord, John, they're neighbors and kin, we've been harvesting together since I was a child. John, did I just kill them all by my just being neighborly?"

"Don't think like that, Victoria. Just stay calm."

One of the militia came forward with a box of one-gallon jugs of water and stopped, looking nervously at Victoria. He placed it on the ground and hurriedly stepped back. All of the group with the reaction squad were now anxiously talking amongst themselves.

John could sense the rising panic in the air.

"This is the main pathway up to the reservoir and then over the mountain to Burnett's community. How many roads from here up to the North Fork?" John asked, turning to Charlie.

"At least four."

"Seal them all."

"Her boy, Harold, he came into town twice, he might already be carrying it in spite of his not having contact with the Patricks, but he's close to his grandmother now. What do we do, John?"

"We pray."

PART VII

[T]he whole equation of the world is changing . . .

—General Joshua Lawrence

CHAPTER ONE

He returned home to find Makala fast asleep. There was nothing she could do now, so he left her alone in the bedroom. He poured a tumbler of moonshine, downed it with a gulp, and headed into his office. He let the shortwave heat up then slowly turned the dials.

There was the usual static as he searched, but this time of night was when shortwave was at its best with atmospheric skip. The news, what little that he could pick up, was all bad.

South Korea had yet to report a case, but their military was on high alert, stating that some of their sources in China were reporting a brutal state of affairs, half a dozen cities, including Quanzhou and the capital, on full lockdown. The radio station in Northern California reported that the infection was definitely in San Francisco, which was on full lockdown, with reports it was in San Jose now as well.

All of it bad, all of it, he thought numbly, as he finally turned the radio off, smoked the last cigarettes he had, and then poured another drink.

Can't get drunk, though Lord knows I want to do so, crawl in the bed beside Makala, pull the blankets over my head and just hide. Why does it have to be me to do the deciding? he thought for what must be the thousandth time since the Day. *Until then I had my two daughters, a nice job at the college. I could write some articles about the Civil War in my free time to bring in a few extra dollars and just enjoy life. Enjoy watching my girls grow into womanhood, figured someday I'd be a granddad and enjoy that. In short, I just wanted to live life for the pleasure of it.*

He thought of that line from one of the *Godfather* movies, how every time Michael Corleone thought he was out of the wider world of strife it kept pulling him back into its center. *I never wanted to become the head of this town. I definitely did not want to become part of the fledgling attempt at a republic, let alone vice president. When I resigned and left that, I thought I could hide out here and find some semblance of life for myself.*

"John?"

He looked up to find Makala standing by the office door.

"More has happened, hasn't it?" she asked quietly.

He could only nod, his head feeling an infinite weariness.

She came over to his side, leaned down, and hugged him. "There's one more K-cup out there. Let me brew you some coffee, then you can tell me."

When she finally returned with the steaming mug, he sighed as he took a sip. He passed it over to her and she took a sip as well.

"Tell me everything, dear."

It poured out of him, and she took it in without comment. He even spilled out his darkest musings, that he was almost beyond caring at this point and just wanted to leave with her and Genevieve and hide someplace.

"You can't do that. You know that, don't you?"

He just stared at his mug.

"You know of course why you have to be in this, John. There's no way out."

"Pray tell, why? We could just pack it up, grab Genevieve from the school. I know of more than a few abandoned cabins up in the mountains, we can just hole up and let this thing run its course."

"No."

"Why not?"

"You know why: you are the leader everyone turns to with this. You know that."

John did not reply.

"It's because you never wanted it. Somebody a long time ago said that a leader who wanted to have power should never be trusted, let alone followed by others. The only leader that truly matters is one of the rare few who doesn't want it, doesn't seek it. That's the one to turn to in a crisis. My dearest John, that's you and no one else."

He still couldn't speak.

She leaned over again and hugged him, as if he were a child who needed to be comforted.

"Get a few hours' sleep, I'll join you," she said.

"We both are needed downtown."

"There's not much we can do over the next few hours. Charlie set up the roadblocks, he's the one who should handle that. I'll send some medication up to the Stepp family come dawn. We catch it early, maybe they'll be okay."

He looked up at her, questioning.

"John, I've been thinking, we might as well use the stockpile up front, at least with the possible cases we know. I got a call after you left that Laura Carson is holding steady, so the medication must still have some vitality left in it."

"There could be twenty, fifty cases ready to explode, according to Victoria Stepp. If so . . ." And his voice trailed off.

"It's one in the morning, John. We both need sleep. We'll sort out what we can come dawn. So till then, the doctor is ordering you to get some sleep. Okay?" She laughed softly. "Maybe I can help you relax." She helped him to his feet and led him into the bedroom, where they finally fell into an exhausted sleep.

They managed to get several hours of sleep, until the phone started ringing at four in the morning. There was no coffee left in the house so John put some herbal tea on while Makala grabbed a quick and freezing shower, then John followed suit while she dressed. Coaxing a small fire in the stove, they blackened what was left of the bread and poured some honey on it to at least sweeten it.

This time John's car wouldn't start. Following Charlie's example, he jumped up and down on the bumper several times, not really understanding why, but the starter finally caught. Trailing smoke, they drove to the town hall.

As they pulled into the parking lot, they saw Charlie sitting outside in the half-light of early dawn, leaning back in one of the rocking chairs that lined the outside of the building. The other chairs were filled as well with exhausted militia. Charlie slowly stood up and started over to the car as John and Makala got out.

"Charlie, would you please knock off for a while," Makala said, going up and first giving him a hug.

"I will," he gave a weak smile, "someday."

"How many more cases are confirmed?" she asked.

"Last count, at least eight. We ran a dozen doses of the remaining Cipro up to our line outside the Methodist church as ordered for the Stepp family. The word from the girl is that her grandmother definitely has it. Coughing, fever rising fast."

"What about the older boy, what's his name, Harry?"

"Harold. So far nothing."

"He's the one to watch the closest," Makala interjected. He had been in town, interacted with God knows how many people. "If he's got it, it could be bad. Now, what else? How's Laura?"

"She seems okay," Charlie reported. "They're locked up in the infirmary, but her husband, he's coming down with it."

"Damn all." John sighed.

"Dose him too," Makala announced.

John looked over at her. He knew what she was doing. They were going to run through the few doses they had left, in the hope of stamping it out before it spread farther.

"Anything else?"

"Well, you can imagine word spread like fire up on the North Fork. Several people tried to leave over on the old Camp Eden Road. Our militia turned them back but it got tense. They said half a dozen more are sick.

"What I worry about there is that they head north," Charlie continued. "That's the old road up to Forrest Barnett's people, up toward Burnsville. No way we can block off all the old fire lanes up there."

"Let's hope their mobility is limited. Last I heard, the only old cars up there are the ones that run on charcoal. No way they can climb over six-thousand-foot mountains."

"Horseback, then."

"I know. I know."

Forrest was an old friend and ally. John couldn't leave him in the lurch and just hope for the best. They did have a radio link, but days might pass between contacts, dependent on the solar panels Forrest used to charge his radios.

"Have you been trying to reach him by radio?"

"We've been on it starting a few hours ago. No response—they're most likely just asleep."

"Have someone on our radio link constantly from now until we reach him with a warning to seal off from the outside world."

"Okay."

"Anything else?"

"Thankfully, no."

"Just wait," John mumbled under his breath, as if some sort of vengeful god was listening.

They sat in silence until Alice came out of the phone office.

"Makala, you better take this," she announced, the worry in her voice obvious.

Sighing, she went in. When she came back out five minutes later, her face was ashen. "They are reporting cases in Asheville. That was the Mission Hospital. That's all they would say."

John stood silent. His hope that this was all triggered by the Patricks, coming from Virginia and triggering the scare here, had just gone out the window.

It was to the west of them now as well. Given the squalid conditions that were so prevalent in Asheville, with those who after five years were barely surviving, it meant it would spread, and spread fast.

"Now what?" Charlie asked.

"We seal off to the west now as well. Seal off and pray."

Makala simply collapsed on one of the rocking chairs and sat lost in thought. Finally, she did stir. "There's nothing else we can do, John," she sighed. The touch of resurgence that he'd seen in her last night was draining out of her.

Alice was holding a note pad, scanning through the night log.

"John, Ernie called an hour ago. You know how he is, always so darn self-important. Says he wants to see you as soon as possible."

John looked up at her. "Did he say what it's about?"

"Nope, you know him. But he said he had to see you now. I told him he'd maybe have to wait awhile for you to get back. You can imagine his response."

There were times with Ernie that could drive him to distraction, but then again . . .

"I said you'd call, but he wants you up there."

CHAPTER TWO

Charlie had allotted five more gallons to John from the nearly finished stockpile of gas and diesel, but the car was definitely dying as he chugged the last few hundred yards to the top of Ernie's drive.

Maggie was out, wanting to jump on John and play, but for once he tried to ignore her. As he came to the top of the porch stairs Linda was already greeting him with some coffee, which he gratefully accepted.

"Ernie's in his lab, at least that's what he calls it."

Thanking her, he had to step over the frames of half a dozen old computers to squeeze into Ernie's lair.

"You're going to thank me for this, John."

"It better be good. I'm dealing with a lot of deep shit in town that won't wait."

"Well, a few days ago this seemed all-fire important to you, and I've been working on it ever since."

John was so tired he wasn't sure for a moment what exactly Ernie was so excited about.

"Sit down, check out this screen, that one to the right."

The font reminded John of something from twenty years ago. He started to read.

Calling Shangri-La, this is J for L . . .

He scrolled down; the transmission seemed endless.

"What is this?"

"Like you wanted, I've been trying different frequencies for Raven Rock. Nothing, and frankly I can only CQ someone for so long before I get bored to death."

"CQ?"

"Ham operator lingo. Means you wanna talk to someone."

"Oh."

"So I figured, why not? Still had a lot of old email addresses, from after we took Raven Rock and had things up for a while. So I put those on repeat loops, then for the hell of it just tried anything related to Shangri-La. Found out, by the way, that was the old name FDR gave to Camp David.

"You were closed-mouth about it, but I kind of figured that's who you were trying to reach. I'm not so dumb as people think at times, John, I was a damn good software coder in my day. You know I worked on some problems with the shuttle and—"

"Ernie," John snapped.

He could hear Linda chuckling in the next room.

"What?"

"Not now! Stick to the moment. What have you got?"

"Jeez, all right, we got this," he announced triumphantly. He hit a few keys and pointed to one of the other monitors.

This is L. What can I do for you J . . .

"Holy shit," John whispered.

"Yeah. It could be somebody just spoofing us for the hell of it. But the URL for the return looks like a Pentagon address—prewar, but still."

John sat down next to Ernie, staring at the screen.

"Anything else?"

"Yeah," Ernie said, and punched a few more keys. The first line with a time stamp was his Shangri-La signal.

The next line was time-stamped forty-five minutes ago:

This is L. What can I do for you J?

The line was repeated several times, stamped shortly after 07:13:10, then 07:14:00, then 07:14:45.

Then one more line.

If this is J, what is your military serial number? No number, nothing more to say. Try at 0900 exactly.

John found he was actually trembling slightly.

What the hell was his serial number, damn it? Of course he remembered his old social security number, but no one had asked for that kind of identification in decades.

"John, maybe . . ." Ernie started.

"Ernie, just shut up and be still. I need to think."

What was it? He thought back to basic and OCS. What was it? He looked for a memory, a sergeant in his face, some ridiculous questions, the favorite of all drill sergeants back in the day: "All right. What's your serial number!"

He grabbed a pen on Ernie's desk, pushed some papers to the center of the cluttered space, and jotted the string of numbers down.

Was that it? He wasn't sure.

There was nothing else to do but wait for the next thirty-five minutes.

"Ernie, I have to ask. Could you just leave me alone until after nine? I have to think."

"John, maybe I can . . ."

A withering look from John silenced him.

"This keyboard, is it hooked up?" he finally asked.

"Yeah, just type away. I'm so glad I could help, John," he added sarcastically.

John wanted to scream a few choice obscenities at him but held back.

"Thanks, Ernie. Just close the door on the way out, will you?"

Just as the door was about to close, Linda poked her head in. "Good for you, John," she whispered conspiratorially. "Now, more coffee? We still have some."

"Please."

"Anything to go with it?"

"Maybe later, not now, I need to think. Please don't disturb me for anything, Linda. Okay?"

Linda quietly opened the door again five minutes later, left the coffee, and withdrew. With a few sharp words she silenced Ernie, who went off in a huff.

The twenty-five remaining minutes dragged on like an eternity, reminding him of long-ago days of staring at the clock, wishing for the last five minutes to tick by in school.

Maybe he should call back down to the town office; so much was going wrong today, more things were most likely happening. He heard the phone ring in the next room, a loud, old mechanical sound. A hushed comment. Good old Linda taking the message but not disturbing him.

It could be nothing, John realized. He had zero love for Lawrence, yet he didn't know if it even was Lawrence. It could be anything, some damn kid in a country where computers still worked, who was playing with him. It could even be the Soviets, it could be some twelve-year-old with a computer that still worked. But something told him it was not any of those things, and he had to figure what was the game to play now.

The minutes ticked by, and then, just a few seconds before nine, John typed in what he hoped was his serial number and hit the Return key.

Long seconds passed, thirty seconds, a minute. He was tempted to type it again but stopped himself. Chances were it wasn't anything legit; what good would his serial number do in this world now?

What type of cigarettes did I give you and how many? popped up on the screen.

He actually smiled slightly, figuring what the hell.

One carton of Dunhills.

Smoke them all yet?

Nearly every damn one. John smiled ruefully. *Thanks for getting me hooked again.*

Of all things an *LOL* appeared next. Nothing for a moment, then . . .

I type slow, John, how are you doing?

Who wants to know?

You know the answer. We last parted in a tunnel, I assumed you were staying, but you resigned and ran off . . . Not very polite of you.

I made my choices.

Wish you had stayed, we could have worked together.

Really?

Tragic about Scales, he was a damn fine general.

And president, John reminded him. There was a pause, and he sat back to finish his coffee.

So why did you contact me, John?

Shall I play a game and ask for you to provide a reason?

I'm not a game player, John. Let's cut to the chase here.

Cipro or some other specific treatment for the plague.

Now there was a long pause of several minutes. This was the long shot, most likely a dead end, but it was at least worth trying.

Why ask me?

Lawrence, with all that you have stockpiled down there, I think it's fair to assume that you've got antibiotics on hand, quite a large store perhaps.

Why do you want Cipro?

I think you know.

Enlighten me. Like I said, let's not play guessing games.

We have plague. Started three days ago, a family from Virginia carried it in. We're trying to contain it but it's starting to look bad. So I'm asking, do you have medication to stop it?

A pause and then a single word.

Yes.

John was not sure how to proceed. Then he decided he might as well just tell the truth.

It's here in Black Mountain. This morning in Asheville. Without meds it will explode over the next week. He hit Return then waited. There was no response.

He tried again. *You can help us, Lawrence. I'm asking you to help us.*

The response took a while to appear.

Why?

"Damn you," John said under his breath, "don't make me beg." He typed, *You know I'd help if things were reversed.*

I'm not you, John. I offered you something, a role you can help me with. You walked away. Why should I help you now?

I'm sensing your answer is no, John angrily typed in. *If so, may God forgive you, Lawrence.*

John hit the Return key a final time. He cursed as he stood up, and in a fit of anger, threw his coffee cup across the room, spilling what was left inside and shattering the mug. Seconds later Linda opened the door.

"John, what's wrong?"

He was suddenly embarrassed at his explosion and just stood there, trying to control the part of him that was on the verge of tears of rage. This whole damn thing, all of it was pushing him to a breaking point.

"Sorry, I'll clean it up."

"Don't you worry about that. Come out to the kitchen and I'll pour you something a bit more bracing." She gave him a sympathetic look. "Ernie is sulking in his office upstairs. I'll keep him away from you."

"No, I'll be okay. But yeah, I could use something to calm down with."

As he stepped away from the computer a new line appeared on the screen.

How many doses you need, John?

"God in heaven, thank you," he whispered. He motioned for Linda to close the door and sat back down.

How many? How many? He hadn't even thought that out.

Five thousand, he typed in.

Another pause.

I'll want something in return, John.

Ask it.

We'll talk about it later today. Is your interstate clear to land a plane?

Yes, you'll have a mile or more for landing.

1600 hours then, Black Mountain interstate exit. Five thousand doses. Until then.

John sat for long minutes in silence, uttering a thankful prayer. Whatever Lawrence wanted in return, he held the cards now, and whatever they were, John knew he would have to play them. He realized the alternative was simple: the town would be dead.

CHAPTER THREE

By 15:30 that afternoon the situation was going downhill.

The west end of town past the Methodist church was descending into chaos. People kept coming to the barrier lines set up on the various roads, asking for help, asking to be let in, and over by the Lake Eden Road, an armed group had almost exploded into violence. They were turned back only because Charlie threatened to fire in one minute without warning if they didn't immediately disperse.

For John, it was horrifying to observe how in a few short days, a community that had held together through numerous crises was unraveling in the face of the plague.

"We better get down to the interstate." It was Makala, by the doorway.

He had spent the last several hours writing down some messages to Charlie, to his classes with assignments to keep them busy while locked in their dorm rooms, and then a note to Makala if things went bad.

Without a word he got up and joined her. After he completed his new routine of jumping up and down on the bumper several times, the car roared to life. Chugging down through the center of town he noticed it was strangely still, except for the reaction team in the fire department parking lot, fully suited up with bulletproof vests, weapons resting beside them. It was a helluva sight, John thought. The town might very well turn on itself if this crisis deepened, and all that he'd worked for would be finished.

Coming to the exit ramp for Interstate 40, he drove up to just before the merge started and parked. He had told no one else, other than Makala and Linda, what was hopefully about to happen. If it was all a mirage, a dark game played by Lawrence, there was no sense in getting people's hopes up.

He pulled out his pocket watch. It was 15:50.

Makala stepped out of the car and John did likewise, the two of them alone and waiting.

"From what you've told me about him I have to ask, why would he do it?"

Why indeed?

"I'd like to think that there is some sense of common decency in the man. Call it the old concept of helping a brother officer, though that sounds foolish, doesn't it?"

She didn't answer that. Her face was pinched with exhaustion and worry. "You know if he doesn't come through, we're at the end of our rope. We're out of antibiotics, John. In a week, especially with Asheville to the west of us down with this, we'll be overwhelmed."

He couldn't reply, there was nothing to say.

She cocked her head and looked up. "Hear it?"

"No, your hearing is better than mine."

"It's a plane!"

The world had been silent for so long that a lone engine in the distance stood out clearly; now he heard it as well.

She turned, facing west, shading her eyes, and repeated. "It's a plane."

John had a flash memory from childhood of the television show with Tattoo shouting, "The plane, the plane!" and he actually started to laugh, partly at the memory of it but also with the flood of relief that washed over him.

Swinging in from the west, what looked to be a twin-engine turboprop came down low, curving around the bend in the interstate below it. It lined up, landing gear down, and touched in, engines roaring as it braked to a stop. The air was suddenly thick with the smell of jet fuel and smoke, the roar of the engines near to overwhelming John emotionally, filling him with memories of a world where man had crossed the sky with ease.

Makala had an arm around John, and was actually shouting with delight.

"My God, we're saved, John. God bless them!"

John tried to contain his emotions. Yes, if that plane did contain the medication needed they were saved, but the question came back to him. What would Lawrence ask in return?

The hatch down at the back of the plane opened, and there was a frozen moment as two military police in tactical gear stepped out first. They stopped at the bottom of the stairs, obviously on alert for any possible threat.

And then the next person came out. It was Lawrence, in uniform of course, sunglasses on and hat pulled low. The way he walked . . . for a split second it reminded John of something. It was MacArthur, that look that was almost imperial in its swagger.

He swallowed the thought, stepping forward, extending his hand, Makala by his side.

"John, damn good to see you again," Lawrence announced loudly.

John restrained the instinct to salute, and Lawrence finally extended his hand; again that nearly overpowering grip.

"I assume this beautiful woman beside you is your wife Makala."

John offered the introduction, adding, "She is our chief medical officer, in charge of all medical concerns for our community."

Lawrence took her hand politely. "Then I assume it is in very capable hands, Mrs. Matherson."

"Makala would be fine," she replied smoothly, and John could see that the first impression was not a good one.

An awkward silence ensued until Lawrence turned and looked back at the two MPs. "You can offload the boxes over by the car," he announced.

"And they are?" Makala asked.

"One thousand doses of Cipro."

"One thousand?" she asked. "John said there'd be five thousand doses."

"I misspoke when chatting with John. It's a thousand for now."

The joy she was showing a few minutes ago hardened.

"Two doses a day, for proactive use in those showing signs of infection. Three to four doses a day for those displaying symptoms." She calculated in her head, though she'd already gone over the numbers countless times. "It won't be enough. A minimum regime is seven days from exposure, fourteen or longer if there is onset. Sir, that means we can maybe treat a hundred people at most, if we stretch it and hope for the best. The outbreak is probably spreading on the west side of our town. This won't be enough."

"Do you prefer then that I just skip delivery?" he said, his voice now cold.

"No, of course not," Makala replied, trying to contain her frustration. "But I thought . . ." She fell silent, sensing this was not the time to argue.

"We'll talk about it more later," he said. "I'm certain a sufficient supply can be found."

"Of course," she replied in a monotone.

"Miss Makala, I would love to talk more with you, find out how you are handling this, but John here and I need to talk some business first."

"In other words, you'd like me to excuse the two of you."

Lawrence just smiled, and John now felt an annoyance over the dark sunglasses that made it impossible to read his eyes.

John looked over at Makala and forced a smile. "Let's get the medication loaded in the car, I'm sure those MPs will help you. I'll meet you back at the town office once we're done here. Okay?"

Regaining her composure, she hugged John closely, whispering, "Be careful, love," then went to supervise the loading of the car.

"I sense she can be a hard person at times, John."

"That she can be," he replied.

"Let's get back in the plane, there's much to talk about."

Turning, the general climbed back into the rear of the plane, John following. The interior was plainly appointed in standard military style, but did have two oversized leather chairs with a small desk between them, a heavy laptop computer on the table, and a sideboard, which Lawrence opened as John sat down.

He produced a bottle of prewar scotch and two glasses, and without asking, poured John a drink.

Sitting back in his chair, he took the sunglasses off, his gray eyes narrowing, and looked at John appraisingly. "You ran off on me back in May. I didn't appreciate that."

"You had what you wanted, Raven Rock. And with it the collapse of our attempt at self-governing. Therefore why should I have stayed?"

"You know that Bob Scales killed himself. It wasn't natural causes, as was leaked out afterward."

When he lost Raven Rock to Lawrence, what was left? Being kept on as some sort of token?

"It was the honorable way out for him, God rest his soul," John finally said.

"But were you honorable? You were the vice president. It was your duty to stay on for what could have been next."

"Our attempt at a renewed government was failing. And don't speak to me of duty. Last I remember, an official elected or appointed to high office has the right to resign. It used to be that he did so if his sense of duty, his honor, dictated that there was no other reasonable response. Bob offered me a way out, to return back to my home where I belong. That became the higher obligation, and I took that obligation as my duty."

"Noble, but what a waste."

"What's that supposed to mean?" John demanded.

"We'll come to that."

John looked out the window. Makala was now in the car, and he had to smile as he saw that one of the MPs had the hood open and the other was jumping up and down on the bumper. The Edsel started up in a cloud of smoke and Makala turned it about and drove down the exit ramp.

"Why only a thousand doses, Lawrence?"

"Why not?" He gave a smile that John didn't like one bit.

"Damn it, you're playing some sort of game."

"Don't insult me. We'll scramble up more if things work out, and get them down here pronto."

"What do you mean, 'If things work out'?"

"We'll come to that."

"You heard my wife. A thousand doses will not even be remotely sufficient if this thing is spreading here, which I assume it is. Beyond that, they now have an outbreak in Asheville."

"Why be concerned for them, John? You can't save everybody."

"Call it compassion."

"John, compassion be damned in the world we have now."

"I kind of figured you'd say something like that."

"Let's just get down to the way it is, the way it will have to be if we are to survive."

John helped himself to another ounce of scotch and sat back and waited to hear what Lawrence would say next.

"Was there anything in my book collection that made you think?"

"Of course. What's on a bookshelf is always a good indicator of the person who owns them."

"Nietzsche, for example. 'That which does not kill us makes us stronger.' Would you say that applies to you? You've survived more than most."

"But I never lost my humanity, if that's what you mean."

"How many people have you killed, John?"

He remembered the drugged-out punk he had helped to execute back when all this started and the old man he blew down yesterday with a shotgun blast. "Drug-addicted thieves mostly. That's it."

"Bullshit, John. You've killed hundreds, more likely thousands. As you took over Black Mountain you ordered the borders sealed. Those first months, thousands of people were on the road, starving, sick, begging for a bowl of soup for their children. But you sealed the border to let them die."

John recalled the woman who still haunted him at times. The executive type who was reduced to offering her body to John for just one meal. When he refused her, he knew it meant she would be dead in a few more days, most likely raped by the side of the road and abandoned.

"That posse you fought, how many did your people kill?"

"We had to, there was no alternative."

"All right then. At the end of the fight, you ordered the execution of some who were left. I heard you were so enraged that you ordered one of them to be strung up and then put a sign of warning around his broken neck."

"Had to."

"Ah, the cruel reality, kill or be killed. And doing it made you stronger for the next one. How many more have you killed since that posse? Ten, a hundred, a few thousand? You didn't pull the trigger anymore, but they did die by your orders."

"Damn you, what are you driving at?"

"You're a very proficient killer, just like anyone who is still alive after five years of madness. And with each killing, you come away a bit stronger than you were before that killing."

"If there is some sort of moral lesson in this, just come out with it."

Lawrence smiled and sipped his drink. "Again, we are not all that different, you and I."

"I'd like to think not."

"John, what do I represent?"

"I really don't know much, other than that you, and those with you, survived for five years hidden in those damn tunnels and bunkers while the rest of us struggled and the vast majority of us died."

"Would it have been any different if in the days after those of us, as you say, who hid, had come out from out shelters, opened our warehouses, and told the world, 'Here we are, let us help you'?" Lawrence actually laughed sadly. Then got up and reached back into the sideboard.

"You know, I almost forgot, I brought a little present for you." He pulled out a fresh carton of Dunhill cigarettes.

John could not help but look at them covetously.

"Not a bribe, John, just a present to an old friend." And he tossed the carton over.

It fell onto John's lap, but he didn't pick them up.

"Oh, for God's sake, no game here. No smoking on the plane, though, let's just step outside." Without waiting for a reply, Lawrence stepped out of the plane. A moment later John followed, reluctantly carrying the carton of Dunhills.

He felt like an idiot at that moment. Lawrence had hit a weakness. *What difference does it make if I have one now or not? He knows I'm craving them, but damn it all,* he decided, and lit one up.

"This really is a beautiful place," Lawrence announced, having donned his sunglasses again against the late-afternoon glare. "I really do long for topside. Sure, we take breaks back at Camp David."

He smiled as he caught himself. "I mean Shangri-La. As a boy I would go off hiking for days at a time. I grew up in Pennsylvania, you know. Little town tucked up in a fold of hills next to the Appalachian Trail. We'd hike it all the time. Those were happy days, and at this moment I miss it terribly."

John stood silent, the way Lawrence was lost in the moment, the forest around him an explosion of colors, the mountains, layer after layer, the view stretching for fifty miles and disappearing in the dark blue-green haze of the Smokies. There was at least a moment of peace, all that was going on in the town a half mile away forgotten.

"There's a reason for what you're doing, Lawrence. Why the game with the medicine? And, frankly, why are you playing this game with *me*?"

"Well, John, you see, I want you to come back with me to Camp David."

"You implied that back in the spring. Why is it different now? My place is here, not up in your underground maze. The answer was no then, and it's still no now."

"Okay, my friend. That's your answer? Fine." He turned and started back for the plane.

"What about the medicine? Do we still get the extra doses or not?"

"Think hard, John. I think the answer to that is obvious, isn't it?"

"Damn you to hell, Lawrence," John snapped.

Lawrence turned back to John and stood for a moment, his eyes hidden by the sunglasses.

"You son of a bitch," John said softly.

"Maybe I am, but then again, John, I'm the one in control here, not you."

There was a long moment of silence.

"Twenty thousand doses, delivered tomorrow," John finally whispered.

"Ahh, now we haggle. Why not thirty, fifty? Last I checked our inventory it's in the millions, by the way."

"Bastard."

"Cursing at me won't change the paradigm here, with you or other things as well. You have something I want, I have something you want."

"And it's me, is that it?"

"John, to be frank, the whole equation of the world is changing. Like it or not, you are one of the numbers in that equation. You are somebody, John. Your reputation far exceeds this small corner of the world. So if that's worth twenty thousand doses of a life-saving drug, so be it. When someone has what you want, you bargain."

"Or you just take it."

"Not that crude, John. But remember. I don't bring in more medication in the next day or two, in two weeks' time half this little precious town dies. It's that simple."

John took out another cigarette, lit it, took a puff and then, looking at Lawrence, he threw it to the ground, and the rest of the pack along with it.

"Give me till tomorrow morning."

"No can do, John. You're not the only thing I'm dealing with. Two hours. I assume, of course, you've got to get your pretty wife's consent."

John stared at him, fuming but out of options.

PART VIII

A good and healthy aristocracy must acquiesce, with a good conscience, in the sacrifice of legions of individuals, who, for its benefit, must be reduced to slaves and tools. The masses have no right to exist on their own account: their sole excuse for living lies in their usefulness as a sort of superstructure or scaffolding, upon which a more select race of beings may be elevated.

—Friedrich Nietzsche, *Beyond Good and Evil,*
Section 258

CHAPTER ONE

It was a twenty-minute walk back to the center of town, and what greeted him was barely controlled chaos. Outside the town office was an ever-increasing crowd of people. They were not yet threatening but they were obviously upset, and at the sight of John turning the corner half a dozen all but blocked his way.

"I think my wife has been exposed, John."

"Mr. Matherson, can I have a minute . . ."

He tried to brush them aside as Charlie came up to him, looking even more harassed and exhausted than the last time they'd spoken.

"John, we've got to talk . . ."

"Just get me inside, and where's Makala?"

"Inside with the meds."

"Take me to her, we'll talk later."

As John forced his way to the door, which was guarded by one of the militia, the crowd surged around him, still shouting questions. The guard managed to hold them off so he could make his way inside. John turned the corner of the hallway toward the meeting room and saw Makala. Bottles of medication were strewn across a table in front of her, several of her infirmary staff helping.

"All right, remember, ten five-hundred-milligram doses, tell them to give a pill every twelve hours. Someone take two bottles up to the Camp Eden Road . . ."

She trailed off when she saw John.

"We need to talk now," John whispered as she came up to hug him.

"Yes, I figured."

They ducked into the bathroom to get some privacy.

"He wanted you to go back with him, didn't he?"

John could only nod his head.

"The bastard. If you don't?"

"He cuts off the medication supply."

"Oh Jesus," she said wearily.

As he stepped out of his home, for what he feared could be the last time, John looked back at the garden where his Jennifer rested. He put his flight bag down and went to the garden and stood there for a moment. Makala hung back, deciding it was of course best to leave him to his thoughts.

It seemed to John just yesterday that Jennifer would snuggle in his arms at night with Rabs the Rabbit and he would tell her a story, then Mary would gently pluck her up and take her to bed.

He of course had nothing but love for Genevieve and Makala, but at times a dream would float up to haunt him in the hour before dawn. *I have this life now, a daughter who I love with all my heart, but the memories of a before-time still hurt now and then,* as they did at this moment.

He bowed his head. "Sleep well, my sweetness," he whispered, and then went back to the car, where Makala waited.

"You think it best I don't stop and see Genevieve?"

"No, better not," she replied softly. "She won't understand. Once she's back home, I'll find a way to explain that Daddy's on a trip far away but will come back to us soon."

"Okay then," he sighed. Throwing his bag in the back seat, he got up front, with Makala driving. She hit the starter and the car rumbled to life.

"Wish the damn thing was really dead," Makala announced, trying to laugh as she put it in gear and they went out the driveway.

He had expected her to put up a fight about this but she had instantly agreed: he had to go.

The equation, to her, was terribly simple. As if it was some sort of old-fashioned barter or trading deal. She had offered John the choice of not going, but then what? That question went unanswered. One week from now, people by the dozens, and then hundreds, would be dying. It was the equation of one community leader in exchange for the life of a town.

They rode in silence down Montreat Road, and to avoid the growing crowd at the center of town, she turned onto some back streets.

When they merged back onto the road to the interstate, the plane was at last visible, engines idling and blowing the rich scent of jet fuel. A small crowd had gathered to watch, obviously wondering why the plane was here. Makala drove up the exit ramp and came to a stop. She was suddenly in John's arms, crying uncontrollably.

"You're not coming back, are you?" she sobbed.

"Don't say that, I'll find a way out of this."

"I don't trust that bastard. If he had any sense of honor, of humanity, he'd give us the drugs and leave you here. This is just straight-out blackmail, John."

There was nothing to say. Of course she was right.

"John, there's a lot more to it, you know that. Where did the plague break out? We pretty well know it was Virginia. How far is that from this Camp David? And China, the same time in China. There's a link to it and you know it."

"Yes."

"John, if you can find out why . . ." Her voice trailed off. Nothing more needed to be said.

There was a knock on the passenger-side window that startled both of them. It was one of the MPs.

"Sir, we're leaving, with or without you, in five minutes. I'm ordered to get you or leave, so what will it be?"

The tone was like that of someone following orders. It rankled John.

He broke the embrace.

"Stay in the car. Okay?"

She nodded her head.

"There should be a full shipment tomorrow. You've got work to do. Tell Charlie he's in charge of everything now. Kevin Malady, if he is up to it, is second in command. He'll know what to do."

He paused to think; there were so many things to consider. What next?

"Sir, one minute or we are leaving."

He gazed at Makala for a final moment, forcing a smile. "I'll see you at sundown soon enough, my love."

Sitting in one of the bucket seats behind the pilot, Lawrence in the copilot seat, they started their takeoff run, eastbound on the interstate, quickly picking up speed.

Out the window, John got one more glance of Makala, standing rigid by the car. He knew she was still crying as she raised a hand in farewell when they roared past.

How many have done just as she did through the ages. That final wave of farewell and then turning away. From the most ancient of days, of women standing on a fortress wall, or lining the road out past the town gate, to parades and troops, who for a brief instant of glory had that parade while bedecked with flowers. Always the same parting, and so rare the blessing of a coming back.

The plane lifted off, soaring upward, turning to weave through the high mountain pass, then banking over sharply, a quick flash of Ernie and Linda's house at the top of the pass, then they turned northward, the last rays of sunset illuminating the western sky before they flew into the clouds and darkness.

CHAPTER TWO

There was a terrible sense of disorientation as John Matherson finally switched on the light above his head, then shielded his eyes from the glare. He sat up, trying in these first seconds to get his bearings.

The room had no windows. The walls were adorned with some motel-like prints of mountainscapes. There was room for a desk, a few chairs. His clothes were folded over the chair where he'd left them.

How long ago? He wasn't sure. The flight from Black Mountain had been completed in near total silence. Lawrence flew the plane for a while, taking over from the pilot, then, handing controls of the plane back, he had walked to the rear. He motioned to offer John a drink, which he declined, so Lawrence just stretched out in the leather chair and went to sleep.

John didn't care to converse with the two stoic MPs, and he was too full of adrenaline to sleep, so he had sat alone, occasionally looking over the shoulder of the pilot. No answers there as to where they were going, other than a heading of 325 degrees, north by northwest, which was enough for him to assume they were bound for Camp David.

In spite of his racing thoughts, he finally just settled back in his seat and nodded off as well, until he was awakened by the plane touching down.

The buildings next to the single runway were unlit, but there was a guard detail out, and by the time the engines were barely shut down Lawrence was up on his feet.

"Get some sleep, John, long day tomorrow." And he was out the door, the guard detail falling in behind him. The MP who had summoned John to the plane was out the door as well, carrying John's flight bag, and with a curt "Follow me." He escorted John into one of the buildings, which housed an elevator. Producing a security badge, he held it to the keypad, punched in a long string of numbers, then stepped back as the elevator opened. He motioned for John to step in.

The drop felt like it would leave his stomach behind, and a minute later had whisked him to God knows where.

Another guard was standing in the hallway when the elevator opened. There was a whispered conversation, the flight bag was handed over, and this new guard motioned for John to follow.

The whole thing with its evident layers of security and secrecy was just starting to annoy John. He was tempted to ask the guard where they were going, but he sensed this wasn't the person to get any answers from.

It was a long walk to another elevator, what felt like a short ride up, then another empty corridor. In his army days John had visited an aircraft carrier as part of a short exchange familiarization program, and this reminded him of that: the endless corridors that seemed to go on forever, archaic numbers and letters stenciled on doors that only the initiates would understand.

They passed another side corridor that had the scent of food wafting from it. He was hungry but felt that could wait for now.

At last there was a short flight of steps, the hallway beyond becoming wider, the bare metallic walls giving way to standard paneling. A collection of photos and prints hung on the walls, the typical military style from the 1960s. He always thought them to be slightly ludicrous, since all the men's faces looked almost identical, rock jawed and determined to win victory, be it at Yorktown, San Juan Hill, or the Bulge.

They stopped at last, and the MP opened a door. "Your quarters for now, sir," he announced, depositing the flight bag inside the door.

John stepped in, the MP not following.

"Sir, if you want something to eat, head back down the corridor to just before the flight of stairs. This time of night they should still have some sandwiches and coffee."

"Fine, thanks."

"I have to advise you not to go beyond the stairwells back there or up ahead. This is a restricted area and you must stay within it."

"Just great, thanks for the advice."

"Good night, sir." Closing the door, the MP left him alone.

Hell of a welcome, John thought. Part of him was at least expecting something, anything beyond a "cold food at the end of the hall, sir" greeting.

He wondered of course if this was all part of some elaborate game, some sort of psyops to see how he might react. The touch of paranoia in him suddenly made him wonder if there was a camera hidden in the room, and in the next room over people were watching him on a monitor.

He finally decided the hell with it all. Taking off his outer clothes, he crawled into a bed that was at least somewhat comfortable and tried to drift off to sleep. But it wouldn't come until a few hours before dawn.

CHAPTER THREE

A loud knock on the door finally stirred him awake. The room was pitch black and, fumbling around, he finally hit an overhead light switch and shielded his eyes from the glare.

Another knock, this one louder.

"Yeah, yeah, give me a second, will you?" He stumbled to the door and opened it.

To his surprise, it wasn't an MP. It was, of all people, Staff Sergeant James Harrison, though it took John a moment to place the man.

"Good morning, sir, I got breakfast waiting for you, then a meeting topside in thirty minutes with General Lawrence."

"Sergeant? Just what the hell are you doing here?"

"All in good time, sir. Unless you want to do this meeting in your shorts, I suggest you get dressed."

"Yeah, okay," he muttered, and after getting shirt, pants, and shoes on he went to the head. Looking in the small metallic mirror, he rubbed his week-old stubble, thought it was starting to look too much like most of the men living on the edge of things, but the hell with that, it was a reflection of how things were.

He rejoined the sergeant and they took the short walk to the

small cafeteria, which looked like a comfortable setting for the officer class on a military base. He was greeted by the scent of real
eggs, real bacon, and real coffee. He was starving, and after a quick
prayer of thanks, of course remembering Makala and their baby, he
set to with a will. Harrison went behind the counter, drew a large
cup of black coffee, and sat down across from John.

John ate in silence. Of course he was filled with questions about
how a man he thought loyal to General Scales was here in this place,
but he didn't ask.

Finished with his meal, he instinctively reached for the cigarettes
in his breast pocket, but then realized he had thrown them down
on the ground in a display of contempt for Lawrence. He now re-
gretted it.

With that, to his surprise, Harrison drew a pack from his own
pocket, opened it up, got one out for John, and leaned over the table
to light it for him.

"A bribe, is it?" John asked suspiciously.

Harrison just smiled. "The general felt you'd want them, so he
passed a carton to me this morning for you, and told me to make
sure you were well fed."

John just stared at Harrison. On one hand, he was glad to see
a familiar face of someone General Scales trusted completely, but
then again, the sergeant was obviously working for "them."

As John stared at him, Harrison tossed the pack on the table and
John saw a slip of paper sticking out of the open end. Harrison sat
silent, staring straight at John.

He pulled out the slip of paper and palmed it and surreptitiously
read:

*Can't talk here. More than a few loyal to what our old general stood
for. Talk later. Trust Y.*

John looked back at Harrison, who was smiling. John crumpled
up the note, mixing it with a paper napkin, and casually tossed it
on the table.

"Another coffee, sir?"

"Yeah, Sergeant."

Harrison swept up the plates and napkins, carrying them to the back counter, then returned with another steaming-hot cup.

"Last I saw you, you were working as a cook in Raven Rock. Why still here?"

"Well, sir, after this new group took over, some of the team left, but for a lot of us, what the hell, we were offered jobs and decided it was best to take them."

"Understandable," John said.

"Besides, what was there to go back to, know what I mean?"

"Maybe that's best," John agreed.

John looked into Harrison's dark features, almost blurting out the truth, when his thoughts were interrupted by a major coming into the room.

"Vice President Matherson?"

He had not been called that in months. He was no longer the vice president of anything, and being addressed that way caught him off guard.

John stood up, looking coldly at the major. "You have him, that's me."

"Would you please come this way. General Lawrence is ready to meet with you now, sir."

There was a defiant streak inside John at this moment that wanted to tell the major he was going back to get a decent sleep and to call again later, but he knew that was just childish defiance.

"Let's go."

"Mr. Matherson?"

It was Harrison, who tossed the pack of cigs over, and a pack of matches.

John nodded his thanks then followed the major down the long corridor to arrive at yet another elevator. A bit of a stomach-dropping lurch as it whisked them up, and when it opened John was startled by the heady scent of the wet leaves of autumn. He stepped out of the elevator and walked down a short corridor and into the mists of a mountain morning.

The sun was already up, casting golden shadows through the trees, most of them maples turning golden red, a few birches of bright yellow, and several hickories of muted gold.

CHAPTER FOUR

"Beautiful spot, isn't it?"

John turned to see Lawrence approaching alone.

"I love coming up here when it's morning like this. That scent in the air, hardly a breeze, the cooling mist gradually burning off. Good day to be alive, John."

John did not reply, but yes, Lawrence was right—it was a beautiful morning to be alive. However, it filled him with longing for his own morning ritual instead, with Makala sitting across the table just making small talk about what the day would bring.

"Let's take a walk, shall we?"

They started up a paved pathway through the trees, so that for a few seconds they were lost in mist, and then Lawrence led him into a glade where sunlight was breaking through.

"Where are we?" John finally asked.

"Oh, I should have told you. Camp David, of course. You can't see it from here but there are the original cottages that Roosevelt once used. Kind of amazing, isn't it, the path we're on, it was paved so FDR could use it with his wheelchair. There are photos of Kennedy on this same walkway, head bowed in conversation with McNamara. If the trees could whisper back as to what was said. McNamara, now there was a case study in failure."

Curious, John could not help but ask why.

"Near universal praise for how he counseled for restraint with Cuba," Lawrence said, almost as if delivering a lecture to a class, "but with Vietnam, he created a military disaster. You know, when I was at the War College, I read some case studies, one of them a General Bennett, an Omaha Beach officer who made four stars. He was part of a strategic study group, back dealing with what to do with Vietnam.

"Their assessment, don't, for God's sake don't."

"Don't what?" John asked, his curiosity aroused.

"Bennett said it was the wrong war, in the wrong place, and with the wrong enemy. There were far bigger fish to fry rather than support a corrupt regime. Anyhow, McNamara wanted that war, his war, so he finally fired that study group and replaced them with some yes-men generals who said, 'Oh, go ahead, you'll win it in less than a year and be a hero.'"

"And you think . . . ?" John asked.

"Halfway right. Only fight a war you know you can win, and don't fight it unless you are really willing to fight it out to the finish you know you can achieve. So yes, I'd have agreed, wrong war, wrong place, wrong enemy."

"But we didn't stay out of it."

Vietnam was before John's time, but when he did go into the military, he saw the wreckage that was left behind for a generation or more.

"So don't fight, or fight. What would you have done, John?"

The last thing he'd expected this morning was going off on a tangent about a war lost half a century ago.

"No answer?"

"What would have been your answer?" John countered.

"Ah, trying to learn more about me? Well, today's the day we need to do that. So okay then. I would have ended at the start."

"How?"

"When we decided to go in, there was that horrid moment of realization that rather than acting on a cadre of political types, fight it to win in the opening move. We convey through back channels they have a week to think about it and damn well come to terms. If not, a week and a day later, Hanoi and Haiphong will cease to exist. And most importantly they absolutely know we have the resolve to do it and damn the political blow back. Result, no Vietnam War."

For John it was a history lesson to be debated in a classroom, but he knew more than one veteran of that conflict who felt the same.

"Nixon finally did do that, with his bombing campaign in 1972, and it did bring them to the table at last, and most of what was left of our surviving POWs were released, but by then the rot had taken hold of a once-proud military. They sign a peace treaty, we get our prisoners back, which was all we cared about at that point, and then the communists resumed the war, took the country, and went on to murder millions in Vietnam, Laos, and Cambodia.

"So therefore," Lawrence sighed, stopping for a moment in their walk, "the answer goes back to the beginnings. There was the mistake. If you are going to go to war, you have to show absolute resolve, a killing resolve both to your enemy as well as to your own people.

"We did that in World War Two, at least in the Pacific. You must have heard that famous quote from Admiral Halsey, who when surveying the destruction at Pearl Harbor announced that by the time we had finished with that fight, the Japanese language would be extinct.

"You know, John, from start to finish, that war, for us, World War Two lasted a thousand days. Think of it, a thousand days from the smoking wreckage at Pearl to two cities obliterated in a split-second flash of light and a thousand ships anchored in Tokyo Bay."

"So you're telling me what?"

"If you don't have total resolve to win, and are not willing to do whatever's necessary to win, in the end you will lose." Lawrence turned away and continued on up the pathway, the fog gradually melting away.

"That was our mistake in the war with Germany. There were two enemies there, and Germany was one. The real enemy beneath it all was Russia." He shook his head and repeated it. "Russia. Maybe later we'll talk about that and what to do."

Was this walk just going to be a history lesson? John didn't think so. He realized he was learning details he could use to gauge this man.

"Then there's nine-eleven, of course. Now there was a real cluster for you."

"How so?"

"Remember President Bush standing in the smoking wreckage of the World Trade Center? Remember what he said?"

"Basically."

"It was mealy-mouthed nonsense, John." There was a touch of anger in Lawrence's voice. "Oh, he said that we were going to find out who did it, and pay them back." He scoffed. "Pay them back? I remember that moment clearly. What I wanted at that moment was Winston Churchill, not some Mr. Rogers–type character."

John said nothing.

"Come on, we knew who did it and who supported them doing it. What the hell do we have a CIA for?"

"And then what?"

"Nuke the bastards. Nuke the bastards so that for the next hundred years if one of them even whispers, "Let's attack America," the others would beat him to death. Result: terrorism stops, no Iraq and Afghanistan bleeding us dry of a trillion dollars."

John looked at him, surprised how vehemently he spat out those three words.

"Would the world have howled over such a response? Oh, undoubtedly, but would they have retaliated? And I mean Russia or China. Hell no. In fact, I think the Russians who already had their own problems with Islamic terrorists would have silently cheered."

"Nuke who, Lawrence, who?"

"Half a dozen tacticals in Afghanistan would have finished it there. Tell Iran to turn over the following terrorists or Tehran is next. If they knew we were dead-set serious and not just bluffing they would have folded with the message that if they even twitched the wrong way, they're next.

"The same goes for Iraq, though we should have finished that back in 1991 with Bush number one. John, it is a principle of war back to Hammurabi and even long before. It is nice to be loved and respected, but far more important to be feared." He paused and looked over at John. "Of course you might see it different? Or do you?"

"Do you honestly care about my opinion?"

"Actually I do, considering what I'm going to be asking of you."

"Uncorking the nuclear weapons is fraught with danger."

"And look who finally did it. The terrorist states and North Korea, that's who. We know that now. And look at us now, John." Lawrence continued down the path, showing no signs of slowing. "One final point, and that is Rome. Why did they survive for a thousand years? Think of it, we didn't make it much past two hundred, a fraction of the time they lasted. It was because of the might of their legions.

"You know the quote, I believe it is from the Roman author Tacitus, describing an enemy reaction to Rome: 'For they make a desolation and they call it peace.'"

The way he spoke the quote was unnerving.

CHAPTER FIVE

The trail ahead broadened out into a spacious lawn, dark green and obviously freshly mown. Beyond, there were several neat single-story cabins, each painted forest green. Interestingly, the cottages had camouflage netting hanging from the trees that flanked them.

Half a dozen comfortable lawn chairs were arranged on the lawn with a table between them, a sergeant standing to one side, saluting as the general approached with John.

"Sir, we've got coffee, tea, or something a bit stronger if you wish?"

"Tea for me, Lapsang with some honey. John?"

"Coffee, black, is fine, Sergeant."

They sat down and the sergeant set their drinks before them, then discreetly withdrew.

"I assume you're back in the habit, John, so feel free."

John lit up and they sat in silence for a few minutes, Lawrence looking around at the trees. The last of the morning mist was evaporating, and it felt like it would be a warm autumn day.

Lawrence looked up at the camo netting. "During World War

Two this was a regular armed camp, the entire facility concealed with netting and other tricks."

"Why use it now?"

"Why not? Amazing what photo recon is today, just about count the hairs on your head."

"Little paranoid now, isn't it?"

"Ever hear of the rods of God?"

"No."

"Just launch from space a ten-foot-long titanium rod as thick as your finger, boost up its speed. Very efficient way to kill someone and not leave a trace of who did it."

"That *is* paranoid."

"We've done it," Lawrence said, sipping his tea, but did not elaborate further.

"Can we finally get down to it?" John asked. "It's about time I got some answers. The fact I'll cooperate with you holding the issue of medication over me, that's a given, and I'm getting tired of all the mystery."

"Okay, let's lay it out then, John. I want you to be part of our new government."

"Oh, great, just what I was hoping for."

"Hear me out, indulge me, okay?"

"I got nothing else to do."

"Your government was preordained to fail, John. It was a nice idea, reestablish a republic the way it used to be, model it on the government that ultimately did fail to protect and was turning into a nightmare bureaucratic mess if ever there was one."

"It was still the legitimate government."

"Really. How so? At least the Founding Fathers carried a reputation into Philadelphia, most of them signers of the Declaration, most of them heroes of the Revolution. And they had Washington. They had George Washington, John, and that carried them through more than any single thing to the creation of a new government.

"What did you have? You were trying to build on the survivors of the worst disaster in our history, in fact in the history of the world. Up to three hundred million dead. And on that you wanted to build a new government, of, by, and for the people?" He chuckled sadly.

"It was a pipe dream and you know it. Scattered pockets of survivors, struggling to stay alive. You know in 1790 there were about fifty thousand people living in New York City, remember for a while it was our capital. Know how many are living there today?"

"Maybe fifty thousand again, but I assume less."

"The city is abandoned, except for the tribes of thugs— cannibals, some of them—warring in their gang-like enclaves. There's some who live full time underground in the subway tunnels, regular troglodytes who come out at night to hunt for food, usually human derelicts. I hear Central Park is reverting to jungle ruled over by some chieftain who calls himself Jeremiah the Prophet. He crucifies his victims then eats their hearts." He sighed and fell silent.

"New York of George Washington, the financial capital of the world for a while, and that's what's left. In 1790 you had anchor points for this new country of America. The cities that Hamilton wanted for commerce; farmland for the taking that Jefferson wanted. What, pray tell, did your republic have to build on? Take New York City back, hunt the vermin down, and make that your capital one day. John it's never coming back."

"At least an ideal, if given a chance, Lawrence."

"So you had your thirteen original states again, and add in coastal Maine. West of the mountains, from just about where we are here, clear to the Pacific? No one would recognize you. You were a thousand, two thousand miles away and their concern was far more immediate, like trying to put a crop in, guard it with your life and hope it grew. The cities are ghost towns, or nightmare realms. I know a few places like Fargo, Helena, even Omaha had gotten some semblance of normal back, but then again, why acknowledge you when they had their own little fiefdoms to try and rebuild from?

"Then there's the West Coast. Well, what was left there sold their souls to China, and be damned to the rest of us. So that was it, John, and I hope there's enough of a realist inside you to know that."

John wanted to argue his points. That at least what they offered was a chance to reconnect, and from there to eventually rebuild; even if it took a generation, it was a start. But for the here, the now, Lawrence's cold words hit hard.

"So again, why me?"

"John, you were indeed known beyond the borders of your little fiefdom. After all, you were the vice president of the Republic and people knew that."

John said nothing, wondering if there was sarcasm in the general's voice.

"By the way, how did you take that position, let alone General Scales becoming president? Were there elections, a constitutional convention perhaps?"

"You know the answer as well as I do."

"You took on those roles because you said you had those roles. You had a secure base, at least for a time, at Raven Rock. You drove out the civilian bureaucracy the same way Christ cleared the temple of the moneylenders.

"You had a few pockets then of what could pass as a new beginning up here, in Roanoke where the army had secured a base, at least for a time. Some civilians clustered around what was left of the navy in Charleston, Wilmington, so you said they could decide at some meetings, Scales was something of a hero, and he was shooed in and your friend cast your name as a vice president and that was that. Did you ever actually have at least a senate meet face-to-face?"

"You know the answer to that," John repeated sadly.

"Oh, you tried, but how in hell were these so-called senators to travel from Augusta, Maine, and or even your Black Mountain,

North Carolina, when travel on roads was still at risk of banditry? So you said the meetings could be virtual.

"How many actually had computers running again? Oh, you did have some shortwave radios scattered about so at least you tried, feeble as it was."

"At least it was an attempt, a start," John argued.

"Ultimately doomed to failure."

"So let's get to the point, then, damn it," John snapped as he lit yet another cigarette, then motioned for the sergeant standing in the background to refill his coffee.

"It's early in the morning yet," Lawrence announced, and looked over to the sergeant standing a discreet distance away, "Sergeant, how about a bit of scotch in my drink, and Matherson's here." The sergeant nodded in agreement and brought over a bottle. "John, it's time for a fresh reboot on this whole thing. We've decided that a republic, we're calling it the Third Republic, will happen."

"Third Republic?"

"Gives it a nice historical touch. The First Republic was the original one, the second was your attempt. The third, which *will* take hold, is ours."

And the third republic was wiped out when Germany took France in 1940. John wondered if the irony somehow connected.

"Why do you say *we*?"

"Because, John, of course there's more than myself in this."

"I was waiting for that."

"The job is there for you, John. You'll be appointed president of the Third Republic." Lawrence smiled. "With all the ranks and privileges thereof." Then he shook his head. "Just kidding, of course."

"A figurehead then, is that it?"

"Don't be so cynical. You were already widely known, you are respected, and you are damn good at what you do. You were our first choice when this issue finally came up."

"Again, *we.*"

"Oh, come on, John, you expect I'm running this all by myself?"

"You know, Lawrence, I've wondered of late just how much of a hand you really have to play. So far I've been taken on a quick whirlwind tour of what? Fifty, seventy-five miles of tunnels; seen a few hundred personnel; was promised I'll get twenty-five thousand doses of antibiotics in exchange for my soul. You could be bluffing, you could be a hollow nothing the same way you claim we were at Raven Rock."

Lawrence put down his drink. He stood up and walked for a few yards, and then turned back.

"Don't insult me too much, or my word, John Matherson. Yes, there's a *we.* I'm in command up here at Camp David, and now Raven Rock, but believe me, sir, far under Washington long ago, the bunkers were built for Armageddon. We have over five thousand personnel in place, not even completely sure what the CIA built on their turf, but it is real.

"You play along, becoming the face of the new government, a voice of reason, a voice that will be respected, and you have a place in this new government. I'll be frank, though. Do otherwise, or play me otherwise, and you'll just disappear."

The velvet glove was finally off the mailed fist.

"The same stands for your little prospering village. I'm good for my word—a planeload of antibiotics will touch down there in less than three hours if your answer is a firm yes. Answer in the negative and the plane will be turned around, no more antibiotics, and in a few weeks most of your town will be dead."

"At least you're finally being up-front," John said coldly.

"We shake hands on this, even if you say it was under duress, you will be of genuine help for the betterment of so many things. My teams here have resources not seen in the continental United States since before the Day. Medications, of course, hospital units, public health teams. And of course real security at last. We can spread out over time to wipe out the last of the bands of brigands and bring about a real return to law and order. When we do, good people will flock to us because we represent a return to actual law rather than your half-hearted failed attempt."

"Just one final question, then."

"Go on."

"The plague. Where did it start?"

There was the slightest of hesitations.

"Your guess is as good as mine."

"Did the Fort Detrick biowarfare research center have something to do with it?"

He was met with silence.

John stood up, holding his mug, and went up to the sergeant. "Pour a good stiff one, Sergeant, will you?"

With drink poured, John just walked off, while Lawrence went back to his chair and sat down.

John wondered if some animals being led to the slaughter felt like this. *I could make the moral stand, refuse; my town, Makala, my children, they die. Agree, but try to sabotage them in some way? How?*

All that was left was to sell his soul to them and try to somehow do what is right.

Or . . .

He walked for an hour or more, lost in thought.

CHAPTER SIX

When John Matherson returned, he went up to Lawrence and wordlessly shook his hand.

"Good, John, I knew you would see the plain hard truth of it. Relax now, take the day off. Hard to believe, but if you like golf we have a driving range Eisenhower put in. Or get some sleep."

"First, some questions," John demanded. "Look, Lawrence, you've forced my hand and I have to play it, if for no other reason than you have me by the short hairs, and the life of a community I love, and my wife and children, rests on what I do."

"Yes."

"So if I don't have the truth, or find out later you lied, then why cooperate now?"

"Fair enough."

"The plague. You started it, didn't you?"

Silence for a moment.

"What makes you think that?"

"Too many coincidences, Lawrence. The big one being Fort Detrick under your control. I held just the shadow of a doubt that no one would be so insane as to release such a deadly toxin, but when I turned to you and asked for the antibiotics there was no wait."

"And?"

"Oh, come on, Lawrence, something was going down at Detrick months back with those guards in hazmat out front. Some sort of alert, maybe."

"Or drill," Lawrence replied.

"Or drill."

"So you figured it out. Good for you, John, tell anyone else?"

"Not yet."

"Not ever, John."

"How's that?"

"Just that: you're part of us, remember. John, I can play you so easily if I must, even frame you up if need be. There are a dozen ways I could do it."

"Straight answers, just for once."

"All right. You know Fort Detrick, long before it was linked to Raven Rock, was one of our centers for biological warfare research."

"Yes."

"Then just before the Day, administrative responsibility for Raven Rock was turned over to Detrick. John, can't you put two and two together on that score?"

"The government that took over Raven Rock wanted that card in their deck. To control, if need be, the nightmare, the threat of biological weapons."

"Precisely, that's a main reason China never went down on us in the chaos after the Day. And since we were behind the government we now had two counterforce strikes in our arsenal. The nukes at sea, the boomers, and the brew frozen away but ready to be thawed out if ever needed."

God, what have I got myself into, John thought morosely. He lit another cigarette and just held up his glass to the sergeant, who quietly refilled it.

Lawrence signaled the sergeant to hand him the whole bottle of scotch and poured himself a drink too, a very large one. He took a long sip and sat silent for a moment.

"There's no backing out now, John, you're in for the entire game. Realize it now and live with it the way I live with it." He took another sip. "If I even sense you are playing a different game . . ." His voice trailed off.

"I'm a dead man."

Lawrence looked at him and smiled sadly. "Okay, John, the truth . . ." He paused as if for dramatic effect. "We released the plague two weeks ago. Actually, there was only one planned release, a remote area over toward Lexington, Virginia. But somebody apparently screwed up, and there was another release at our former base in Roanoke."

John could not find the words to reply.

"The particulars. Lexington was a small, controlled release. A band like the posse you fought had seized control there a year ago and settled in. It was a horror show, from what I heard about them. They had taken over the campuses of Washington and Lee University and VMI.

"I had friends who graduated from VMI, in fact one of them now sits on what I'll call our committee. He was the one who suggested our first test run should be there.

"John, they were practicing human sacrifice like the Romans. They would take prisoners and let them fight to the death on the school football field. The winner survived until the next game, but until then he was pampered like the gladiators of old. Told if he won ten fights he was free. John, there were some nutjobs that volunteered to do it, just so they could eat and drink their fill and there were even some willing girls to wait on them. Of course what they were eating," he paused, "well, you know what that was. So we quietly sealed the area off with some Special Forces types and sent in the plague, simple enough to do. It pretty well wiped them out in less than a month."

"But it would spread from there."

"No, John, we had it controlled, we knew the protocols. Hell, the people we had, some of them had been at Fort Detrick for decades, they knew what they were doing."

"Still . . ." John could come up with nothing to say so he waited for Lawrence to continue.

"Oh yeah, I almost forgot to mention, we've had the vaccine for years, and well stockpiled."

"What? You mean you could have," he was actually flustered, "you could be in Black Mountain now, today, inoculating, and that would really end it?"

"The second part of my equation with you, John."

He took another drink and John wondered if this man was the rare type, like a Churchill, who could consume hard liquor like it was water.

"Yeah, I'm drinking a bit much these days. Who wouldn't?" Lawrence said, then shrugged it off and went back to his story. "So, the test program worked for what we wanted. Wipe out a nest of scum without a shot being fired. Have the area sealed off, put the bug in place, let it run its course. The few who were left afterward . . ." He again laughed softly. "Well, disease-weakened scum are not much of a problem to deal with. Hell, John, you executed your share of prisoners after you beat the posse. By the way, what did you do with their wounded after the fight? Patch them up and send them on their way with the admonition to go and sin no more?"

John did not reply.

"You shot them all, didn't you? There was nothing else you could do. It was either your wounded got what treatment you could provide or not. Share it with barbarians or treat them as they deserved. How many did you execute thus, John?"

Again, he could not reply.

"So there you have it. We freed some prisoners who miraculously had not yet caught the plague. Our research showed a lucky minority did have some natural immunity in their genes, the same way all of us do for different diseases.

"Remember the Indians of the New World and smallpox? It's estimated that ninety percent who were exposed died horrible deaths, while at that point with the European population maybe seventy-five to eighty percent would survive. Same thing here with this pneumonic plague.

"So, that was going to be our test run, but then this second outbreak hit at Roanoke. Somehow, someone got exposed—we think it was a broken vial that wasn't reported, but we'll never really know. Just that cases exploded shortly after our little test up in Lexington was done.

"It almost got ahead of us. Most of Roanoke is a dead zone now. Used to be five thousand people there, and the thousand or so who were left of Bob Scales's old military base. It broke your way, of course, when one of their personnel stole a car, put his family in it, and took off, beelining straight to your town."

John couldn't contain himself any longer. He wanted to hit Lawrence, even kill him, but to do so would accomplish nothing. The polite, drink-serving sergeant was just a few yards away, and he did have a sidearm. John knew he would use it if John threatened—let alone took—Lawrence's life.

He got to his feet instead and just walked off again, heading down the path that led to the grove of trees that had so enamored him just a short hour ago.

There's nothing I can do, John reasoned. *Rage won't change anything.* Flat-out refusal could very well mean taking a bullet, thereby abandoning Makala and so many others, leaving them to die horribly.

Conspire against it? How, how to do that?

There was no answer. He remembered a late-night ethics discussion at the War College long ago. Scales had presented a scenario. You are an officer in the Wehrmacht, a soldier schooled in at least some semblance for the rules of war. You encounter an SS unit executing Russian prisoners. What do you do, when to act overtly will be futile? The questions compounded quickly. What about civilians, and what about seeing a trainload of Jews and knowing their fate? Can you stop it? And perhaps more importantly, how will you maintain your own soul, your own sense of ethics in the face of such wrongs?

It was so easy then, the armchair discussion in a comfortable classroom in a comfortable college-like atmosphere. And now he stood alone, looking up at the red and golden maples that seemed an eternity away from the madness of this world.

There simply was no answer.

Numbed, he finally walked back to the cottages, where still Lawrence sat, drink in hand, eyes half closed.

"How do you live with yourself?" John asked, sitting back down.

"I became a realist a long time ago, John. You never really have. You still cling to a belief system that died on the Day—in fact, long before that day."

"Damn you, Lawrence."

"John, be careful whom you choose as your enemy, because that's whom you become most like." Lawrence smiled at that one. "Nietzsche had another thought worth considering. It utterly contradicts your extreme eagerness to advance and protect the well-being of people who, frankly, contribute nothing to the world's intellectual and material progress, those ignorant drudges that constitute the great unfortunate mass of humankind. Do you know what Nietzsche said we owe them? Nothing. He said that they are, at best, the superstructure and scaffolding, on which we, the Übermenschen, are to build our culturally and technologically superior world. Their only purpose is to provide raw labor, which we will require to build our brave new world, and when they can no longer perform those tasks, all they deserve is the grave, and our job is to hasten their journey into it as quickly as possible."

"For the moment, my only concern is keeping them alive."

"In the end, John, that's what it always comes down to—what happens to them? How do they survive?"

"Agreed."

"I always knew that was your position, and I'm already on it, John, not just as a favor to you. Let's just say with this accidental release we had to think a bit farther ahead for the moment. Kind of fortunate that Black Mountain figured in this equation.

"We really didn't want it to explode southward, that just didn't fit the paradigm of the moment. If it got into what was left of the population centers in Greenville, even Asheville for what's it's worth, those regions were mostly pacified and potentially useful. Atlanta, well that's a different story and you know that; in fact that was one of the places we were considering next.

"So, fortunately for you, we'll draw a line starting with you. If we stop the disease there, it secures, for the moment, the interstate corridors of I-40 and I-26."

"Secure how?"

"Just exactly what we are doing even as we speak here. I've sent a plane with twenty-five thousand doses of antibiotics and a thousand of the new vaccines for you and yours. And that should contain it. John, we were caught a bit off guard with it breaking out like this, but we'll contain it. It still actually fits what we've planned."

"You keep talking about *we,* your plans."

"We intend to reorder the paradigm, this drifting into the night ever since our asses were handed to us five years ago. John, America is forever finished as any kind of power. You yourself know that even if your Republic had worked, you would have been relegated to the status of a third-world power, the only thing left to guard us, the remnants of a navy reduced to four boomers as sentries and a couple of bases on the coast that were a shadow of what we once were.

"We'll never in our lifetimes be a power again, that's finished, the American Century is finally over with. Fun while it lasted, but fraught with paradoxes that eventually doomed it. But there was an answer all along that you now see. Disease is now the weapon of choice. It was in ancient times."

"Monstrous."

"Ah, John, you have to transcend old prejudices. Burn people alive by firebombing cities. Which is worse, dying in your bed after a brief illness versus being burned alive like the tens of thousands in Dresden and Tokyo? What's the difference, the enemy is dead, even if he was mostly civilians, old people, children.

"So here's how it will go. We're containing the outbreak from Roanoke. We're setting up an enclave in Newport News, we'll need the people there. The one area secured, of course, is our center of operations around here. The rest of Virginia from Washington south down to you. Well, let's just say it will spread and that's it." Lawrence took another sip. "It'll be reseeded south of you. Atlanta area, of course."

"Why Atlanta?"

"Why not? There's not even the semblance of a civil government there anymore. You and I both know that when it hit the fan after the Day, Atlanta turned into a hellhole, the gangs, the thugs running rampant, and when there were no more at least halfway decent people to live off of anymore, they turned on each other."

"I don't know how much more of this I want to hear."

"Wake up, John," Lawrence snapped, coming to his feet. "Civilization is dead, long live anarchy until something new arises. Those who work here know what the answer is and, like us or not, we are the one chance left to bring some semblance of that civilization back again.

"Now, John, do I have someone shoot you because you still cling to a past, or do we go on from here? You are well cast for this, John."

Again he thought of Makala, his friends, his world, what little there was of it, and could only nod his head in agreement.

"Just one final question," John asked. "China."

"John, what do you think?"

John simply waited.

"There's a meeting here at thirteen hundred, John, some of our brass, you'll find it interesting. Meet-and-greet sort of thing for you. You might as well hang topside till then, walk in the woods, clear your head, you still got a long day ahead of you. . . ."

PART IX

If you want a picture of the future, imagine a boot stamping on a human face—forever.

—George Orwell, *1984*

CHAPTER ONE

Right on schedule, Sergeant Harrison appeared at noon, carrying a lunch tray with a ham sandwich, some chips, and a glass bottle of Coke, and set them down on the table.

John sat down, motioning for the sergeant to join him. After saying a short prayer for guidance he ate in silence. Harrison was quiet as well.

"Can we talk here without others listening?" John asked.

"Sir, I assume everything is bugged, best to think that way."

Again, a long silence. John felt like this was the same old routine: he had questions to ask, Harrison knew he had questions to ask, but neither would bring it up first.

John decided it was time to talk about something positive for a change. "I have some good news for you at least, Sergeant."

"And that is?"

"Your daughter is alive, your wife as well."

Harrison just sat there, stunned.

"When I returned back home last time, your name rang a bell for me. Turns out your daughter Yolinda registered at my college a year ago. Your wife teaches now at our elementary school."

Harrison drew a careful breath in and then slowly exhaled. "Don't bullshit me, sir. Please don't."

John tried to remember details, anything specific he could say about the two, but couldn't.

"You just have to believe me. Remember, you told me a bit about them back in the spring. I know it's a long shot they got through it all, but they did. Please believe me."

Harrison was still silent, but then John saw tears trickling down his dark cheeks. He fought to control his emotion, not moving or saying anything more.

"I'd like to believe you sir," he finally replied.

"Why wouldn't you?"

"This place. Why they allowed me to stay on. My records show I'm just a cook. I took care of General Scales, was loyal to him, that's all they know."

"I assume you are a lot more."

Harrison just smiled.

"Let's take a walk," John announced. Getting out from behind the table, he lit a cigarette and casually strolled into the woods, Harrison following respectfully a few feet behind, almost like a well-trained adjutant carrying a general's papers.

"Is there anything further you can tell me?" John whispered, feeling it was safe to talk in the wooded glade.

"Just that the general told me that if there was one person to trust in this mess it was someone in the navy, Admiral Youngblood. He's old school."

"Is he here, at Raven Rock, I mean Camp David?"

"Heard from a source he's at the meetings taking place right now. You might find a friend there in all this madness."

"That's it?"

"There's other stuff, but I don't think it's healthy for us to just go wandering off, sir. Maybe at some point later."

The major who had escorted John at the start of the day was waiting by the table when they returned from their short walk.

"Sir, we're ready to start, you better hurry."

John followed him back to the elevator, and minutes later he seemed to be again in the bowels of Camp David, though even now he wasn't fully sure if that was the case.

Again the long corridor, he thought, going off in a different direction, and then to his surprise a brightly lit concourse. In the middle was a large bunker, a completely roofed-off and enclosed structure of solid steel, the entire building actually mounted on springs as thick around as his arm.

MPs were at the door. They checked the paperwork carried by the major, then announced John should go inside and then to the end of the corridor.

Ascending the few steps to the entry, John could see the doors were heavily reinforced steel. There was a small viewport in the middle of the door, the crisscross pattern of a Faraday cage evident. The MP by the door took hold of it and pulled it open, obviously with some effort.

As the door closed behind him John felt a cold chill over the entire thing. All of this. *What am I doing? I don't belong here.* Lawrence could snap his finger and have him eliminated, and he felt there wouldn't even be a second thought to it. He was someone useful for the moment. He would become the face of this new government until he was no longer useful, and then be set aside.

Playing their game was all he could think of, driven only by the thought of what would happen to his family—and to the town—if he didn't. That, and some sort of ingrained character matrix—who he was and who he had always been . . . even before the Day.

As his eyes adjusted to the glare of the overhead lights he saw that Lawrence was waiting for him, while talking softly with a woman in civilian Washington-type garb.

As he approached, Lawrence, all affable, smiled.

"Mr. Matherson, should I say Speaker Matherson, I'd like to introduce Dr. Lisa Hanson."

The stern, attractive woman nodded at him. She appeared to be in her late forties. Her black knit business suit was immaculately pressed. She stiffly took his hand.

"So this shall be our speaker," she said. "Is that what he will be known as?" The hint of sarcasm was clearly evident.

"I prefer Professor or Dr. Matherson, or if we are into rank I was once Colonel Matherson."

Back home he was often called "President Matherson" since he was president of the local college, but he saw no point in bringing that up.

"Lisa is CIA."

John said nothing.

The tableau held for a moment, and Hanson managed to force a thin ghost of a smile. "Doctor, then," she said. "Remember that old movie, *Dr. Strangelove*? Are you that sort of doctor?"

"Hardly, but still, the title will do."

"We better go back in, we were on a quick break just now."

Like anyone who had played in this strata of government, he found himself wondering: if the meeting was going on before his arrival, what did it entail?

As John stepped through the door his eyes had to adjust again, this time to a semidark aura, lit by computer screens and a full-length high-definition screen dominating the far side of the room. If Hanson's movie reference was meant to imply some sort of comparison to a set from a Cold War film this was it; even more so than the war room at Raven Rock.

Whereas Raven Rock had a definite 1960s feel to it—complete with old push-button phones and bare fluorescent lighting—this room was high-tech. Comfortable leatherbound chairs, two razor-thin monitors with a keyboard at every desk. The phones were still landline, not Wi-Fi, and he instantly knew that was for security reasons. All of it felt subdued, even hushed.

A general was up at the front podium talking, but as the door opened a message instantly flashed on the main screen and the ones at the desks.

UNSECURED ENVIROMENT.

The door closed behind the three latecomers, Lisa walking over to an empty desk and sitting down, Lawrence and John standing in the back of the room.

"I think we can secure the room again," Lawrence announced, looking to the back corner, where several enlisted personnel were behind half a dozen screens and control boards.

The warning sign flashed off.

"Dr. Hanson, I think we can wrap up your remarks later, if that's fine with you."

"I was about to make one final point," Hanson replied sharply.

"Of course, ma'am, in due course, in due course. But I want to take a few moments now to introduce, ah"—he hesitated—"Dr. Matherson, who will now be our government spokesperson and acting president of the new Third Republic."

There was no applause. If Lawrence had wanted any, the audience didn't seem to know it.

"John, anything to say before we resume?"

"Nothing, General Lawrence. I know my place here, so why bore these people with some useless platitudes?"

There were an awkward few seconds until Lawrence motioned for John to take one of the empty conference chairs and walked to the front of the room.

"I think Dr. Matherson has just made himself clearly understood, and we can accept that," Lawrence said.

"I think he just told us to go screw ourselves," Lisa snapped.

There were several nods of agreement.

"I think he should hear the rest of this plan, at least," someone announced from the other side of the room.

"Admiral Youngblood, if you say so."

Youngblood addressed the general. "If somebody is going out there as our front person, which is an idea you cooked up, Lawrence, let's hear what he has to say. For that matter, when was the last time we heard from someone beyond our own inner circle? It's getting us into the jam we are now facing, a complete nightmare of a scenario, so let's just have it out."

John gazed at Youngblood and put on his best face of appearing to be disinterested in this man. This was the same man who had sat with him and Bob Scales back at Raven Rock before it fell and just moments ago, a sergeant whispering to him that Youngblood was a straight arrow to be trusted. All he could surmise was that Youngblood had been playing both sides all along. He was here with these people, and four months ago sat with General Scales as a trusted resource. What was he really? John wondered.

"Admiral, if you are getting cold feet then damn it, just say it," another shadowy figure announced.

John actually inwardly smiled. He had presided over hundreds of meetings in his day, especially the town ones after the Day, and sensed there was deep dissent dividing those assembled in this room.

"All right then, we'll go over it yet again," Lawrence said. "Dr. Matherson, if you'll excuse us and wait outside . . ."

"Damn it, I think he should stay," Youngblood retorted. "I want someone who once held responsibility, even if it was for this so-called republic which was destined to fail. I would value the views of someone outside our circle."

"He should go." It was Lisa, her voice cold, distant.

"You haven't answered my question," John said, coming back to his feet. "If I'm to represent this body, just what the hell is it that you are doing now, today?"

"He deserves to know that," Youngblood replied. "He'll know soon enough, so why not hear it from us? We're the ones who designed it, God save us."

"I think not," Lawrence snapped.

"Damn it, what the hell, why not tell him? If he's in with us, well and good, if not, he knows the price.

"Dr. Matherson," Lisa continued with a calm icy intonation. "I assume General Lawrence briefed you on the outbreak of plague in Virginia."

"I did," Lawrence interjected. "The planned release in Lexington, the accidental release in Roanoke."

"We are about to do the same," Lisa Hanson said. "More planned releases. New York City for one, to finally clean out that nest. Atlanta will be another, and so on, half a dozen releases over the next month."

John sat in silence, barely able to fathom the enormity of their plan.

She punched a few keys on her computer and looked at the screen. "The population centers—I should say, what were once population centers—will have an estimated eighty-five percent die-off. Current population estimates for the targeted areas are actually less than two million total, and we expect the surviving population by January to be less than two hundred thousand."

"Why?" John asked, keeping his tone neutral.

"Reestablish control, John. It will be a pliable population that is left, ready to receive appropriate medications, inoculations, and to gladly accept the order we bring. Appropriate administration will be brought in. Not like those ridiculous attempts immediately after the Day. This time it will be backed up by the resources we have here. And from that, we'll need your help to rebuild into a single viable entity. From there, further sites will be selected through the following year, out to the Mississippi. The residual populations will welcome us with open arms."

"And they'll never know who did it?"

"We blame the Chinese, of course," she replied with a trace of a smile.

"If someone talks?"

"Who will believe them?"

This is sickening, John thought, but said nothing.

"Dr. Matherson, it's the only way left, and you will come to understand that. It is the most humane way we could think of to finally bring back order to what once was our country."

"John, we're going to have to break some eggs to make a better future," Lawrence said softly. John remembered that was what the despised Duranty of the *New York Times* once said about the Ukrainian famine. Looking at Lawrence he wondered if the choice of those words was deliberate and realized instantly they definitely were.

"Okay, then," it was Youngblood again, "tell him the rest."

"That's an entirely different operation," the marine general snapped.

"Like hell, it's all out of the same poisonous bottle. John, we're the ones who've placed the plague in China."

John had already been coming to assume that, but to hear it so baldly spoken of . . .

"That was your operation, Admiral, not mine," Lisa said calmly.

"Some of my people helped place it there, yes, but it wasn't just my doing. You ordered over my resistance and I wish now I had stopped it," Youngblood replied, looking over at Lawrence. "You used one of my assets, the remnant of a Navy Seal team, to release the plague in Quanzhou without my cooperation or foreknowledge."

Lawrence stood silent, and John could sense by the murmurs in the room that not everyone, let alone a majority, were in accord.

"Damn it," John snapped. "Just out with it, will you? I'm supposed to be some sort of spokesman now. Just say it."

CHAPTER TWO

"Two weeks ago, in the port of Quanzhou," Lisa Hanson announced, "an airborne, extremely virulent form of pneumonic plague was released into the population."

"By whom?"

"We had one of our few Navy Seal teams left infiltrate and they released it. Unfortunate, but it killed them, too."

John wondered if that was planned us well, to leave no witnesses to come back and haunt later.

" 'Released it'?"

"You'll have to ask our biowarfare people how that was done." She looked over to one of the other two civilians in the room, who was silent, not saying a word.

"The navy helped."

"Something I was not aware of, damn it, until after the fact," Youngblood shouted.

"Regardless, it was done. Quanzhou was chosen because it was across the straits from Taiwan, and easy enough to place blame there. It apparently jumped to Beijing within twenty-four hours, most likely by high-speed train, and then spread outward from the station with hundreds of people who were now carriers."

"Youngblood, you get too emotional over some of this," Lisa said dryly.

"How bad?" John asked.

"How bad what?"

"What is happening now, today?"

Again Lisa tapped some keys and stared at her screen. "On the board?" she asked, looking at Lawrence.

Lawrence nodded and stepped to one side. A few seconds later a map of China was up on the main screen in front of the room. Its regions were color coded from deep blue to various lighter shades, light pink on up to deep red, and numbers were displayed over each of the regions.

"We estimate ten million dead so far." Quanzhou was now high-lighted, the province all in deep red. Several areas next to Quan-zhou were colored various shades of pink, as was Beijing. Lisa was rattling over statistics for each.

"It appears to be catching China by surprise in spite of their massive biowarfare research, research we knew about even before the Day. That whole Wuhan lab disaster wound up costing all of us, but it was contained. This will not be." Lisa looked around the room, commanding everyone's attention. "The plague variant cre-ated, actually some time ago at Fort Detrick, is highly mobile. The accidental outbreak in the western North Carolina region proved that."

"That's where I'm from," John said.

"Unfortunately, Matherson," she replied. "But we're getting good data on it now."

"They can't develop the resources quickly enough to stop it," Lawrence said, "other than the old routine of quarantine and isola-tion, both for individuals and entire cities and regions. They most likely have a vaccine, same as us, but half a billion doses? I seriously doubt that."

"The Chinese will resort to what we never could," Lisa Hanson said. "We know that they've sealed off all of Quanzhou, with a military cordon that has been given orders to shoot to kill any who try to get out. Problem there is that personnel in that cordon are now falling sick themselves, with the sick being pushed into the death zones to die.

"Beijing is the same, everything in lockdown. Upper echelons of government, of course, are dosing with antibiotics. If they do have the vaccine it'll go to the party cadre, the rest of the populace . . . End result, by the end of the year, analysis is a quarter of a billion people will die, China will descend into chaos and that, as they say, will be that. A year from now, the only capable nuclear armed force left will be the new Soviet regime east of the Urals. When the time comes, we will handle that as well."

She looked over at John. "I know what you're thinking, Matherson. Curse me, hate me, but it will not change the outcome, so be a realist. It's been done. It was that, or sit in our bunkers and underground systems until we too ran out of food and then drifted into the night. So I rest my case."

"That which does not kill us makes us stronger," John said, paraphrasing Nietzsche and looking straight at Lawrence.

And Lawrence smiled in return.

"And now our asses are in the garbage-grinder," Youngblood snapped.

"I really think this should be addressed later, Admiral," Lisa replied.

From the way she was taking over the meeting, John sensed that it was she who was the one who was really in charge of this group, not Lawrence. That had some interesting implications. Did it mean that Lawrence was as much a straw figure as he wanted John to be?

"Why not now, Ms. Hanson?" John asked.

She did not reply, but her look of smug self-assurance was telling.

"It's the real reason we're here, isn't it?" Youngblood pressed. "Perhaps a nice little diversion with Dr. Matherson and then afterward we resolve to kick the can down the road until tomorrow and see what happens. Is that it?"

John noticed an exchange of glances between Hanson and Lawrence, and that somehow confirmed it. Hanson was the one in charge and Youngblood was definitely the loose cannon.

"I call for adjournment," Hanson said. "We'll take this up later in a secured environment. Meeting is now adjourned."

"Bullshit," Youngblood snapped. "You avoid this, in another twenty-four hours we really will be at war."

John could see the other generals in the room sitting frozen in place.

"I think the admiral should be heard," one of them said softly.

"I said the meeting was adjourned," Hanson announced, far more sharply this time.

John looked from her to Lawrence, who stood silent to one side. The generals in the room shifted uneasily as Hanson stood up, the other two civilians in the room following suit.

"Just what is it then?" John spoke loudly enough to be heard by everyone. "What is it you're so afraid of, damn it?"

Hanson stopped at the door and turned back, silent and unmoving.

"It is going out of control, Dr. Matherson," Youngblood snapped, voice filled with anger, "China knows. Do you even remotely think that they are going to sit back now and not retaliate? You are a ship of fools. What the hell are you going to do now!"

Hanson stepped back into the room, setting her briefing papers down on a table.

"There's only one answer left to us now, and I said it from the beginning if it went all the way. Quick, hard, and clean. We tried to take them out with the plague. I don't think they have any direct evidence, the unfortunate death of the Seal team cut the link on that. We will stand innocent, even offer some vaccines for their leadership if they don't have them. Make it clear, though, that if they even twitch in the direction of a nuclear retaliation we have four boomers still out there, that's twenty-six launch tubes per boomer, each tube holds up to eight independent warheads of 300 kilotons each. Do the math. That's close to a thousand nukes we'll rain down on them. So no, gentlemen, they'll hold their revenge.

"We've wasted enough of my time for today, we'll reconvene in the CIA complex tomorrow morning at 0900. I prefer there anyhow, I think it's more secure. Good day, gentlemen."

She stalked out, the heavy steel door closing behind her and her two assistants, leaving the room in silence.

"She's blaming us for the problem," Lawrence said coldly.

Admiral Youngblood leaned over to gather up some papers and hurriedly tucked them into his attaché case.

"Dr. Hanson is most likely right. Gentlemen, there is only one way we can act now," Lawrence said. "You'll recall it's what I said we should have done from the start."

No one replied.

"Admiral, if it goes all the way you know what the decision will have to be, and I expect you to act accordingly."

"Of course, Lawrence," Youngblood said, a note of dejection in his voice. "I'm going back to Charleston and yeah, it will be taken care of."

Youngblood started for the door. As he stepped in front of John, he stopped and looked at him appraisingly. "Mr. Matherson, we need to talk further. With the plague in the region, even if contained, we need to review precautions further in the Carolinas and you are the one to go to."

Youngblood looked over at Lawrence.

"I think it best, Mr. Matherson, that you go with me."

"Why?" Lawrence asked.

"Because I want him with me for the next few days, that's why. If he's the new front person, then it is time for him to be the front person."

"John?"

He did not reply.

Lawrence, after a moment of contemplation, simply nodded his head.

PART X

The sin ye do by two and two, ye must pay for one by one.

—Rudyard Kipling, "Tomlinson"

CHAPTER ONE

It had been a strange, almost surreal flight to Charleston aboard a navy twin turboprop. John had flown in one years before when he had taken the flight to the admiral's carrier off the Atlantic coast.

They were ensconced in cramped bucket seats with no real padding or insulation from the roaring engines. Last time he'd flown in a navy turboprop, it had left him with a throbbing headache.

Back at Camp David, once they had left the elevator, Youngblood had a very brief conversation with him. "Not a word till you get on the plane. Gather your gear if you have any, act like everything is okay. If not on the plane in thirty minutes I leave without you. Okay?"

John did as suggested, packing his few belongings and the carton of smokes. A major escorted him back topside and then it was a short hop by Humvee to the airstrip. Not much to his surprise, Lawrence was there, talking with Youngblood.

They shook hands as John approached, Youngblood boarding the turbo prop as its engines started to turn over, and the plane roared to life in a cloud of smoke.

"John?"

Lawrence stood rigid, sunglasses on against the afternoon sun making it impossible to read his emotions.

"I'm trusting you."

John said nothing.

"If I thought that you would betray us . . ."

He fell silent for a moment.

"Youngblood is going to be the major player in this if things unravel and Hanson has her way. Frankly, I hate the bitch, but she's the face of the CIA now. It's a reason I want you with him for the next few days."

That was a revelation he, in fact, suspected.

"Youngblood will play the bluff game with the Chinese, they'll back down. Frightful as it sounds, the plague will serve them well. Cut the population down to a level they can manage. I'm surprised they didn't do it to themselves years ago. You've been reading up on your Nietzsche since we talked, I know that. They'll see the advantage in the end, that we did them a favor. They don't want a nuke exchange, that will blast them back into the Stone Age, for what? Revenge? Hanson, though, I half think she would be willing to go all the way. I hope not."

"So why not kill her?" John asked, even forcing a flicker of a smile as he spoke.

Lawrence actually laughed softly.

"Kill off the head of the CIA and not be found out? Chances are she is thinking the same about me. Our own balance of terror if you will."

He fell silent for a moment.

"Got your cigarettes packed."

"Yes."

"Why if you're coming back in a few days?"

John inwardly froze. Lawrence was right, why pack the carton? He had no reply for a moment.

"Suppose the Chinese do launch, where am I then? Might as well indulge my habit till the end."

"They'll fry Charleston as well. That will be at the top of their priority."

"I'll die smoking, then," John said evenly.

Again silence.

"Don't screw me, John, I have a very long memory, you know that."

"I know that, Lawrence. Believe me, I know that."

What he did next struck John as strange. He drew to attention and actually saluted him. "I'll see you tomorrow, Mr. Speaker."

Without another word, he turned and walked away, leaving John to wonder, just who was this man?

Going up the narrow steps of the transport plane, Youngblood was waiting for him, looking back out the door as a crewman started to close it behind John.

"I wasn't sure if he was going to shake your hand as a send-off or shoot you dead."

"I thought the same."

"All right, Matherson, let's get the hell out of this madhouse."

What the hell have I gotten myself into? John wondered.

CHAPTER TWO

The last time he was on a CV-71, the USS *Theodore Roosevelt,* was back a decade before the Day when, as a newly minted lieutenant colonel, he had been invited to spend an exchange week with the navy to observe carrier ops at sea. He had even been offered a chance to go aloft in an F-18 for a half-hour "ride," but turned that one down with a smile after hearing stories from the other four army officers who'd experienced it and swore the only purpose of the flight was for the navy to have some fun pulling some radical maneuvers until the poor souls in the back seat puked, and then pull eight-plus g's until they passed out cold.

He remembered something of Youngblood from that excursion. A no-nonsense man, intolerant of officers too impressed with themselves to relate to the enlisted personnel. At least one meal a day, every day, no matter what the situation, he'd eat with the lowest ranks, insisting they just voice their opinions flat out. He struck John then as the type of leader men could truly respect and not just pay lip service to, salute, and mumble an oath behind his back when out of earshot.

It was nighttime when they landed at the base near Patriots

Point where the *TR* was docked next to her illustrious forebear, the carrier *Yorktown,* a World War II ship that was a museum until the Day, and had since then served as a community shelter and hospital.

To John's surprise, as they took the short drive from the base to the *TR,* he could see where parts of the town were actually lit up, and as they approached the mammoth bulk of the carrier, he could see why. It was lit up as well, with strings of heavy cables arcing from the ship down to pylons carrying the electrical power from the ship, generated by its nuclear reactors. To John it almost seemed profligate to the extreme. Enough electricity to light some of the streets, public buildings, and even private dwellings. Charleston was still something of a functioning city, even if reduced in population to a fraction of its former self.

A marine guard escorted John onto the carrier, and then they started, just as he remembered, climbing endless stairs and marching through interminable passageways. The marine at last opened a hatch, announcing that it was the admiral's quarters, and left him.

Admiral Youngblood's compartment was well-appointed, as John had expected it to be as a carrier with a record of continuous service going back several decades. Dark wall paneling, brass fixtures, a portrait of Teddy Roosevelt, naturally, adorning a wall—John had to smile after one look at the man with that historic grin that almost shouted "bully."

A steward came in, actually dressed in whites, asking John if he wanted something to drink and offering scotch or bourbon. John remembered the long-ago prohibition forbidding alcohol in the mess, which any officer of sufficient rank found excuses to ignore. John refused, opting for a Coke, which was soon produced and even had ice in it, another luxury.

Just as he sat down the door opened and, old habits still within him, John stood up and even came to a semblance of rigid attention.

"Dr. Matherson, sit down, damn it. We're both tired. Have you had a drink?"

"Just a Coke, sir."

"Whiskey and water for both of us, if you want." This time John gladly agreed.

A few minutes later the drinks were on the table. Youngblood took off his uniform jacket, tossed it on another chair, then reached into his pocket and pulled out a cigar case, opening it up and offering one.

"They're actual Cubans, don't ask me how I got them. Care for one?"

"Actually, no," John replied, but he motioned to his breast pocket, which held what was left of the pack of cigarettes he'd opened that morning.

"Go ahead, you look like you need a smoke and a drink."

"That I do."

"Tired of getting jerked around?"

"That's about the size of it."

"What do you think of Lawrence?"

"Is he the one actually in charge of that madhouse up there?"

"Hardly, John. He's just a front, though maneuvering all the time to come out on top with that madness up there."

"To what end?"

"Their power—it's Lisa who is pulling most of the strings."

"CIA?"

Youngblood laughed. "It was maybe called that once. Actually she was a direct advisor to the president just before the Day. Never saw her in the news, but then again that was true of many of them, especially those who are left."

"So what exactly is happening?"

"War with China, full-scale exchange within the next two days, more than likely. Two days from now, this city, what precious little is left of it, will be a crater half a mile across, as will every other city east of the Mississippi."

"You need to explain this to me, sir, the whole thing is beyond me and I just feel like a pawn getting bumped back and forth. I still don't even know why General Lawrence was playing his game for me."

"Oh, that's easy, John, think about it. You'll get set up as the new president, or speaker, or whatever damn title they were giving to you. The shit goes down, and when the smoke clears, you are to blame. Your first act was the plague in China, and it's your fault, all of it."

"I think I need another drink," John said his voice tinged with anger. "All of this so I can become the fall guy."

Youngblood opened the sideboard and looked up. "Scotch, or bourbon?"

"Scotch, please."

"Bourbon man myself." Returning with two bottles, both of them already opened, he poured John a drink.

"I've been through a lot of this stuff the last couple of weeks." He poured a glass for himself and held it up. "To Armageddon," he said with a wry smile.

"The crew down in those bunkers," Youngblood announced, staring into his glass. "Yeah, all that stuff Lawrence most likely told you about the secret facility built starting in the 1950s is true enough. In the years just before the Day they became an entity unto themselves down there.

"Lisa Hanson was one of the masterminds of this. Lawrence wanted to let it run its course. Let things go a bit farther, then we finally step in, use Scales as a figurehead. But he took the honorable way out, and Lawrence then figured you'd be a good choice.

"Meanwhile, there was a whole other plan afoot to use the plague. It was Lisa and her side who pushed through the plague idea within our own territory and Lawrence agreed, a final taking down a notch, till what was left of the population were nice and manageable, then come out of the shadows. Got that?"

There was almost too much to absorb. John poured a little more scotch for himself then nodded for Youngblood to continue.

"They wanted to use the plague here to wipe out bands of brigands, or for that matter some group or other who didn't want to be taken over. Give them a dose, let nature take its course, clean up afterward, with the population now nice and subdued. But China? Oh, that was Lisa's brainchild." Youngblood downed the rest of his drink and poured another, and then relit his cigar.

"Why stop with our own little problem populations? Let's go for the whole ball game and end it once and for all. So, China it was. They had their little fluff-up with us back before the Day with a nice variant of flu that killed a few million. Well, why not pay it back and kill a billion people, John? It's really simple if you have the right demonic brew.

"She got Lawrence, who I think was reluctant at first, I mean killing a billion people deliberately would have been even much for a Stalin or Mao, but he finally agreed. Just do the whole damn thing at once, here in what was our country and to our key rival. The fly in the ointment was the probability that China would, of course, trace it to us and go berserk. But Lisa argued even if they did, what could they do in reply? They nuke what is left of us, we nuke them, then it's the old mutual assured destruction game. Well, mutual assured destruction or not, I believe China will take the risk of a first strike and that then is the endgame, my friend.

"So, leave a lot of dirty fingerprints that point to Taiwan, South Korea, even the new Soviets. That's why they planted the first dose in that city close to Taiwan. I'm not privy to all the inside madness but assume you'll see a sudden outbreak up by the old Russia border. I mean what the hell, Lisa and company couldn't just leave the Soviets as the only other major power. God damn, John, it really is crazy.

"Might have worked, damn them. But the Chinese aren't idiots.

They have their assets here. We think a couple of deep moles, maybe even inside Camp David, spilled the beans. They also caught some of our provocateurs, I'm told we had some deep mole Korean agents working for us and well, of course, if captured they were convinced to talk about it. Therefore, as we talk, it's late morning over there, and they are broadcasting to the world that the plague is our fault and it'll be payback time."

He sighed sadly.

"And it is our fault—the fault of that crew that has been hiding for years in those bunkers and tunnels, hatching their plots and counterplots until even the darkest fantasies get turned into realities.

"So that's the short version of it all. Needless to say, the Chinese have had their own plots, there's even rumors they encouraged the EMP strikes, and for our paranoid bunch, that was reason enough to get even."

"So what's next?" John asked.

"As we speak, China is laying full blame for the plague on, and I quote, 'militarist warlords hiding in the shadows.' In the few hours since we came down here, China is demanding full surrender of our remaining military assets, including this ship right here in Charleston. They already have some pretty potent stuff in what was once California, standard assets but nukes as well, being organized to deploy out here to the East Coast."

"Do you think they will actually go through with an attack?" John asked.

"Your guess is as good as mine but I think they will, I mean what other alternative is left? They've been moving airborne units there for some time now. So that's about it."

"We still have the boomers, those nuclear strike subs out there, don't we?" John wondered. "That's been a counterforce ever since the Day. One asset they couldn't touch. There's four of them, at least that's what I heard."

"Yes," the admiral confirmed.

"I understand they actually answer to you, is that true?"

"Yeah, you could say so, John."

"Couldn't that still be the counterthreat?"

"We have three now, John."

"What?"

"During the flight down here I received word that all contact with one of the boomers, the *Texas,* stopped. We think they got it. John, our deterrent is fading fast and the Chinese have gone light-years ahead of where they were just ten years ago with their sub forces. We used to have at least one nuclear-powered attack submarine guarding each boomer. Not anymore. Anyhow, as we sit here talking, they're hunting down our remaining nuclear deterrent.

"So I don't know. Sure, we have some deterrent and nominally it is still in command. I was willing to defer to Bob Scales. You see, I knew him long before the Day and respected and trusted him. I think, as well, that's why they were pushing you forward, John, someone I just might listen to as well."

John said nothing, though he was touched by Admiral Youngblood's compliment.

"But after Scales," Youngblood hesitated, "died, I started to doubt who I was in bed with. Anyhow, be that as it may, that is where we are at."

"What do you think will happen?"

"At the moment I just don't know. The Chinese are great bluffers. They've been doing it for centuries and often get their way. They are economic hegemonists, John, they gain through economic warfare.

"But this time, they have us dead to rights. We did it—or I would prefer to say Lisa Hanson, and General Lawrence, that cabal of trolls in their bunkers and tunnels did it—and they overplayed their hand and now the bill comes due.

"China is demanding surrender of what assets we have left. Okay, we refuse. Frankly they can lick us conventionally in a fortnight if they so choose. We are not going to be some nation in arms the way we were in the Revolution with a patriot behind every tree taking a potshot at the Redcoats until finally they just say the hell with it and go home.

"I'll ask you this. If suddenly you had Chinese airborne units coming down around you, would you fight?"

"Maybe we would."

"Come on, John. Your town up there in the mountains. How many died in the last five years. Eighty percent?"

"Something like that." And he realized that even as they talked, there was still the plague at their doorstep.

"Maybe you personally would be willing to fight, but the rest of the folks in your town, the small villages left that struggle day by day to survive? I think not. Besides, what would you fight with? I think what modern weapons you even still have are depleting out. Are you back to black-powder muzzleloaders yet?"

John could only nod in confirmation.

"This time? Let the Chinese pass out some rations, definitely some medicine with the rightful claim that your own so-called government unleashed it, then move on. There'll be nothing really to fight for, let alone with. So your town, your college, just goes on as before. Maybe even salute an old flag we once cherished from time to time and then just drift into the twilight of our world."

He sat back morosely, nursing his drink. He had smoked the cigar to a stub, and now lit another.

"Anyhow, tomorrow will tell. Tomorrow we'll see what those benighted fools say and see how the cards fall."

"What do you think you'll do, sir?"

"They may want to order up World War Three. I mean the real World War Three, and not just the EMP—meaning, a whole shithouse full of nukes. Of course, they could also throw another EMP at us."

"Beat the dying horse to death?" John asked.

"They might very well order me to launch an EMP strike or outright send up 800 plus nukes against China and they'll retaliate in kind."

"And—?" John asked.

"I won't do it," Admiral Youngblood said, his voice barely a whisper. "We launch that, in six hours our entire East Coast will be glowing embers, and don't think they won't do it. They are so enraged that I can't blame them."

"You have three commanders of ballistic submarines out there, sir. Are they completely loyal to you? Suppose you tell them not to launch, but one of the three goes ahead, taking their command over yours?"

"I know. I had four ballistic commanders, and I guess now only three. Those vessels have been out on patrol for going on five years. That would make any man or woman squirrelly. Oh, there was a time when if you got to command a boomer, you were vetted and vetted, the only ones left a tough, grim elite, who would salute, follow orders to the letter, and never go off the reservation.

"Since the sixties when they first put to sea, the public was absolutely assured that never would a nuke be launched except by command of the president, or the proper designated authority in the line of succession.

"But now? No matter what was said about protocols, that only a president could give the launch codes, blah blah blah. Those commanders out there—and God alone knows how many sleepless nights I have had over this for five years—in the end all along, they have the capability to launch, they have had command without relief. Stay out as long as you can, sneak back into port for resupply, try and keep your personnel intact as the world goes into chaos, and then head back out again for another four-to-six-month patrol.

"Shit, it would have driven me crazy long ago. So that's the status there. The three surviving captains know they are being hunted.

Think of that pressure. If they get an order from Lawrence that this is it, go ahead and launch on China and let's get it over with once and for all, do you think at least one might do it?"

John could not answer.

"I'm almost certain at least one of those three men still out there would do it, empty his launch tubes, then come home, discharge his crew, then either shoot himself or drink himself to death."

"The order would come from Lawrence?"

"Oh yeah, those men out there are hard-core military. They would tell Hanson or anyone else to go to hell. But this damn general, I think definitely one, maybe two of the three will salute and unleash at his command, glad that the years of waiting, of doing nothing, are finally over and they can go home."

"But you are in the loop, and if you said no?"

"I no longer can be sure, I just can't be sure."

Long minutes of silence followed, John watching carefully as Youngblood, lost in thought, stared into his empty glass. Eventually he mumbled, "Let's get some sleep, Matherson. There's an extra bed in the back room. Sack out there. I need some alone time for a while. Okay?"

John stood up and on an impulse, offered a salute to Youngblood, then left him to his silent contemplation.

Try as he could, sleep would not come. At some point in the middle of the night he heard Youngblood get up and leave the room, and he could picture the man almost like a ship's officer of old, walking the deck wrapped in thought until the coming of dawn.

He remembered a fragment from a poem how one faced "decisions and revisions which a minute will reverse."

There's nothing I can do in all this. It is so far beyond me, John thought. For too long now, he'd felt as if he was in the back seat of a runaway car, or in a plane without a pilot. *Why the hell did I get dragged into all this? Before, I at least felt I could do something.*

But now? He felt as if he was watching the final curtain coming down on this world and himself. And yet he felt as if he was pushing through the darkness to find some sort of light. He remembered once talking to a writer who said the most awful moments in his craft were when his story had a thousand possible paths, and none of them worked.

He finally dozed off into a dream world, where strangely he was walking up his driveway path, Makala and Genevieve were out the door and coming toward him, but he just couldn't reach them.

The dream drifted, moving softly like a bank of fog on a mountain slope, just undulating slowly and then cloaking the mountain in darkness.

"God help me," he whispered, coming awake. He sat up and turned on the room light, then walked back out to the conference room. It was dark except for the single light by a side table.

Opened on the table was a book, and picking it up he saw, of all things, it was a King James Bible. It was dog-eared, more pages folded over to mark other pages, some passages highlighted with a red pencil.

He had a sense that the Bible belonged to Youngblood. It had the feel to it of a book repeatedly turned to, and he thought that was a good mark for the man.

When he was a boy, and it was something he still did at times, he would just randomly flip the book open and see if there was something to be found within. He did so now, and, unable to sleep, unable to think any more about all that was closing in, he sat down and started to read.

It was an hour later that John opened the door to the corridor outside the admiral's suite. A solitary marine guard was leaning against the wall, fast asleep while still standing.

John touched her lightly on the shoulder and the young woman came awake with a gasp.

"Sorry, sir, I mean, I wasn't asleep, sir . . ."

"It's all right, marine. I won't tell."

"Really, sir, just had my eyes closed and—"

He forced a smile. "It's our secret, just if you could tell me where the admiral is."

"He's most likely in the CIC, sir."

"And that is?"

"Combat Information Center."

"And where is that, please?"

"I'm not supposed to leave my post but if you follow me, sir, I'll show you the way."

She braced herself, obviously shaking off her drowsiness, and led him through the maze to the uppermost decks. She stopped at a bulkhead door and cracked it open.

"We'll keep our secret," he said with a gentle smile. She smiled back and then hurriedly returned to her post.

The control center was a maze of computer monitors and switch-boards. He expected it to be alive with activity as he stepped in and looked around, but it was empty, except for two sailors keeping silent watch on their computers. It seemed strange how silent it actually was. Youngblood was sitting at the far end of the room. The cigar he was smoking offered the only light, other than from the few monitors and the first shifting of the sky from darkness to a deep indigo blue.

John wordlessly walked over to join him. Youngblood saw him approach and motioned to a chair next to him.

"Couldn't sleep, John?"

"No, sir."

Youngblood looked back out the window. The carrier's long flight deck was below and pointing to the east. There were no longer any planes on her; they had been stripped off long ago. A faint band of red lights at the bow end of the ship broke the darkness.

"From the first time I put to sea, as a midshipman on my first summer cruise," he smiled, as if lost in a happy memory, "this was the watch I most deeply loved. The hours between darkness and dawn. I guess all sailors do—watching the horizon out there on a calm night at sea, looking for the first ghostly glimmer of the sun, the first sense that 'the dawn comes up like thunder,' as Kipling wrote, even before you can truly see it.

"I loved the tropical seas, the trade winds sweeping down the deck, warm and seductive before the heat of day. You'd always find a couple of sailors up by the bow, having a smoke, yarning a story. I learned a hell of a lot in those days when a chief petty officer, one of the men who really did run the ship, would welcome me to sit and chat, and often to learn.

"There's not more than a few hundred left on this ship now. Barely enough to keep things running, but up on the bow, I know at least one or two are up there keeping silent watch. I used to go and join them, even when I was an admiral in command of this ship, the flotilla keeping watch around us. There was always something new to learn, if only of my humanity, my need to be a leader who reasoned, and not just commanded."

He sat for a moment and watched the sky again before continuing.

"Oh well, so here we are, you and I. The world is crashing down around us, John. The Chinese are moving fast now. Three hours ago we got a message that they are hitting Taiwan with a missile strike, a barrage of several hundred, non-nukes so far but that is coming, declaring that Taiwan was one of the players in starting the epidemic, and they will invade in force unless they surrender."

"Will they?" John asked.

"Unlikely. They'll fight, and it will be bad."

"And regarding us?"

"It's on a knife's edge. Lawrence is already up, he's waiting for Hanson to reply to his request to be ready to fire off an EMP on China. Orders are out to the boomer, and it's the commander that has me worried—he's off Guam and should receive an ELF message starting at twenty-three fifty-nine Zulu time. That will most likely be the message to go. We still have one of those ELF transmitters on Guam."

"You have to refresh me on Zulu."

"That's nineteen hundred our time."

Even then it took him a few seconds to translate to 7:00 P.M. Eastern.

"So that's it, then. We spend the day trying to bluff them that we mean to do it, they dicker back don't you dare. And then so it goes till the clock runs out and we see who craps first." He looked over at John. "I think, Matherson, if you want, I can get you a flight on a small plane back to Black Mountain, to your wife and daughter. 'Cause if this goes down within a day, two or three at most, it spins out of control and this place will cease to exist."

"And what will you do?"

"Stay here, of course." There was a flash of anger in Young-blood's eye, as if John was implying he would run and hide.

"Sorry, I know you'll stay. What I mean is, do you have any alternative that you can think of?"

"No. I think the players up at Camp David, the Pentagon, and McLean had their scenario thought out and gamed long before we thought of it."

"And that is?"

"They bluff to the last minute, and if China then agrees to leave where they are hiding alone, China can have the rest of the damn country—lock, stock, and barrel. China will go for it. It'll be plague-ridden anyhow and sooner or later the Chinese will give up on occupying it and then one day they'll crawl back out.

"But if China goes nuke, they'll retaliate in kind while staying safe thousands of feet underground."

"If China does have leads on our underground warren, why don't they take it out?"

"They know, of course everyone knows, about Raven Rock, but

Camp David, Fort Detrick, and the CIA, I don't think they know. John, a nuke can do a lot but to get them they'd have to have precise coordinates down to a few dozen yards to make a hit count even with a megaton worth of punch to crater it so deep that even if those below survive, it'll be months, maybe years, before they can claw their way out. So, Hanson, Lawrence, and crowd know they'll survive, even if what's left of us is turned into a wasteland."

"I assumed that was the scenario," John said.

"They would rather rule in hell than serve in heaven, John."

"Those years of reading Milton weren't lost on you," John said dryly.

Drawing a deep breath, John stood and stared out the window at the dawn sun that was slowly surmounting the eastern horizon. Down at the end of the carrier deck he saw a lone person stand up and bow his head for a moment, as if in prayer.

"Perhaps you're making a Faustian bargain, sir. If you go through with it, however, we might both end up in hell, when this is done. Unless—Unless we—" John paused.

"What is it?"

"We nuke them first."

"The Chinese? If that's your solution, you're as mad as the rest of them."

"No, damn it, that's not who I mean. We nuke our own underground world—Camp David, Raven Rock, Fort Detrick, and McLean. That's the Faustian pact we make with the nations we've harmed. We agree to end the violence . . . *on their behalf.* They don't need to attack us. The bad guys have been incinerated."

There was a moment of total silence.

"My God, you are crazy, John. Nuke ourselves! To what end?"

"Think about it. It's a move no one in this world expects, and I think it is the only solution. Remember that movie, *Fail Safe*? By accident we nuked Moscow. The president, in atonement, sacrifices New York. It is the only thing that will prevent a global holocaust.

"That is what I am saying we can do now. We, ourselves, can wipe out that nest of vermin that took us to this edge of darkness. Leaders who would murder a billion or more with plague—what redeeming value do they have left?"

Youngblood looked stunned, staring off at the slowly rising dawn.

"Listen to me, sir. It is the only alternative left to us. We have to be willing to make a sacrifice as did Abraham but for us we will indeed make the full sacrifice on our own soil as an act of atonement. We then turn around to the Chinese, explain why we did it, send whatever aid we have left, and hope, just hope they see reason. If they will accept that sacrifice and not attack, either conventionally or with nukes, it ends here and now."

"And if we do all that and they still don't see things our way?"

"We push the button and the hell with the consequences."

"Would you be willing to do that?"

"I honestly don't know," John admitted.

"I wouldn't," Admiral Youngblood said.

"Let's pray you don't have to ask me that question a day from now."

"Why does the strike have to be nuclear?" Youngblood asked.

"Two reasons. The first, to show that we really mean to cleanse ourselves with fire. The second, I doubt if we have any weapons left, other than nuclear, that could do it. The one caveat is this: it will have to be very precise, within dozens of meters at most from the targets, and I assume that will mean a ground-burst weapon."

"You're asking for a truly prodigious bunker-buster," Admiral Youngblood said.

"I know," John replied, his voice now cold. "Our decision is very much like Abraham's choice. To atone we must sacrifice. Downwind from the explosion, the fallout will contaminate a lot of people— several hundred thousand at least. They will sicken hideously and die horrendously. But, Admiral, what alternative have we left? It's like that stupid trolley car ethics question: don't throw the switch, five people die, throw the switch and only one dies. So which will it be?"

Another long silence.

Finally the admiral looked up, gave his answer, and John felt like a mass murderer.

CHAPTER THREE

The float antenna, sent up from the depths of the Atlantic and attached to the submarine *Tennessee,* finally went online. There had been several hours of anxiety before receiving an acknowledgment. *Have sent the ELF for Tennessee to deploy the float.* There was the question did the sub even receive the signal, and secondly, would he obey? If the sub commander thought he was being actively tracked by the Chinese, protocol was to stay down and stay silent. And sending up the float, attached to several thousand feet of wire, was all about announcing to the Chinese, "Here I am, come sink me." If there was an actual war message it would have to go through the ELF or not at all.

"Admiral Youngblood, this is Scott Hancock, USSN *Tennessee,* security code . . ." and a long minute followed of numerical strings to confirm for both Youngblood and Hancock they were indeed talking to their counterpart, and that neither one was under any kind of duress. Then a final exchange of one word from each of them, known only to the two of them, as added insurance.

"Okay, Scott, we're secure."

"God damn it, Vincent," Scott exploded, "what the hell are you doing? I receive word the Chinese might have nailed the *Texas,* so I'm going extra deep, top level of securing, and you come blasting in with your ELF telling me to send up a surface float and stand by? Are you crazy?"

"No, Scott, I'm as serious as a heart attack. For the next few minutes you are to stay calm, listen carefully, and then act on my orders."

"That float antenna was a tool of last resort, Vincent, so this better be good."

John, who was silently listening in, could detect obvious strain in Scott's voice. He jotted down a quick note and slid it in front of Youngblood.

High strain, is he reliable?

Youngblood looked over at John and nodded.

He jotted a second note: *Will he follow orders?* and Youngblood quickly wrote back, *The only one I think will.*

"Great," John muttered softly.

"Scott, I have a priority order for you. It will seem to be madness, and believe me, it damn near is, but we have to do it or we are all dead men."

"That serious?"

"Yes."

"Does it involve my assets?"

"Yes, Scott, yes it does."

There was a long silence and then finally, "Go ahead," a pause, "sir."

"Scott, I will be passing launch codes and coordinates to you once you confirm you will follow my orders. You know the situation here. There is no semblance left of a real government. I do have one person in the room with me, and he was vice president under Bob Scales, so I'll say he is what is left of a legitimate government. Do you understand me?"

After a long silence, they finally heard: "Go ahead, Vincent."

"You have been out of the loop, of course, for the last two months. There has been a coup."

"Oh Christ."

"Yes, oh Christ. You know the rumors. The group is based in the D.C. area. I think you know who I mean. We talked about it last time you were in port, two months ago."

"Go on."

"I don't have time for all the details now. If we survive this you'll have to trust me to tell you then. Now, I'll ask, do you trust me in what I am going to do?"

"Give me a minute, Vincent."

"We don't have much time."

"You want me to ask my weapons officer and XO if they will follow protocol?"

"Yes."

"They're here with me, Vincent. You know them. We have a lot of time down here to think and talk about a lot of possibilities. You're about to ask me to launch my package, aren't you? On whose authority? Remember, there was a time that unless it came from the president or his duly appointed successor I was to refuse."

"You don't know him, but as I said, he was chosen as our vice president by Bob Scales, and now he might be all that's left of what was once a government. And yes, for what little it is worth, he presented me with this scenario and I have come to agree."

"Oh hell, Vincent, it was basically down to you and me anyhow. But the three of us down here must concur to launch."

"Scott, my people will be sending up the launch codes. You will release one ballistic missile, five of the warheads are to be activated, the other three are not, and will be dropped inert into the Atlantic after the missile is launched."

"Five of the eight warheads are to be hot," the sub commander confirmed. "Targets?"

Youngblood rattled off the precise GPS coordinates for the Pentagon, McLean, Fort Detrick, Camp David, and Raven Rock. . . .

"Jesus Christ, Vincent, you have gone insane!"

"I'm dead serious."

"And if I refuse?"

"Then a real war will be on your head, Scott. Let's call it Abraham's sacrifice. If we don't do this, far worse will follow."

"Give me the codes, Vincent, but I've gotta to think on this damn hard. You know what you're asking of me."

"Yes."

There was a pause for a moment and then Scott was back on, his voice urgent.

"We're being tracked, damn it! I'm cutting the antenna and going deep."

"Scott, you have to do this," Youngblood shouted.

There was no reply.

John looked over at the techs running the communications. One of them cursed, then looked over at Youngblood. "Signal's been cut."

"Because of what, damn it?"

"Either he cut the wire and started to run deep . . . or the Chinese got him."

"Can you tell the difference?"

"Not yet, we no longer have sonar arrays working out there, sir, to tell us if there was an explosion."

"How long before we know?" John asked.

Youngblood said nothing, getting up from his chair and walking out of the CIC and to the open bridge. John wasn't sure if he wanted to be alone, but decided to follow, and came up to his side.

"They're designed to move fast once they get an order to launch. The assumption was that if it came to this, we would be in a hot war and minutes counted. Once the new coordinates are programmed into the missiles, they could launch within minutes if given the go-ahead. With this plan, though, he'll have to recalibrate a missile with new coordinates and make damn sure it's correct. Twenty minutes maybe, half hour at most. From launch to impact, if he does launch, we're talking six minutes or so at that distance."

He pulled a cigar out of his jacket pocket and lit it. John smoked one of his cigarettes.

"If the Chinese are on his tail, which we have to assume they would be, it's going to be a tense few minutes, a very tense few minutes." He raised his cigar and blew out a long stream of smoke. "I don't know, John, but this I'm sure of: more than a few will forever damn us for doing this."

The minutes ticked by as they stared out at the ocean. John knew they were blind to what was happening now.

There was nothing more to say. All they could do was wait.

CHAPTER FOUR

This is the BBC Home News. It is midnight London time, and here is the news.

It has been reported that this afternoon, at 1800 Greenwich Mean Time, there were at least two, possibly up to five nuclear detonations in the eastern United States near Washington, D.C. This shocking turn of events is still confusing. We received a broadcast from the American naval base at Charleston. The order was reportedly given by a serving admiral of their navy to put down an attempted coup by rogue military and civilian agencies that apparently had an active underground base in the greater Washington, D.C., area.

So-called authorization for this unprecedented action came from what claimed to be remnants of the former government of President Robert E. Scales, and was acted upon by a John Matherson who was known to be the vice president of that government.

Needless to say we are receiving a number of contradictory reports that we will attempt to sort out in the coming hours. The one reliable bulletin received in the last hour is that the Chinese

government has said it will not, repeat, not, move assets into the
eastern United States, that, and I quote, "the bandit coupists who
have released a deadly plague on our nation have been punished
severely and we applaud this decision and for the moment refrain
from further action."

And now a report by our correspondent in Charleston, South
Carolina . . .

The twin-engine Greyhound turboprop touched down with a bone-jarring lurch, an instant later full-throttling in reverse, so that John jolted forward, to be restrained by his shoulder straps.

The crew chief came aft, giving him a thumbs-up, then popped the side hatch open.

John unbuckled and stood up. After thanking the chief and shaking his hand, John slowly walked down the steep ladder and into the early-morning light.

He had called ahead and she was waiting beside the Edsel. Stepping back from the plane, he watched as the crew chief snapped off a salute and climbed back in. Pivoting a hundred and eighty degrees, the plane went to full throttle, raced forward, and finally lifted up into the morning sky. Banking sharply, it headed back to Charleston.

He walked up to Makala and tried to force a smile but couldn't.

"You must be exhausted," she said softly.

"Beyond it, actually," was all he could say.

"Get in the car, we'll go home. The kids brought over eggs, bacon, real coffee, and a good bottle of prewar scotch."

She helped him get into the passenger seat, and as she closed the door he realized the windshield was completely gone.

"What happened?" he asked.

"Oh, just finally knocked it out, it was falling apart anyhow."

"Oh."

"John, how are you?"

"News here first?"

"We got it under control. That Lawrence came through on his promise—actually sent fifty thousand doses of Cipro, and a thousand vaccines the morning after you left. We lost thirty-five people up on the North Fork, but it's contained, I think."

"Good." He closed his eyes wearily.

"John, I have to ask. What happened? Ernie and Linda came over, they've been monitoring the BBC. Everyone is talking about it. John, what did you do?"

"What had to be done."

"You said on that interview with the BBC that you made the choice of Abraham, except this time God insisted that a sacrifice must be made. Do you really believe that?"

He took a moment to think that over, just staring off through the missing windshield, then took a deep breath before answering. "We hit the place with five ground-burst nuclear warheads of two hundred fifty thousand kilotons each. That's twenty times more powerful than Hiroshima." He didn't think he would be able to talk about the horror he'd helped unleash, but now that he was pouring it out, he couldn't stop.

"They were ground bursts, Makala. On CIA headquarters at McLean, the Pentagon—" He paused for another deep breath. "What was the Pentagon. Camp David, Raven Rock . . ." Another breath. "And Fort Detrick. That was the hardest—about six thousand civilians lived next to it, in what was Frederick, Maryland. Beautiful old town that, wonderful history, used to go there with . . ."

He fell silent and swallowed hard.

"It's now inside a crater a thousand feet across and several hundred feet deep."

He pulled out a cigarette and lit it. Makala sat quietly next to him, waiting until he was ready to continue.

"Well, they never knew who hit them. The ones downwind,

though. The wind was such that Philly and New Jersey will get the fallout. They'll never know. It's most likely falling like flakes of snow right now, radioactive snowflakes . . ." His voice trailed off again and he took another drag of his cigarette.

"It said on the BBC that England says they're sending aid to us and China, God bless them."

"If you heard my broadcast, you know why."

"I heard it, the whole town heard it."

"And?"

"They think you're a hero."

John laughed sadly. "Oh, a lot of those down in the deeper holes most likely survived, but it sure must have rattled their fillings. Key thing is, they're down there, but we smashed all their communications, and blasted them in so deep it'll take months to dig out, if at all. Maybe, just maybe, they'll just turn into troglodytes and if so, fine and the hell with them."

He went back to his cigarette and she knew enough to be silent as well, simply resting a hand on his arm.

"Maybe someday I'll learn to live with what I did. It really was the only alternative left. They were going to push it all the way, and believe me, it would have ended a thousand times worse. I'll take what comfort I can in that. Can you understand that, Makala?"

"Of course, and so does everyone here." She reached down and squeezed his hand.

"Okay." John let out a long sigh and closed his eyes again.

"The kids are putting on their premier performance of *Our Town* tonight. They want you as their guest of honor."

And with that, John dissolved into tears.

She let him cry it out, offering to hold him, but he shook his head.

He thought of Abraham. He wondered, if God did not stay his hand, would he have still worshiped him? *But my hand could not be stayed, someone had to be sacrificed.*

He thought yet again of Lawrence. Was he indeed mad? Or at

some level did he really believe his was the only way out of it all, mad as it was? He knew that man would haunt him for the rest of his life. Just who the hell was he really? He wondered now if indeed in some twisted plan within a plan, Lawrence knew that John just might betray him, and let him go anyhow to fulfill a vision John could not begin to divine.

"That which does not kill us makes us stronger," John whispered at last.

He still had Black Mountain, Montreat, the world he had loved even before the Day, which in the end he did protect, and that was something after all.

He wiped his eyes and cleared his throat. "Let's go home."

"A couple of the kids are at the house babysitting Genevieve. They even are heating up water so you can have a darn good hot bath."

"Splendid."

Makala hit the starter . . . and nothing happened.

John slowly got out of the car, jumped up and down on the bumper, and got back in.

Nothing.

"It looks like the old Edsel is dead at last," John said with a rueful smile, and then they embraced . . .

He was indeed home.

ACKNOWLEDGMENTS

This is the page where authors get to say their thanks to all those who made your latest book possible. The list could be a long one. Across the fourteen years since the first book in this series, *One Second After,* was published, I've interacted with hundreds of people, from fellow citizens concerned about the topic of EMP to top officials in government, the power industry, and military. To even begin to list even a few would take page upon page. Perhaps the fairest thing is to express, instead, their concerns, which can best be summed up as this: the federal government is failing utterly to take some kind of action to protect our nation from the existential threat to our nation's security. We currently are spending a trillion dollars on so-called "green energy" but we see nothing being spent to protect the grid from the threat of an EMP attack. The previous administration was at least moving in that direction, acknowledging the threat as real and starting to act. The current administration abandoned those efforts. It is nothing short of criminal to do so.

This, however, is a time for acknowledgments and my thoughts go to Dr. Peter Pry. I always referred to him as the "Godfather" of this issue. For thirty long and at times bitter years it was Dr. Pry who testified before Congress, to the Pentagon, to any who would listen. It was Peter, more than any other, who inspired me to write *One Second After.* I'm a novelist; I took the hard science taught by Peter and others and tried to turn it into a tale that above all else would cause an awakening. Dr. Pry passed away several months ago, I fear in part from simply overworking himself in trying to get the word out. I hope my humble efforts were of help to him. George Noory, another acknowledgment for him, host of the long-running late-night radio show *Coast to Coast AM,* devoted a program to the memory of Dr. Pry where I shared the microphone. I think both of us were near to tears in remembrance of a true American citizen in a just cause. A thanks as well to former Congressman Roscoe Bartlett, who during his long tenure in Congress tried mightily to raise awareness and legislative action. Thankfully, Roscoe is still with us, but unfortunately is still waiting for action to be taken.

Another thank-you goes to Commander Bill Sanders of the Navy, who was one of our country's top experts on nuclear strategy. A darn good friend and advisor who wrote the afterword of my first book on the subject. We would often joke in a macabre way that no one wants our nightmares, they are simply too scary. When you write about this stuff, you do have to learn balance to lead a good and happy life in spite of the concerns.

The next acknowledgment is for Linda Franklin. Yes, the model for my Linda Franklin in the novels, along with her husband, Earl "Ernie" Franklin. Linda's story is a remarkable one. Born into Southern rural poverty, a kindly aunt took care of her tuition in Vanderbilt, where she earned a degree in mathematics. I recall a dinner with her, dated exactly to July 20th, some years ago. It being July 20th, I raised my glass in a toast to Apollo 11. Linda replied, "I helped write the TLI programs for that." Me: "You mean the Trans-Lunar Injection math." And she beamed proudly.

Linda spent more than a decade in the 1960s doing the math— not the software, but the actual complex mathematical formulas—

for the Mercury, Gemini, and Apollo missions that would then be coded. Don't get it right there, and you don't have the right software that became the triumphs of those glorious days for NASA. Yes, there was a movie made about it a few years back that featured several African Americans that deserve credit, but Linda was part of that team for ten years as well.

Sadly, this is being written in late March of 2023 and by the time it is published, Linda will be gone from this earthly abode. Launch well, Linda, as you head off to the heaven you so richly deserve.

Of course, on the business side of writing a book there are always genuine acknowledgments to my never-tiring agent, Eleanor Wood; Robert Gleason, my never tiring and always inspiring editor; and Tom Doherty, who has been the best darn publisher in the world. Not many writers get to say that about their publishers and editors, but it is indeed well meant here.

And a final acknowledgment to Mary Frances Flora. You have been a beautiful part of my life for a year and you show such remarkable patience with this writer, who on too many nights says, "Just let me finish this chapter," and then I'm still at work at two in the morning. And, oh yeah, who can forget our goldendoodles Chloe and Abby (I call her Abby Normal from the movie *Young Frankenstein*). They are such joys and such company when writing away; both are asleep by my desk and, like any good dogs, will cheer even the darkest day.

In closing, perhaps a bit of an acknowledgment to you, the readers who are still buying these books. I pray we help band together in growing numbers to finally bring government action to the threat of EMP and get the job done.

William R. Forstchen
March 2023

ABOUT THE AUTHOR

WILLIAM R. FORSTCHEN is the *New York Times* bestselling author of *One Second After, One Year After,* and *The Final Day,* among numerous other books in diverse subjects ranging from history to science fiction. Forstchen holds a Ph.D. in history from Purdue University, with specializations in military history and the history of technology. He is currently a faculty fellow and professor of history at Montreat College, near Asheville, North Carolina.